THE CLOSEST THING TO HEAVEN

"How do you know anything about me, Hawk?" Sienna asked as she pulled away from him. "What do you really know? I think you're really describing yourself. There's something that haunts you, Hawk, that makes you see me the way you do. I am far from some pure, perfect vessel. I've got my problems like everybody else."

"No, you may not be perfect, Sienna Russell"— Hawk walked over and put his hands on her face— "but there is something special enough in you that out of all the human beings walking this earth, you were born as the last Stonekeeper. That's damn special," he said, staring into her eyes with a fiery intensity as his mouth slowly descended toward hers, "and probably the closest that a man like me will ever come to heaven."

Eboni Snoe
The Passion Ruby

ARABESQUE
BET
BOOKS

BET Publications, LLC

To my mother, Ruby Thomas Coleman Williams, and my father, Willie Williams. You have forever been an example of strength and stability. Love and thanks.

A profound thank-you goes out to Valeria Jenkins, owner of Val JaVaughn Modeling Studios of Memphis, Tennessee, for her expertise in photographic design and makeup.

ARABESQUE BOOKS are published by

BET Publications, LLC
c/o BET BOOKS
One BET Plaza
1900 W Place NE
Washington, D.C. 20018-1211

ISBN 0-7394-1590-5

Printed in the United States of America

One

The wooden board creaked beneath Sienna Russell's high-heeled feet as she shifted her weight. She closed her eyes and adjusted the black netted veil just as the whitewashed double doors opened before her. Taking a deep breath, she stepped forward, away from the haunting spiritual hum of the unfamiliar relative in the funeral procession behind her.

The country church was filled with flowers, but Sienna barely noticed them as she kept her eyes focused straight ahead. Stiffly, she walked past wooden pews speckled with an overwhelming number of unfamiliar elderly people.

A barrage of thoughts tumbled through her mind as she led the procession, but uppermost was the funeral itself. She never would have imagined Aunt Jessi would want a funeral. She didn't even know Aunt Jessi believed in them. During the few years that she had lived with her great-aunt, the older woman had never attended church or even spoken of God. Yet, she had also never thought Aunt Jessi would sell the house and the land to strangers. Sienna recalled it was the earth and nature that Aunt Jessi seemed to worship. That's why the call from the attorney's office had come as such a surprise. Aunt Jessi had recently sold the land to a developer, and Sienna was the sole beneficiary of that sale. It was the attorney who had informed her of the funeral.

Finally, a white-gloved Mother of Mt. Zion Baptist Church directed Sienna into the first pew. As she eased into the aisle and sat down, she was glad to feel the smooth, cool wood beneath her. Moments later, the pew was filled with three women who the minister said were Sienna's distant cousins. The youngest one, a middle-aged woman with a large mole near her mouth, eyed her openly, turning up her nose at Sienna's pillbox netted hat and tailor-made black suit. The cousin's obvious displeasure with Sienna's presence only added to her discomfort.

Sienna wondered why the woman disapproved of her, and she glanced at the trio once again. Although their skin had been baked in the southern sun, it was still fair, and their hair, which was worn in simple styles, was wavy to straight in nature. Sienna could tell from their postures that they were all of substantial height and girth, and she felt dwarfed beside them on the pew. Comparing her own dissimilar features, it was hard to see these women as her or Aunt Jessi's relatives.

Sienna placed her hand on the thick, textured bun at the back of her head. Like Aunt Jessi's hair, her own curled into tight, spongy ringlets when washed, and both their skin tones were more a mellow brown than yellow. Sienna's petite frame was curvy but slim, her facial features a balanced design of large, almond-shaped brown eyes, a small nose, and lips that were neither too wide nor too thin.

From what she remembered about her mother, Sienna used to see her face reflected in Aunt Jessi's. More than once she had wondered if her mother, had she lived long enough, would have grown to resemble Aunt Jessi.

From the moment Sienna had arrived at the church in Campbell, Alabama, she had felt totally out of place. Not that anyone had said a word against her. It was their eyes that told the story as she took her place at the head of the procession outside the church door. Although she had spent two years of her life in the small town, there was no doubt she did not belong there and probably never had.

Sienna's thickly lashed, dark eyes stared through the small veil at the open casket only a few feet away. For years after her mother and father were killed in the train accident, she had lived in an orphanage. Then, almost as if by an act of magic, she was told she was being sent to live with a relative, a great-aunt by the name of Jessi Thompson. Sienna was nearly grown by then, and her stay on Aunt Jessi's small farm which was a hodgepodge of country living, had been far from easy. Her aunt had been a silent, distant companion. When she did speak, sometimes it sounded like parables . . . quite difficult for a teenager to understand. For a while Sienna had wondered if all elderly people spoke in measured, poetic terms.

Her two-year stay on the farm had been a far cry from the noise and activity at The Children's Sanctuary, which was in an urban setting. But in the end she, too, had come to appreciate the land and the woman who had become such a large part of it. For Sienna it was a discovery of a great-aunt she had never heard of and a kind of living she had never known.

Full of emotion and memories, Sienna looked down at the bangle on her wrist. Aunt Jessi had given it to her the day she left for college, toting all the possessions she owned in a tapestried doctor's bag. That day Aunt Jessi had come out on the porch to say goodbye. She did not hug or kiss her. It was simply not her way.

"This is yours, Sienna," she had said as she gave her the intricately carved silver bracelet she always wore. "Remember the things you've seen me do or heard me say. One day, just like that bracelet, they will be real important to you."

A mournful chord on the organ pulled Sienna out of the past, and she watched a group of women behind the casket rise from their seats and begin to sway and sing. "I'm goin' up yo-onder to be with my Lord."

For nearly thirty minutes, Sienna joined everyone at Mt. Zion in the service for Aunt Jessi. Cries of "Amen" and "Yes, Lord" rang out as the minister preached a heated sermon, acknowledging Jessi Thompson had been "slow to join the flock, but yet her heart was pure." The women on the pew with Sienna sobbed openly when the casket was closed and the benediction read.

From the congregation's reaction, it was obvious to Sienna that during her last years, Aunt Jessi had changed from her solitary life to a life closer to the community of Campbell and the people of Mt. Zion. Sienna felt a unique sense of sadness, coupled with rejection, that her random attempts to communicate with her aunt over the last year had gone unanswered.

It wasn't long before Sienna found herself standing alone out in the churchyard beside Aunt Jessi's grave.

"So, you must be Sienna?" an elderly voice called from behind her.

She turned and faced one of the women who had sat on the pew beside her. It was obvious the woman knew the answer to her own question but had finally decided to talk to her. Sienna was glad she had.

"Yes, I am." She gave the woman a sincere smile. "And who are you, may I ask?"

"I'm Hattie. Hattie Lawson. Jessi was my third cousin on my father's side. I think we were part of the reason Jessi moved back to Campbell. Although for years you never would have known it, because we never saw her." She rubbed her hand over her silver-grey head. "You staying for the dinner?"

"I didn't know there was one," Sienna replied truthfully. "Am I invited?"

"Sure. Everybody who attended the funeral is. You just come on with me."

The little room attached to the church was buzzing with activity when Sienna and Hattie arrived. Several long tables had been pushed together and covered with white paper tablecloths. In the rear of the room one table was set up away from the others. It was ladened with dishes ranging from ham and fried chicken to sweet potato pie and peach cobbler— a virtual potpourri of food supplied by the women of Mt. Zion.

Soon everyone had filled a plate and taken a seat. Sienna sat near Hattie, who introduced her to her daughters Annie and Janice.

"I had heard that a young girl had come to

live with Jessi several years ago. It's a shame that
back then we were not close enough for me to
get to meet you. And of course, during her last
days, she spoke quite a lot about you." Hattie
spooned in a mouthful of potato salad. "But she
lived to be eighty-one years old . . . and taking
care of her own self until the last couple of
weeks. That's better than a lot of folks get to do."

"To be honest with you, I'm really amazed,"
Sienna chuckled lightly. "I didn't know I had
any other relatives outside of Aunt Jessi. She
never said a word about you."

"Well, that don't mean we ain't her relatives,"
Janice threw in abruptly from across the table.
"As a matter of fact, the way things were before
she died, you would think we was her only folks.
Me and Hattie took care of her. Bathed her. Fed
her. Did everything but go to the bathroom for
her."

Sienna took a long look at the woman who had
shown her disapproval of her during the funeral,
her gaze focused on the mole before she turned
away.

"I guess I can understand how you must feel,"
she said softly. "I wrote several letters to Aunt
Jessi over the past year, but I never got an answer.
And of course she didn't have a telephone. During the years prior to that we had kept in touch,
but I didn't have enough money to come—"

"Humph." Janice rolled her eyes and rounded
her shoulders. "You don't look like you were doing too bad to me. We heard you owned your
own business. Sellin' all kinds of strange stuff
like stones and old African and Indian things."

"Yes." Sienna attempted to keep the conversation pleasant. "It's called The Stonekeeper and

I do sell a lot of different kinds of things, but
I've only had it for two years now. It takes a business at least that long, if not longer, to become
stable."

"Yeah, I'm sure," Janice replied, then looked
into the distance before eyeing Sienna again. "I
just think you're feeling guilty 'cause you aban-
doned the old woman. You could have come and
saw her if you wanted to, but you just didn't."
She leaned forward across the table, wagging a
finger at Sienna. "And you don't deserve to be
no benefish-ciary from the sale of that property,
either."

"All right, Janice," Hattie said, putting her
fork down. "That's enough now. You have said
all you need to say . . . even if you got more
you want to say. You need to be respectful of
the dead. And let these issues of the living rest,
at least for today."

Janice's eyes looked a little remorseful, but
her jaw was rock hard. She leaned back in her
seat and murmured to Annie. "We all know she
been marked, anyway."

Sienna watched as the quietest relative stared
at her, wide-eyed.

"What did you say?" Sienna asked Janice.

"You heard me."

"No, I didn't," Sienna replied shortly. "If I
had heard you, I wouldn't be asking you to re-
peat yourself."

"I said we all know you been marked."

"Janice, don't start that mess," Hattie warned.

"Now, Mama, you know I'm right," Janice insisted. "Aunt Jessi told all about it when she was
'bout out of her mind. Said she was born with
a mark between her breasts. Said it looked some-

thing like a crystal. She said she was like some other women from the past who had the same thing." Janice's voice got louder.

"Shhh." Hattie waved her hand at her daughter as she looked around the room. "Hush now. These folks going to start thinking some awful things about the family if you don't quiet yourself."

Hattie looked sheepishly at Sienna.

Stunned by the woman's outburst, Sienna placed her hand against her body, shielding the mark she had had all her life.

"What else did Aunt Jessi say?"

Janice's nostrils flared as she eyed Sienna.

"I don't want the people of Mt. Zion thinking there's something wrong with us 'cause of you." She squinted her eyes. "But I'll tell you this"— her voice lowered until her whisper turned into a hiss. "She said you was destined to be involved with all kinds of things. Stones. Folks in foreign countries. Some of the things I couldn't even make up in my wildest dreams. And I'll tell you what else she said." Janice looked smug. "If you don't do what's cut out for you, you might just end up dead somewhere."

Sienna rose from her seat and backed away from the table, unaware that all eyes in the room were upon her. She was shocked by Janice's words, but more so by the apparent pleasure that accompanied them. She felt a need to get away from these people who claimed they were family, but actually seemed ashamed of her or even to hate her.

With her mind in a whirlwind, Sienna hurried to the door and out into the churchyard. As she fled, she balled her hand up into a fist and pressed it against the telltale mark. Although the car was only several yards away, it seemed as if her steps couldn't carry her fast enough. When she finally reached it she jumped inside, clutching the steering wheel. Sienna held it so tight her palms turned yellow, contrasting strangely with her pecan-colored skin.

Moments later, the sound of gravel grinding against rubber could be heard as she pushed down hard on the accelerator and the small Mazda entered the dirt road. Sienna drove on, without a thought to where she was heading, Janice's words still pounding in her head: *We all know you been marked.*

The subtle truth of the words shocked her, but it was the recurring dream she had had for the last month, ever since her twenty-fifth birthday, that made them more credible. Haunted by Janice's accusations, Sienna replayed the dream in her mind.

She is standing all alone in a desert, where she knows she has been banished. Banished because she refused to do what was expected of her by her ancestors. Then suddenly, in the blink of an eye, two apparently endless lines of ancestors appear, stretching across the desert plain. Fearful, she begins to run between the parallel lines they've created with their bodies. At first she can barely hear the words they are saying, but then they begin to get louder and louder, until their voices become a roar. "Every four generations a Stonekeeper is born with the mark of the crystal between her breasts. It has been the same from time remembered by the elders, ending with the millennium." By now she is covering her ears to block out what they

are saying. Suddenly, she reaches the end of the
line and Aunt Jessi is there. She wants to stop,
but her running has gathered so much momen-
tum that she can't. The next thing Sienna
knows, absolute terror is engulfing her as she
flounders in midair beyond the edge of a cliff.
As she falls she can hear Aunt Jessi crying out
to her: "You are the last of the Stonekeepers,
Sienna. It is your legacy. Do not fail."

Thud! The loud sound, followed by a hissing
noise, jerked Sienna back to the present as the
Mazda hit a deep hole in the middle of the
road, causing her to swerve recklessly. Moments
later the car rested up against the trunk of a
weeping willow tree, and Sienna emitted a loud
moan as she looked out the window into a cloud
of green leaves. She was thankful she was not
hurt and that the country road had been de-
serted, ensuring no one else had been involved.

Still shaky, she climbed out of the car, but
Sienna knew what she would find even before
she looked. A flat tire. She sighed heavily. Although she had a brand-new spare in the trunk,
she had loaned her jack to her good friend and
employee, Dawn, the day before yesterday.

Feeling taxed beyond belief, Sienna walked
through the shroud of tree branches and
glanced around. As she surveyed the surrounding land, she saw a small pond bordered by an
apple and a plum tree that looked vaguely familiar. Then realization began to set in. This
was the field just east of Aunt Jessi's place. It
was only a matter of cutting across the nearby
field and walking beyond the line of trees, and
she would be at the edge of her aunt's property.

Just the thought of seeing the old farmhouse

brought a smile to Sienna's face, for it was the only place she could remember outside of the orphanage that she had ever called home. To come back to it under such sad circumstances made Sienna hesitate, but a strong desire to see the house one last time overcame her.

Sienna recalled it was at least two miles between Aunt Jessi's house and the nearest neighbor, but she figured if she walked along the road long enough, someone would come by who would assist her. She knew the folks in Campbell had their ways, one of them being never to neglect a person in need.

She began to walk, and as she did her spirits began to rise. Perhaps it was the beauty of the sunny autumn day, for all the trees had begun to change color. Deep in thought she progressed in silence, her high heels working their way into the fertile soil, her veil gently blowing in the breeze. Her pensive mood made her stop and reach into her large purse, from which she extracted a mini tape recorder. Because of the dream and Dawn's prodding, Sienna had made it a habit over the last month to record her dreams. It was only after Dawn couldn't convince her to write in a journal that she had compromised with the more spontaneous method. Yet as the days had rolled by and the meaningless dream began to haunt her, the recorder had become a therapeutic sounding board.

Sienna looked down at the hand-held machine, and her full mouth lifted in a wry smile. All of her life she had never given much credence to her dreams, but someplace deep inside she knew this one was different, special, maybe even a warning.

"I attended Aunt Jessi's funeral today," she spoke into the recorder as she walked, "and I think I am on the brink of understanding the dream. I just wonder if I am ready for—"

Abruptly, Sienna stopped speaking as she stared at the new waist-high wire fence surrounding the land nearest to the house. It struck her as strange, for she distinctly remembered Aunt Jessi saying she didn't believe in fences, because the land could never really belong to anyone.

She walked along beside the structure, looking at Aunt Jessi's farmhouse from a distance. It was certainly a far cry from the well-kept premises of her memory. The house was run-down, in fact, with the porch nearly caving in.

For a moment Sienna stopped and laced her fingers through the wire. How strange that Aunt Jessi would allow the house she so loved to deteriorate to such an extent, while at the same time she would buy a new fence to protect it. Sienna's smooth brow furrowed as she considered the inconsistency while she continued to trail her hands along the fence. But the sight of the padlocked gate stopped her all together, and at that moment she knew the fence had not been Aunt Jessi's doing. So who was responsible?

According to the attorney, Aunt Jessi had only been dead for three days, but it appeared the developer who had bought the land had already taken it over. Sienna looked around at the wide countryside and the nearby forest. It was beautiful and quiet, with the nearest neighbor quite a distance away. There were no other businesses in the area, and one would have to go all the way to town for any kind of trade. Why would a large developer want this land, anyway? And even more so, why would anyone feel the need to lock up an old one-story country house, previously owned by a Black woman of little means? It just didn't make sense.

Sienna took the lock and held it, her dark eyes a pool of determination and anger. What was it the new owners had found so valuable that they couldn't even wait until Aunt Jessi's body was settled in the ground?

She bit her lip as she considered the situation, and it didn't take long for her to make a decision. This had been Aunt Jessi's home, and at one time in Sienna's life it had been her home, too. She would not allow the developer to keep her from entering the house one last time.

Sienna removed her jacket, hat, and shoes, tossing them carelessly, along with her purse, onto the other side. From habit, she smoothed the thick, textured bun at the base of her neck as she sized up the task at hand. She couldn't remember the last time she had attempted to climb a fence, but from the size of this one, Sienna believed she could handle it.

For one last time she surveyed the area, making sure no one was in sight. Once confident of that fact, Sienna hiked up her A-line skirt and cautiously scrambled over to the other side. She was pleased when she landed in one piece, with nothing more amiss than a run in her hose, and she gathered up her possessions and headed for the house.

Sienna's buoyant mood had changed; the fence and the locked gate had seen to that. Now her explorations had taken on a more wary note.

She stepped on the sagging porch with caution. Before she approached the door she stopped to listen, making certain there was no movement inside. Once Sienna was convinced, she gave the doorknob a familiar jiggle, bypassing the old lock that had been of little use for many years. Hesitantly, she pushed open the door, surprised to find the worn living area almost unchanged in seven years.

It took only a moment for the memories to engulf her. Sienna placed her belongings on a table as her gaze roamed over the old wall hangings and furniture, noting that even the plants were in their same places. Here, inside, it was almost as if nothing had changed, but of course it had. The main fixture was missing; Aunt Jessi was no longer there.

Sienna made her way from the kitchen to the screened-in porch and finally to Aunt Jessi's room, which was now equipped with the paraphernalia of the sick and aging. A tight knot formed in her throat as she looked at her great-aunt's personal possessions. Aunt Jessi had been the only relative she had known for the majority of her life. Sienna wished she had been there for her aunt during her last days, although they had never really been close. Aunt Jessi's personality wouldn't allow for that.

Sienna smoothed her hand over the sheets on the bed, letting it trail along the antique wooden frame. She had always admired the carved floral bed with its tall posts and massive headboard. Drawn into her memories, she examined the furniture.

"Ouch! Doggone it. What's this?" She drew back suddenly as she encountered an area that was uneven and sharp. With her finger throbbing, she gave the place a closer inspection and was surprised to discover a small compartment.

Sienna vaguely remembered once or twice seeing Aunt Jessi remove a tattered journal from somewhere beside her bed. Could this be the place where she'd kept it hidden?

Carefully, she dislodged the stubborn piece of wood, hoping to discover something that had been special to her aunt, only to find the place empty. Disappointed, she closed the drawer.

A scratching noise outside from scampering squirrels interrupted Sienna's thoughts, and she continued on to the room she had saved for last. Sienna pushed against the creaky door that connected to the living space. She had barely stepped inside to cross to her old twin bed, when she heard a car pulling up outside. Startled, she turned and looked out the curtained window as a blue Cadillac came to a halt in front of the gate. Sienna watched as car doors opened and several men in suits began to get out.

With her heart pounding, she watched one of the men begin to unlock the gate. Sienna realized they were the ones who had put the barrier there. It didn't take long for her to figure out that they would definitely consider her as an intruder. A trespasser.

In an instant, Sienna remembered her things that lay out in the open on the cocktail table, and she made a mad dash to remove them.

Panic gripped her as she ran back, arms laden, into her old bedroom, trying to think of a place to hide. With little time to spare, she turned to close the door when to her horror she saw her hat lying almost in the middle of the floor. She felt compelled to go after it, but the sound of a man's voice right outside stopped her. Stiff with fear, she stood glued to the spot.

"That fence you put up looks like it's worth more than this house," he laughed, and Sienna could hear him move farther inside. "I know I've been gone for a week, and you didn't tell me much about this over the phone, but still, I didn't expect this. I hope you haven't brought me down here on a fluke."

"Don't you worry about that, Carl. This isn't a fluke," another man replied. "And if you hadn't gone off on a tangent about what happened while you were in Indiana, I would have given you a more detailed explanation on our way here from the airport." He paused. "As far as the fence goes, I didn't want anybody getting in here and going through the place before we had a chance. I've got that journal that my cousin sent me right here"—Sienna heard a patting sound. "In a couple of places, the old woman talks about a map."

Sienna's dark eyes widened as she stood pressed against the painted pine door, listening.

"Well," the man named Carl replied. "The emerald you told me your cousin found in the old lady's things was enough to convince me. I just never thought I'd see the day when Curtis and Williams, attorneys at law, of Atlanta, would be conducting big business down in the back woods of Campbell, Alabama."

"It is a trip, isn't it? And if my cousin Janice hadn't been the nosy witch that she was—and always has been, as I remember—we never would have known anything about this. It was a good thing she got close to the woman before she died and was able to convince her to sell to our 'conservation project.' Her sight had gotten so bad, she had to practically help her sign the papers. Can you believe the old broad that lived here? I tell you, from her journal, it seems she's traveled all around the world, but in the end she decided to move back here to *this* town." His tone was sarcastic.

"You know, that's one thing I have to give you credit for, William. You have always known how to wheel and deal. You were able to talk your cousin into just taking some of the money from the sale of the property and leaving the treasure hunting to us. I'm sure you had to do some fancy illegal paperwork to make that happen"— he cleared his throat in a meaningful manner— "since that Miss Thompson thought she was leaving all her profits to her niece. But I have to say, if you told your cousin the truth, she wouldn't have had the means or the know-how to go after any of the stones." He paused. "You know, man, if any of this is true, we're going to be some rich Mother Hubbards when all of this is over. I never saw myself dealing in precious gems, but I surely don't have a problem with it if it's going to deepen my pockets."

Sienna could hardly believe what she was hearing. One of these men was Janice's cousin! And Janice had talked Aunt Jessi into signing something she could barely see, and then had taken it upon herself to remove her journal. A journal, according to this man, that made reference to a map and some precious gems. And on top of all that, this attorney/cousin of Janice's had also had the audacity to falsify some papers, enabling her to receive money from the sale of Aunt Jessi's property!

Sienna could feel both her shock and anger mounting. She would not allow them to get away with this! She would find a way to make sure all of them paid for having lied to and stolen from Aunt Jessi. Her smooth jaw was set with determination. But Sienna knew she would have to be clever, because these men were attorneys. The only way she would be able to accomplish anything would be with actual proof.

The glint of the metallic tape recorder lying within the bundle in her arms stood out like a beacon. That was it! She would tape-record their conversation.

Holding her breath, Sienna removed the tape player from the folds of her jacket, then with excruciating slowness she pressed the button to record.

"Just between you and me, Carl, I think Janice kind of hurried up the old lady's demise when I told her I would make sure she received quite a bundle for her part in the deal."

Carl gave William a rather surprised look, but his back was turned to him as William continued.

"The woman was dead in a matter of three days, after I talked to her. I know Janice said she was old, but—"

"She probably gave the old broad a little help," an extremely deep voice Sienna had not heard before added with a distinctive, hiccuppy chuckle.

Sienna nearly gasped out loud at the incriminating words, and her heart went out to her great-aunt. As she tried to get hold of her rampaging thoughts and emotions, someone else stepped onto the porch and the front door opened again.

"So, have you had enough of nature watching, Hennessy? Or do you prefer for me to call you Hawk, like Carl does?"

"It doesn't matter." The voice was silky, low.

"You're not much of a talker." There was a hint of irritation in William's voice. "You haven't said more than ten words all day."

"I only talk when I have something to say" was the steely response.

An awkward silence followed.

"Ah, ma-an, don't pay any attention to Hawk," Carl chimed in. "He's always been a little strange. You know he'd have to be, to be as interested as he is in hieroglyphics and ancient mysteries like that. So don't worry, he's cool."

"Yeah, well . . ." The man named William didn't sound convinced. "Don't stare at me like that!" he suddenly shouted.

"Come on, Hawk. Don't be trouble today," Carl chuckled to make light of the situation. "At first when we were real young, we called him Birdman. Didn't we, man? He had long, thin legs and knobby knees, and his eyes reminded me of a hawk or an eagle. But one of the main reasons we called him that was because of his karate. This brother could jump and spin like no other in the 'hood, and stories started spreading that he could probably fly if he wanted to."

"Well, I'll tell you what," William said with authority. "Anybody who's working for me has got to show me a little bit more respect. From your attitude, Hawk, you would think we're working for you."

"I am here to look at the map. Nothing more. If you call that working for you, suit yourself." His tone was slightly threatening.

"What in the hell is this?" William's voice rose.

"Just wait a minute," Carl jumped in. "Wait a minute. There's no need for you all to go that way. I knew Hawk was good with old maps and could be trusted. So let's leave it at that."

"All right, just forget it," William acquiesced. "The sooner we look for the map, the quicker we will be out of— Hey, look what we have here!" he exclaimed in surprise. "This is some sharp hat, isn't it? Not at all the kind you would expect to find down here." He paused. "Mmm . . . and it smells strongly of perfume. How long has that gate been out there, Spike?"

"I made sure it went up the day after the old broad died," the bass voice responded.

"That's what I thought." There was a rather lengthy pause. "Maybe the map won't be the only thing we find in here."

Two

Sienna's breath was cut short as she listened behind the door. Desperate, she looked around again for a place to hide as she clutched her jacket and shoes to her chest. With little hope, she decided the only possible solution was an old chifforobe.

She began to tiptoe across the room, when to her horror the recorder went crashing to the floor. Suddenly, the bedroom door swung open, and Sienna found herself on the floor, her belongings flying from her hands. Terrified, she rolled over on her side, only to stare up into the amused eyes of a tall, dark bald man with a scar on his face and a hoop earring in each ear.

Before she could say a word, he had her up on her stockinged feet. Sienna tried to get away, but his grip was like iron.

"You take your hands off me," she spat out as he pulled her into the living area.

"Well, my, my, my, what do we have here?" William purred as his eyes trailed from Sienna's neatly coiffed head to her shoeless feet. "Quite surely, it's not Jessi Thompson's ghost. 'Cuz, honey, if you are, I think I'm ready to go over to the other side."

The top buttons of Sienna's lilac silk shirt had

become undone, revealing a significant portion of her intricately woven lace bra. William's eyes lingered on the exposed area. Sienna's anger began to rise once more, along with her fear.

Never taking her eyes from his, she began to button the blouse with slightly shaking hands.

"So, how about introducing yourself?" William walked up to her, then began to circle about her in a casual manner.

Despite the danger she was in, Sienna found herself furious at the way these criminals had been able to bend the law to suit themselves. Not only had they taken advantage of Aunt Jessi, but they had also hinted at the possibility of her being killed for her property. She knew that for her own welfare she should cooperate, but a stubborn belief in justice egged her on.

"I don't think my name would make that big a difference. You seem to know just about everything I could possibly tell you and more."

"Uh-oh," William exclaimed with contrived awe. "Not only are we beautiful, but we're also brave, aren't we?"

Sienna didn't dare turn around to face him as she stood with her heart beating so loudly, she would swear it could be heard throughout the room. Nearly paralyzed with fear, she heard William's footsteps retreat into her old bedroom, then stop.

"Well, I'll just be damned," William clicked on the play button of Sienna's recorder.

Just between you and me, Carl, I think Janice kind of—

He switched off the tape recorder and crossed over to stand in front of Sienna.

"You were really busy in there, weren't you?"

His pleasing tone had changed to ominous, his glittering eyes narrowing. Roughly, he grabbed her chin and squeezed it. "Who in the hell are you? I want to know and I want to know *now*."

Sienna winced from his touch. She tried not to answer, but the pain was too great. "My name is . . . Sienna Russell."

"Sienna Russell." William repeated the words. "I recognize that name. You're the old woman's niece."

William nodded his head knowingly, then looked at his partner Carl.

"This ain't too good, man." Carl shook his head. "I thought your cousin Janice told you it had been years since the two of them had seen each other."

"Yes, that is what she told me. So it had to be very recently that the little lady here developed a strong enough interest to climb the fence we put up and nose around on private property."

"Private property!" Sienna could not hold her tongue. "Property that you acquired by tricking an old woman who never did you or anyone else any harm." She pointedly looked from one face to the next, her gaze finally resting on Hawk's veiled features. "So all of you should feel really good and manly after accomplishing such a great thing."

"What are we going to do with her, William?" Anxiety laced Carl's words. "She's been in there listening to everything and has the whole thing recorded on tape. And as feisty as she is, she's not going to keep quiet."

"You're damn right, I'm not." Sienna's voice trembled with emotion as she crossed her arms protectively in front of her.

"We're going to have to see about that." William pronounced each word slowly. "Maybe we can help convince you that keeping quiet is the right thing to do. As a matter of fact, I can think of a lot of things that might convince you, and some of them would be a helluva lot of fun. At least for me they will. "Spike . . ." William flicked his finger in the bald-headed man's direction.

Before Sienna knew what was happening, the large man had her up in his arms and was carrying her toward the familiar twin-size bed.

"No! No! What are you doing?" she screamed as he threw her onto the lumpy mattress, then put his knee on the bed beside her. With a satanic grin on his face, Spike's gigantic hand reached for the neck of her blouse.

"This has gone far enough." The low, silky voice reached her from the other room. "I didn't come here to be part of a rape, so you . . . What do they call you, Spike? Whatever your name is, you need to get up off that bed and leave the woman alone."

Spike slowly turned his head in Hawk's direction, then his eyes strained to see his boss.

William's mouth hung open as he stared at Hawk.

"Carl, that's it. I don't know where you picked up this sucker, but I am not taking nothing else off him." He spoke through gritted teeth, then pointed his finger at Hawk. "You shut the hell up. You don't run nothing around here, and I'm about to make your big ass walk back to Atlanta if you don't stop fuckin' with me."

"You heard what I said." Hawk's voice was

low and threatening as he ignored William, his amber eyes never leaving Spike's face.

A hint of a snarl curled the corner of Spike's mouth as he held Hawk's gaze. Suddenly, a ripping noise filled the air and Sienna found her blouse torn open to the waist. Shocked beyond belief, she tried to cover herself while her frightened eyes took in the scene before her.

Spike still held a piece of her blouse in his hand as he spun around, pulling a gun. Although he was fast, the man called Hawk must have been faster, because before she could blink he had crossed the room and pulled William in front of him. He had become a human shield.

Aghast, Sienna drew back farther into the corner of the bed as she tried to use the remaining shreds of material to cover herself. To her, it appeared the man called Hawk barely had a hold on William as he pressed his index finger against the base of his throat. Yet she could tell from the panicked look in William's eyes that he felt in imminent danger.

"Don't point that gun at me unless you plan to use it," Hawk warned as he forced William to walk sideways, his eyes burning with a deadly fire as he kept his target in view.

There was a coldness to his voice that chilled Sienna to the bone, and for a second she thought she was glad he was on her side. For although Spike and William had displayed their sadistic natures, somehow she knew this man, Hawk, had the ability to be cruel in a way few men could.

"And unless you want me to turn your boss into a vegetable for life," Hawk continued, "I suggest you put that gun down."

Sienna could feel Spike's hesitancy as Hawk

and William continued to advance, with Carl standing dumbfounded several yards away. Almost as if on cue, Spike turned and reached for her as Carl made his move on Hawk from behind. All Sienna could do was scream at the top of her lungs as one hand clawed at Spike's face while the other tried to warn Hawk of the impending danger.

The powerful look in Hawk's eyes, as they changed hue from a golden brown to a cloudy green, burned into her memory. Instantly, William's features took on a stunned, frozen look before he fell to the floor, then Hawk spun with deadly grace, kicking and catching both Carl and Spike in his path. On impact, the silver gun whirled out of Spike's hand and onto the wooden floor, affording Hawk the opportunity he had been awaiting.

Sienna felt dazed both from her adrenaline rush and from witnessing the amazing scene that had just taken place. Never before had she been threatened physically, and she felt extremely vulnerable as she clung to the corner in a state of disrepair. By now her shoulder-length hair hid half her face, and her thickly lashed eyes glistened as she studied the man who had assisted her.

His features were like granite as he held the menacing gun in his hand, and it was difficult for Sienna to believe it was this same man who had helped her. She searched for a hint of kindness in his face but found none. Although he created fear within her, Sienna couldn't help but continue to stare, for her fate apparently rested in his hands.

He wore his hair in tiny light brown dreadlocks, held captive at the base of his neck with a strip of leather. The exotic nature of its pulled-back style emphasized his high cheekbones and liberally cut nose and mouth. But of all his ruggedly handsome features, Sienna found his eyes the most unnerving, for surely the color also reminded her of a bird of prey.

His head turned slowly as he surveyed the room, his chest encased in a black leather vest, under which he wore a long-sleeved fitted top. Sienna could tell, as he stood there in his jeans with his long legs apart in a stance of readiness, that he was powerfully built.

Even as she felt her body begin to tremble, Sienna could see the man called William was trembling as well. His well-dressed frame jumped spasmodically as he appeared to become consciously aware. She watched as Spike attempted to comfort his disoriented boss as well as pamper his own injured hand and wrist. Several feet away, the man named Carl lay moaning and holding a protective hand up to the side of his head.

"Throw the car keys over here," Hawk ordered.

The small collection of metal landed with a clatter beside his feet.

"Good. Now you two remain right where you are"—Hawk nodded at William and Spike—"and Carl, I'm going to have to ask you to join them. Now I suggest that you"—for a brief second his amber eyes rested on Sienna, before dismissing her and returning to the men—"go get your coat and cover yourself."

Sienna's fog quickly lifted as his condescending attitude grated on her nerves. Her in-

itial reaction was to balk at his instructions. Who
was he to tell her what to do? As far as she was
concerned, he was one of them . . . an oppor-
tunist who would do anything if it would be to
his advantage.

Her oval chin tilted upward as a set of chal-
lenging words began to form in her mind. Her
small hands and arms clenched possessively at
the bits of material that shielded her. "I don't
know—"

"Look, lady," Hawk cut her off without even
turning in her direction. "That's right. I *don't*
know you, and you don't know me. But at this
time, I don't think it would be too wise for me
to go into any kind of lengthy introduction. So
if you don't want to do what I said, suit yourself.
Maybe being an exhibitionist is your style." His
eyes raked over her, resting on the exposed tops
of her barely covered breasts.

Sienna could all but feel the heat of his gaze
on her body, and her face turned even warmer
from the implication of his statement.

Jolted by his words but not wanting him to
be aware of it, she abruptly turned her back
before inching to the edge of the bed. Then she
used her hands to push herself off before walking toward the bedroom door. If she could only
get through it without him stopping her, Sienna
thought, she could run for the front door and
possibly escape.

"Now don't you get any bright ideas such as
disappearing out the door," Hawk warned. "I
told you to put your coat on, and it's right over
here"—he pointed at her suit jacket. "No one is
going to leave this place before we search thoroughly for that map."

"Did you say *we?*" Sienna's eyes burned with rebellion as she turned slightly in his direction.

"That's what I said." His voice was low and smooth. "Now if you think you could save us some time by telling me where it is, that would work even better."

"I don't know anything about a map," Sienna hissed.

"All right. But I'll tell you what . . . I'd feel much better if you stood beside that piece of furniture right over there. I think it might be a little too tempting for you if you got out of eye range."

For a second Sienna considered making a run for it, but she had witnessed a vivid display of Hawk in action. He was faster than anyone she had ever seen, and her chances of dodging him were slim to none.

"Damn you, Carl," William's voice rang weakly inside the room. "What all did you tell him?"

"I swear I didn't tell him anything." Carl shook his head emphatically, grimacing all the while. "Hell, I didn't know most of the stuff myself until we got in here."

"Yeah, you didn't tell him anything, but still he's willing to tear the place apart looking for a map that he knows nothing about." William placed a manicured hand on his throat before looking up at Hawk with a manipulative gleam in his eyes.

"I've always been a man who knows when it's time to negotiate. . . ." He began speaking in measured tones. "What if I told you we'd give you a cut of what we get from the gems? From what I understand you're a pretty worldly man, doing consulting for museums and all. That's cool." William tried to ascertain how Hawk was receiving him. "But I'm sure you could always use a few lump sums of money just like anybody else."

Hawk took a step back in order to have a clearer view of Sienna, who was fastening her suit jacket.

Calmly, he turned and said, "I don't want any of your money, William."

"You don't want any of my—" Not able to take any more, William exploded. "You just want the whole fuckin' thing to yourself. Is that it? You greedy, yellow-eyed bastard."

A muscle began to twitch in Hawk's honey-toned jaw, and Sienna could see his patience was growing thin.

"Ms. Russell, I think you better take that old clothesline I see beside that piece of furniture and tie up our friends. I don't want Mr. Curtis to get any hasty ideas that he and I both will regret later."

Sienna's hands balled into tiny fists at her sides as she stared at him. Every inch of her rebelled against Hawk's bossing her around, but common sense told her having the three of them tied up would be to her benefit.

For as long as she could remember, it had always been hard for her to bend to authority, especially after her mother and father were killed. As a parentless child, she had felt the ultimate authority of which her parents had so fondly spoken had forsaken her, and she had vowed she would never again allow anyone or anything to have dominion over her life.

Still, Sienna was no fool, and she had to consider how far he would allow her to push him. He was the man with the gun, and although she did not feel he would actually hurt her, she was far from sure.

"I'll tie them up," she finally acquiesced. "But it won't be because I like taking orders from you." She looked at him pointedly. "I want to make sure you understand that."

For a second their gazes met. It was clear in Sienna's wide, frightened eyes that she was willing to stand her ground. But as she looked into Hawk's golden stare she became even more frightened, for there was a burning intensity that she had never seen before.

"You're going to regret this, Hawk," William threatened as Sienna worked at her task. "I don't let anybody double-cross me and get away with it," he spat out.

She could feel his intense gaze on her minutes later as she tied the last portion of the clothesline into a knot. Out of the corner of her eye, she could see his grip on the .38 begin to relax. Then with the confidence of a man accustomed to weapons, he quickly checked the gun before placing it inside the front of his black jeans.

Sienna's knees ached as she rose and stood before him, her dark eyes wondering what he would do next. A familiar rosy hue had descended upon the room and she knew it wouldn't be long before it was completely dark. Sienna tried to conceal the fear that had begun to increase once again inside her. She remembered a time when she had enjoyed the isolation of Aunt Jessi's place, but at the moment she found it to be only a curse.

As Sienna watched, a look she could not describe began to descend over Hawk's features. He turned slowly, then began to stare at the sun that was disappearing below the horizon. In a matter of seconds, a barrage of emotions flickered across his face, ranging from anticipation to fear to anger. Finally, his full lips settled into a determined line, and he turned and walked silently out the door.

For a reason she could not understand, Sienna felt compelled to follow him, and she found Hawk standing like a statue with his head bowed. When he finally spoke, his words were almost raspy.

"Close that door behind you," he instructed without showing his face.

This time Sienna obeyed without hesitation, for at that moment there was something totally strange and foreboding about him that she could not ignore.

"There may not be much time," he announced quietly as he turned and faced her. "I have my reasons to believe that you do have the map and you are keeping it from me."

Sienna was confounded by his words, and her expression conveyed her feelings.

"I told you, I don't know anything about a map. You're the one who came here with them"—she jerked her head back toward the door. "It seems like the three of you have plenty of information, including whatever is in my Aunt Jessi's personal journal."

"That may be true, but the reason we came here was to find the map." He began to walk toward her. "I don't have time to play, Ms. Russell. It won't do you any good to try and hide it from me. Eventually, I will find it."

Sienna looked into his fiery amber eyes, and she was aware of something uncanny about him that she could not explain.

"I told you I don't have your damn map," she said, resorting to profanity out of fear. "So, what are you going to do? Strip me down in order to find it?"

"If that becomes necessary." He stood mere inches from her, causing Sienna to look up to see his face.

Nervous, she held her arm up between them and began to twist the silver bangle Aunt Jessi had given her. "You try to act as if you are different than they are, but actually you're all the same." Her words were breathy as she stood her ground.

"I can guarantee you, Ms. Russell, there are very few people like me." The words seemed to hold a hidden meaning as Hawk reached out and caught Sienna's hand. Stepping back, he gently forced her to stretch her arm out between them, enabling the last dying rays of the sun to focus on the bracelet.

A veiled expression descended over his face as he slowly turned her wrist, assessing the jewelry from all angles.

"What are you doing?" Sienna asked as she looked from his face down to the bangle.

"How long have you had this?"

"What? The bracelet?"

He nodded his head.

"I've had it for seven years. My aunt gave it to me."

"I want to take a closer look at it." His face was a total mask.

The tone of his voice had softened, although

Sienna knew his statement was another order. She also had no doubt that if she refused, he would take the bangle away from her. Vexed as well as afraid, Sienna removed the bracelet and handed it to Hawk. Afterward, she stepped back to put more distance between them.

"Hawk. Man, I know you don't really plan to leave me tied up in here like this," Carl called out from beyond the bedroom door. "You know, you and I go back a long ways. All the way to the 'hood . . ." He paused, as if listening. "I know the way things went down in here earlier, it appeared that I wasn't on your side, but, man, I—I just wasn't thinking straight."

Sienna's body was tense as she listened to the sound of the man's voice pleading from the other room, but her gaze remained focused on Hawk.

With a slow, rolling gait, he crossed the room with the bangle in his hand. In the far corner of the living area, he flipped on an old light, placing the ornate silver bracelet right below the yellowed shade. The minutes seem to drag by as he studied it in silence, and Sienna was painfully aware of the total darkness outside.

"Dammit, are you still out there?" William's angry voice forced its way into the room. "It's too damn quiet in here and it's too damn dark. If you're going to leave us in here, you could at least turn on a light!"

William's enraged words startled her, but it was Hawk's question that caused small bumps to rise on her arms and the hair to stand up on the back of her neck.

"Have you ever heard of a Stonekeeper?"

Hawk seem to position himself far enough behind the light so Sienna could not see his face, yet his view of her was clear.

"S—stonekeeper? What do you— How do you know about that?" She could barely form the question.

They stood facing each other in silence. Finally, Hawk walked back across the room and handed her the bracelet.

"So, you do know something about it." He studied her closely. "How old are you now, Ms. Russell? No. Let me guess. You are twenty-five years old and you just recently had a birthday."

"What? How do you know all this? Did you read it in my aunt's journal?" It was hard for Sienna to comprehend what was going on, so she plied Hawk with questions. "What kind of game is this?"

"Sad to say, this isn't a game, Ms. Russell. Not at all."

Hawk crossed the room and stared out the window into the night.

"It's all there written on the bracelet."

Sienna stared at the ornament that encased her wrist.

"You mean these markings are my name and everything else you just said?"

"No. Your name is not there, but the history of the bracelet is. Your aunt gave you that bracelet for a reason."

Hawk turned and stood in silence before he began to speak again. "I want you to listen to me well. For no matter what you do, this is not something you will be able to escape. What I said earlier is true. I said there may not be much time, and now I know there is not. Before I was referring to something that pertained to me, but now I know this also includes you and a mission that you have been born to. Marked for."

Marked! At that moment the tiny mark in the middle of Sienna's breasts seemed to burn, as her thoughts raced with Hawk's words. For the second time that day, those words had been thrown at her, and suddenly she felt as if she couldn't take any more. Her mind raced with thoughts of the dream . . . of the men who were tied up in the room behind her . . . but most of all, of this man, Hawk, who knew things about her life she had told no one.

"Look, I don't know what this is all about, but I don't want any part of it." Sienna raised her hand between them in a halting motion. "I don't know you from Adam's house cat and I don't want to know you," she spat out. "There is no connection between you and me other than that you have read my aunt's journal. I've had enough of you and your friends. You can do whatever you want, but I am leaving."

Sienna ran and threw open the bedroom door, where she gathered the rest of her belongings. She was headed for the front door when she stopped suddenly.

"I want my aunt's journal," she announced, looking back at Hawk, who stood silently watching her.

"Hey, what's going on out there?" William asked snidely. "Trouble in paradise?"

"I'll tell you where it is if you untie me," Carl pleaded.

Sienna glanced from Hawk to the interior darkness of the bedroom. Feeling bolder than ever because Hawk had not attempted to stop her, she answered Carl's request.

"Tell me first, then I'll untie you." Again she looked at Hawk, her chest visibly rising and falling.

"Carl"—she could hear William say the name between gritted teeth—"I've had about enough of you."

"Hell, I don't want to stay tied up in here forever," Carl lashed back. "Hawk's already got the keys to the car. Even if he untied us, it would take forever to walk to another farmhouse out here in no-man's-land. At least I'd have a chance if I was untied." Then he shouted to Sienna. "The journal is in William's briefcase. I believe it is on that table out there."

Sienna's hands shook as she fumbled with the latches on the attaché. Carl didn't know how right he was, she thought. It would definitely feel like forever walking to the nearest house in the pitch blackness of night. Up until that moment she had forgotten her car had a flat, but she felt she had no choice but to take her chances.

It wasn't hard to find the stack of yellowing hand-bound papers. Hastily, Sienna placed them under her arm and headed out the front door, with Carl's exasperated voice ringing in her ears. "What about me?"

For a second she thought of untying him as she turned and glanced at Hawk, who stood mysteriously aside, a look of inevitability in his eyes. Unnerved, Sienna decided to leave Carl to the mercy of his own actions.

Once she cleared the porch she broke into a spirited run, staying on the driveway and eventually entering the road. She prayed that whenever she reached the next farmhouse it would still be there, not gone the way of so many of the homes that had been damaged several years ago in a tornado, never to be rebuilt again.

Sienna didn't know how long or how far she had run, but she could feel a cramp in her side and her throat had become parched from breathing through her mouth. She was thankful for the bright, full moon that illuminated her way, but she knew it would be different once the road entered the woods. She recalled, years ago, how even in the daytime it had been difficult for the sun to penetrate the natural canopy created by the old oaks and various trees.

Over and over again she caught herself looking back, listening for an approaching car, hoping that one of the residents of Campbell would happen down the old back road. Desolately, as she got closer to the ominous woods ahead, Sienna remembered the road had never been well traveled. She dreaded entering the dark forest alone.

Her steps slowed as she approached the outer edge of the woods, her thoughts suddenly preoccupied with the man called Hawk. Sienna was forced to admit that despite all that had passed between them, she had never really felt threatened by his presence. He had taken it upon himself to protect her, and as she progressed deeper into the darkness, she yearned for that feeling of security again.

No sooner had the thought come to her than she heard the sound of a car approaching. In frightened anticipation Sienna moved over to the side of the road, where she began to wave her arms for the vehicle to stop. The headlights blinded her as they drew nearer, and when the car finally pulled up beside her, she had to blink several times to clear her vision as she leaned into the window of the passenger's side.

"Thank God you stopped! I really need your help. I need to get to a phone right away."

"Sure, I can help you," Hawk replied.

Sienna stood looking into the shadowed face of the man she had just left behind. Nervously, her gaze traveled to the empty back seat. She was surprised to find he had actually left his companions tied up in Aunt Jessi's house. Sienna had wanted help, but she had not expected it would come in the form of Hawk. In silence, she weighed her predicament.

"So, are you going to ride, or continue to walk in the dark?"

She straightened her back and looked at the long, dark road that stretched out before her, then she leaned down and spoke to Hawk once again.

"You will stop at the first gas station or public phone we come to?"

"You have my word."

Sienna's teeth clamped down over her bottom lip as she considered her options. Slowly, she pulled up on the car door handle and climbed inside, sitting as near as she could to the door, her hand placed conveniently on the latch. As Hawk pulled away, Sienna kept her gaze on the window beside her. Within seconds there was nothing to see as the forest closed in around them.

Three

Sienna's uneasiness in the confined space of the car was palpable, and although she sat as far away from Hawk as possible, she could still detect the faint scent of sandalwood emanating from him. She found it strange that a man of such raw masculine strength would choose such an aroma. She always carried the oil in The Stonekeeper and was aware of the aphrodisiac qualities it was said to possess.

Sienna was glad Hawk did not attempt to make idle conversation, for even though they were not enemies, she still could not bring herself to see him as an accomplice, let alone a friend.

After traveling about a half mile they left the forest, and once again the moon cast its generous glow on the fields that lay to the left and right of' the dirt road. When she saw what remained of the farmhouse she had hoped to reach, Sienna knew she had done the right thing by accepting the ride. She realized how desperate she would have been had she arrived there and found the farmhouse in ruins. At that moment she actually felt thankful for the man beside her, whose presence put her somewhat at ease.

"So, you actually left them tied up in the house," she remarked, breaking the silence.

"Yes, I did. But I loosened Carl's ties a bit so it wouldn't take him long to undo them. My goal was to keep them confined for a limited amount of time, not forever." He spoke in a matter-of-fact fashion. "You must have been a Girl Scout back in your day. Those knots were pretty tight."

"I wasn't tying them up so much for you as I was for myself." Sienna continued to stare into the night.

"I know that." For a while Hawk drove on in silence. "I figured Carl would free himself and then the other two. By now they should be starting their trek down the road. It will probably take a good while before they find anyone to help them, if at all."

"Do you think they will come after me?"

Sienna looked at Hawk for the first time since entering the car.

"I think there's a good chance they will. William doesn't seem like the kind of guy who forgives and forgets. You can make problems for him, and I don't think he would appreciate that."

"He deserves any kind of problem I could possibly come up with." Sienna's attractive features contorted into a frown. "And what about you? After rendering him unconscious, not to mention what you did to his partners, he actually threatened to get back at you."

"Yes, I know. And he probably believes I have the map." Hawk turned and gave Sienna a meaningful look. "But I can take care of myself. I also know what I want and what I must do to get it. I won't let a man like William stand in my way. Actually"—his voice became nearly a whisper—"I won't let anyone stand in my way."

Sienna touched the bracelet that was clasped

about her wrist, her mind reviewing the events that had taken place over the past two weeks. Up until her twenty-fifth birthday, when the dreams had begun, she believed the name "The Stonekeeper" had come to her out of the blue, right before she had opened the shop two years ago. At the time it simply seemed to be a clever title for a place that sold a variety of products produced by Mother Nature. Now with everything that had occurred, Sienna wasn't so certain.

She thought of the things Hawk had said back at the house and she wondered what he really did know.

"Tell me"—she took a deep breath—"what do you know about the Stonekeeper?"

"More than I care to know." It was almost as if he were speaking to himself.

"What?"

"More than most people know." Hawk continued to look straight ahead. "Through the years, I've had access to museum artifacts and documents. From that I developed an interest in ancient maps and hieroglyphics. I'm not an archaeologist or anything like that, but I have been a museum exhibition designer. And I've traveled a lot. During my travels I've come across historical objects and documents that make reference to Stonekeepers. Women who are born to a legacy that requires they return precious gems with unusual powers back to their owner, Mother Earth."

"Come on. You've got to be kidding me." Sienna put her hands over her eyes. "And just because you read something like that on some stones or something, you believed it?"

"No, I am not kidding." Hawk paused. "And yes, I do believe it. I've seen proof." His last words took on a haunting note, and he paused again before continuing. "I believe your aunt, Jessi Thompson, was one of them. A Stonekeeper. And if she was, from the markings on the bracelet, she was the second to the last." His amber eyes focused on her. "There would be only one more Stonekeeper after her."

Sienna could feel the palpitations of her heart. "I'm sorry, but this sounds like something out of a movie."

"I guess to the average person it does," Hawk agreed. "But why do you think William and Carl were so interested in your aunt and her property? They would not have gone so far if they didn't really believe in something very strongly."

"And you're saying what they believed was Aunt Jessi was a Stonekeeper?"

"No. I'm not sure of that. But I am sure there was something in your aunt's journal that coincided with William's cousin's conclusions that your aunt had access to unusual precious gems, and that she also possessed a map pointing the way to others."

"It just doesn't seem like any of it could be true." Unconsciously, Sienna began to wring her hands.

"I've come to know there are many things that exist beyond what the average person believes could be true. And if you choose to believe it or not, this is one of them."

"Okay," Sienna chuckled nervously, more aware than ever of the birthmark between her breasts. "So, let's say there is some truth buried somewhere in here. Why would these women,

these . . . Stonekeepers, carry out this legacy?
Was someone forcing them to?"

"I can't say I really know. The only thing I
recall that may shed some light on it is a particular phrase I deciphered." Hawk began to
speak as if he were reading: "Twenty-five rotations mark the start of the powerful winds of
change."

"Twenty-five rotations mark the start of the
powerful winds of change." The words felt foreign on Sienna's tongue as she repeated them.

"You did that quite well." His tone was suggestive. "From what I understand about these
things, the phrase is referring to the earth's ro-
tation around the sun. Twenty-five of them, to
be exact. In other words, twenty-five years mark
the start of the changes in a Stonekeeper's life.
The statement seems to indicate their lives are
swept up by events that are so forceful, so powerful, they cannot fight against them, and they
can't help but be pulled into the current." Hawk
looked at Sienna once again. "There are marks
on the bracelet that show the birth cycle of
Stonekeepers from the time the legacy began
five hundred years ago. It seems the previous
Stonekeeper always dies once the new one comes
into the legacy. But there are no other markings
past the year two thousand. The millennium."

A chill coursed through Sienna as her fingers
traced the variation of marks on the silver bangle. There was no way to ignore Hawk's words
or what the haunting dream was saying.

The dirt road ended and they drove on to a
blacktopped street, with a small cluster of lights
no more than a quarter of a mile away. Hawk
pulled up in front of a gas station with a pay

phone outside. Sienna didn't dare look his way as she searched inside her purse for a quarter. She knew that within the depths of her own eyes, he would see her begrudgingly give in. That would make it real, and Sienna was not ready.

She clasped the cold coin within her hand and jumped out of the Cadillac without saying a word. What had happened to her at the farmhouse was almost more than she could bear, but this new revelation was a burden of an unknown greater kind. Desperately, she felt the need to speak with Dawn, to hear her familiar voice, to talk to someone she knew who could possibly help her make sense of it all. She was like family, and the closest person Sienna had left in the world. Of all the people she knew, Dawn was an open soul who rejected little and examined everything that came across her path with the innocence of a child.

Although it was not cold outside, the tips of Sienna's fingers had become wrinkled because of a chill from within. Placing the receiver up to her ear, she dropped the quarter within the slot and pecked out the numbers she had dialed so many times, her feet shuffling nervously. The dial tone continued to hum. Sienna gave the coin return bar a few good shakes before she realized the phone was out of order. Frustrated, she looked at the businesses that surrounded her, her eyes finally focusing on a man on a pay phone inside a place called Betty's Grill.

In a matter of seconds she started across the street, where several vehicles, including a sheriff's car, were parked outside. She was poignantly aware of Hawk still waiting in the Cadillac. Entering the partitioned glass door, Sienna realized the restaurant reminded her of a mobile home, for the width and length of it were quite similar.

The sounds of dishes clattering and loud conversations filled the air. The space was so narrow that Sienna was forced to walk between the bar stools and the front of the building in order to reach the phone. She was thankful when the man who had been using it hung up as she approached. Once again she dialed Dawn's number. This time the telephone began to ring. As she waited for her friend to answer, a sheriff entered the grill. He joined some people who sat several feet away.

"Hello," an energetic voice answered on the other end.

"Hi. Dawn. It's me."

"Hey, girlfriend. What's goin' on? I've been waiting on you all evening long. We were supposed to get together, remember?"

"I know. But girl, so much has happened." Sienna's voice began to crack with emotion. "I'll tell you what. First, I think I'm going to talk to this sheriff who just came into the restaurant. I just wanted you to know I'm okay, and I should be getting home later on tonight."

Sienna turned just enough to reassure herself that the sheriff was still there.

"Sheriff!" Dawn's voice went up an octave. "Are you okay?"

Sienna heard her friend's concerned voice drift through the receiver, but her attention had become focused on the exchange between the sheriff and the other people.

"Naw, I don' know what the hell's goin' on.

Jake just told me to get on down to Jessi
Thompson's old place."

"I thought they had her funeral earlier today."

"They did," the man in uniform replied. "But
Jake says not too long ago, they got some call
from out there."

"How can that be? Jessi Thompson never had
a phone."

"Yeah, that's right," the sheriff agreed. "He
said he asked the fella where he was callin' from,
and he said he was on one of them cellular
phones."

"Uh-oh. Well, think about that."

"Yeah, and that ain't all." He adjusted the
gun on his hip. "This man claims Jessi
Thompson sold that property to some conserva-
tive group he represents. Jake said he claimed
he was an attorney."

"Sienna. Sienna?" Dawn's excited voice grew
louder.

"I'm here." Sienna lowered her own voice.
"Just hold on for a moment."

The sheriff continued his story, but his
squinty eyes remained focused on one of the
female cooks behind the counter.

"This man says someone was almost killed out
there. And he believes it was Jessi Thompson's
niece who's responsible for it."

Sienna's heart dropped. She quickly turned
her back toward the men, who began to mill
over the juicy tidbit of information.

"Her niece? I didn't think she had any relatives outside of Hattie Wilson, who wasn't really
like a relative at all. Hattie was kin to Ms.
Thompson way down the line."

An older man broke in. "Naw, I remembers some yares ago, Jessi had a niece who came and stayed wit her for a while." A chorus of uh-huhs sounded. "Mus' be talkin' 'bout her."

"Yeah, John, I think I remember that. But what I know for sure is I got to go out there, 'cuz I'm the nearest one to the place. You know, check it out first. Could just be some crackpot or somethin', 'cuz he even mentioned a stolen car. You never know." He shook his head. "But if I find anythin', I'll get on the car phone to Mike, and it'll take a bit before he can get way out there from the station." He paused. "So y'all, even though I'm hyeah, I guess I won't be joinin' y'all in the game tonight."

"That ain't too bad for you, Bill. I had plans for takin' all yo money tonight," a teasing male voice chided.

Sienna held her breath as the chuckles resounded.

"Is that right?" By now she recognized the sheriff's drawl that called out across the room. "Penny, honey. You keep it wome for me, you hyeah?"

She could hear the light laughter of a female before draggy footsteps began to cross the linoleum.

"Dawn." Sienna's voice was barely a whisper. "I've got to go. Promise me you won't do anything until I call you later."

"Sienna! What's going on? Where are—"

She hung up the telephone with Dawn's voice still coming over the line. For a moment she stared at the wall in front of her, until she heard the gunning of a car engine. Mustering all her willpower, Sienna began to walk calmly out of

the restaurant. Once she reached the door, her
breathing became heavy.

Oh, my God! What was happening to her?
Carl or William had actually accused her of trying to kill him!

Sienna turned the doorknob, her hands shaking. As she stepped out into the parking lot, she
looked for the Cadillac that should have been
parked across the street. It was not there! Stunned,
a small gasp was wrenched from her throat. Had
Hawk left her? Had he seen the sheriff's car and
driven off to hide his own guilt?

"Sienna," the low voice called from a space
nearby.

With pure anguish on her face, Sienna turned
and saw the blue Cadillac. Suddenly, it was if
the wind had been knocked from her as she
stumbled toward the car and climbed inside. She
leaned wearily forward against the dashboard.

"What happened in there?"

"Please," Sienna beseeched, "just drive off.
Hurry."

The engine purred as Hawk stepped down on
the accelerator and swung smoothly back onto
the blacktop.

Sienna continued to breathe loudly, as if she
could not catch her breath. Minutes later, Hawk
pulled off onto another dirt road and stopped
the car.

"You're beginning to hyperventilate," he
warned as he reached out a protective hand,
touching her back.

Quickly, he began to search the compartments
of the car until he came across a Brach's candy
bag full of Neapolitan chocolates. Hawk dumped

the candy out, slid over, and handed the bag to Sienna.

"Breathe in here," he directed.

By now Hawk was cradling her within his arm, and just the gentle human touch alone brought on deeper emotions. As Sienna's breathing slowed down, she began to sob quietly.

"What have I done to deserve this?" The words came out between shaky, moanful sounds. "All of a sudden I feel as if I have been cursed."

Sienna's hands replaced the bag in front of her face and her body shook with her tears. She could feel Hawk's body stiffen as if he were in a moment of indecision, then finally he drew her in closer and began to hug her against his broad chest. Just for a second the thought arose in Sienna's mind to pull away, but it disappeared as quickly as it came. She did not have the strength to fight this man who had not harmed her, who had only protected her even though it appeared as if it were against his grain.

Sienna could hear his heartbeat as she rested her head against his chest, and her body rose and fell in unison with the rhythm.

"What's wrong, Sienna?" he coaxed in a soothing voice. "What happened in there?"

"They said that I tried to k-kill someone."

"They who?" He stroked her hair tenderly as he cradled her against him. "They who?"

"Someone at the house," Sienna managed. "They called the sheriff and said someone's nearly dead up there. And that I did it!"

Sienna raised herself up, the tears flowing down her face, and searched deeply into Hawk's masked features. "You'll tell them that I didn't do it, won't you? You'll tell them the truth."

A deep tenderness fought its way to the surface of Hawk's ruthless features as he gazed
down into Sienna's distraught face.

"Of course I will," he comforted her. "You
know I will. But aren't you forgetting something?" He wiped a tear from beneath her eye.
"You've got the tape."

His smooth lips were so close to hers as he
sparked her memory, his breath warm and caressing upon her face. For a moment they just
stared into each other's eyes. Then his gaze
spread over her beautiful features, and she
could tell he missed absolutely nothing in his
assessment. Finally, his attention returned to her
eyes. In silence, Sienna watched as a dawning
realization entered his gaze, causing his eyes to
narrow into slits. She could not read the change
that had come over him, but she could feel it.

"You're right. I do have the tape." She attempted to gather her wits about her. "My
purse. I put the tape recorder in there."

She grabbed her bag from the floor and rum-
maged inside. The small machine was easy to
find. She held it near the window to catch the
moonlight, but Hawk was already a step ahead,
switching on the tiny light overhead. Anxious,
she pressed the play button, anticipating the
sound of William's voice, but none came. Sienna
was overwhelmed with disappointment when
she realized the tape was not there.

"It's not in here." She stared at the machine.

"I guess William didn't take any chances,"
Hawk remarked, his tone conclusive.

"I can't believe this is happening. What am I
going to do?" She directed the question more
to herself than to Hawk.

"I'm going to be honest with you, Sienna, and tell you just what I think could go down. I don't know who's injured back there, but if I had to bet my life on it, I would say it was Carl. They probably had some kind of disagreement and things got out of hand. You are just a convenient scapegoat, and of course they'll be able to prove you were there because of your blouse. There are bits and pieces of it everywhere."

"Yeah, but look at that. I could tell them the truth and my blouse would be part of the evidence."

"That's one way of looking at it, but from what I saw in William today, you're dealing with a deviant mind. One of the first things he's going to say is that you were trespassing on private property. And he'd be telling the truth. You even went so far as to climb the fence to get in. He could say that's when you tore your blouse."

Sienna shook her head. She was accustomed to thinking independently and coming up with her own answers. For the majority of her life, all she remembered was this feeling of having to fend for herself, even within the protective walls of the orphanage. During the two years that she had lived with Aunt Jessi, the same feeling had prevailed. They'd both worked the land and had their individual chores. Although she was a teenager, Sienna seemed to function autonomously. Aunt Jessi had simply served as a guide. But too much was happening too fast now, and Sienna felt as if she were caught up in a whirlwind.

"But you know the truth," she insisted. "You told me you would stand behind me."

"I will if it comes down to that. But you better

believe that when William gets through, both of us will be implicated in this crime, and I will not be your ideal witness. He'll paint me as more of an accomplice than anything else."

"You're right." She stared into the darkness of the night. "This is all so crazy. I feel as if I've just been snatched up inside a tornado. It's almost as if my life is out of control."

Sienna heard Hawk sigh as he slid over, settling beneath the steering wheel.

"It is, Sienna. It is out of control. But once you truly accept responsibility as a Stonekeeper, it will be in your power to control it." His voice was low, almost emotionless, and she could feel the distance he had put between them, not only physically, but emotionally and mentally as well.

"Think about this. I've never met you before in my life, but I know you just recently turned twenty-five. I also know that somewhere on your body you have a birthmark. It is called the mark of the crystal because of its shape. There is no coincidence that your life seems to be raging out of control and you can't stop it. Nothing that has happened to you since your birthday has been by chance. Your Aunt Jessi's death . . . what happened back there at her house . . . my sitting beside you here tonight."

The things Hawk said were heavy, earth-shattering, yet he sat there and announced them in a noncommittal tone. Gone was the compassion he had displayed only moments before. In its place was an aloof coldness that Sienna felt was directed toward her and her situation.

Slowly, anger began to replace fear. Here he sat admitting they would probably also blame him for Carl's injuries, yet he showed no emotion or concern. What manner of man was he? There was something that seemed to keep him from acknowledging his own humanness.

"So, that's all there is to it? You say things that could turn your life and mine inside out, yet you express it like it's nothing out of the ordinary. what kind of person are you?"

Hawk leaned over the seat and placed his face close to hers.

"That's just the point. That's *not* all there is to it. But I've come to understand not to waste energy on things I cannot change, but I'll fight any battle for something that I can. Right now, you need to face the fact that you are a Stone-keeper, and you're being forced to deal with what that means."

"Okay. Okay. So let's say you're right, Hawk." Sienna pronounced his name as if it were some outrageous thing. "What do you have to do with all of this? Are you just hanging around for your health?"

"Maybe." His voice was low.

"Maybe? What kind of answer is that?" Sienna was becoming infuriated. "You are doing your damnedest to convince me of who I am. Who in the hell are you? What kind of name is Hawk for a grown man who claims to have worked in museums and knows about hieroglyphics and such?"

"Actually, my name is Hennessy Jackson. I was given the nickname Hawk. You can say whatever you want about me, but it won't change the fact that we have been thrown together for a reason. Just consider me as extra baggage. I have the skills, knowledge, and expertise for you to accomplish your mission, and in the meantime, I'll be able to get what I need."

"And what is that, Mr. Jackson?"

"I don't think that's for you to know."

The silence that followed was charged with electricity.

"Well, I'll tell you what. Since I'm not supposed to know what kind of stake you have in all of this, I don't think I'm going to buy any of it. Just take me to the nearest Greyhound bus station, and I'll take care of myself from there." Sienna sat back against the seat and stared straight ahead. "There is one in Opelika. You can get on Highway 280, and it will take you straight in."

For a moment Hawk continued to stare at her determined profile, then he finally pulled onto the paved road, his jaw set in a rigid line. Sienna did her best to ignore his unhappy features, for she had made up her mind. If she had to deal with her world falling apart around her, she would deal with it in her own way.

Four

Sienna laid her head back against the bus seat. The sun had started its ascent into the sky, and she realized how much longer it had taken her to get to Atlanta than she had thought. The night had been rough. She had spent most of it in the old bus station. Her shoulder ached where she had laid against it, while drifting off into uncomfortable snatches of sleep on a wooden bench.

Sienna descended the stairs with other passengers traveling from Opelika to Atlanta. She attempted to pull her fingers through the tangled, matted waves of her hair, and she rubbed her eyes to clear them of the vestiges of sleep. Although she felt as if she looked a mess, no one seemed to notice in the busy bus depot.

During her nighttime travel, she had been able to think clearly about what she had to face. In the end, Sienna had decided she would contact the authorities and turn herself in. She was not a criminal. She had never run from the law, and she wasn't about to start. But first she would talk to Dawn.

Wearily, Sienna squeezed into the phone booth and sat on the metal seat. Closing the door, she dialed the number and leaned against the graffiti-covered wall.

"Hello," the strained voice answered.

"Dawn?"

"Yes."

"This is Sienna."

"Uh . . . where are you?"

"I'm at . . . Are you okay?" Dawn's voice sounded almost unfamiliar.

"Yeah. Yeah, I'm okay. I just sprained my ankle earlier, and it's giving me a fit."

"That's what you get for getting up so early. You know you're a late riser." Sienna tried to evoke some of the old spark she was accustomed to hearing.

"Yeah. You're right."

"Dawn, some heavy things have happened to me, girl. I've got to talk to you about it and tell you what I've planned to do." Sienna paused, but continued when Dawn did not respond. "I was going to ask you to come pick me up, but if you've hurt your ankle, I know you should rest. So I'll just take a cab from here to your place."

"Do you think you need to?"

"What do you mean? Take a cab over there?"

"Yes. Maybe that's not a good idea. I . . . all right. Come on."

Sienna stared at the receiver, puzzled.

"Are you sure everything's okay, Dawn?"

"Sure."

"All right. I'll be there as soon as I can. It's real important that I see you."

The line went dead.

Several taxis were lined up outside the building, waiting for passengers, and Sienna took the first grey and black car she approached. It proved to be an excellent choice, for the proficient driver cut her estimated travel time nearly in half. In less than thirty minutes, they pulled up in front of Dawn's apartment building, and Sienna handed him the fare and a tip.

Hurriedly, she crossed the veranda, the need to see and confide in her friend escalating. Sienna felt she had never known true friendship until she met Dawn. Inside the orphanage she had always been a loner, fearful that if she formed any attachment, the person would soon be taken away. In the beginning she had hired Dawn as a part-time employee at The Stonekeeper, and over the last two years their friendship had blossomed.

Anxious, she rang the doorbell several times, with no answer, although she could hear the tones chiming inside. Finally, she tried the knob, which turned easily within her hand. Sienna assumed Dawn had conveniently left it unlocked, since she was expecting her arrival.

"Dawn, it's me." Sienna walked into the familiar living and dining room area.

There was no answer.

"Dawn, where are you?"

After checking the kitchen and half bath, Sienna progressed down the short hallway. She had begun to feel uneasy about the silence, and her brow furrowed with concern. The door to Dawn's bedroom had been pulled closed and Sienna opened it, calling her friend's name once again. As she stepped into the bedroom, she noticed a tape player lying in the middle of the water bed. Beside it lay the amethyst pendant that Dawn always wore, believing it protected her.

Sienna's heart lurched at the sight of the necklace, and almost as if she were walking in a dream, she crossed the room and turned on the tape recorder.

"Hey, little lady. I know you have a fondness for tape players, so I thought I'd leave you this present." The prolonged hissing sound of the tape nearly drove Sienna insane, before William's voice began again.

"It's pretty obvious your friend Hawk took quite a liking to you, and between the two of you I know you have the map. So I came up with a bright idea. Since you both were so eager to be part of our treasure hunt, I'm going to leave the entire job up to you. I kinda like that. It'll mean less work and stress on me. This way we'll play a trading game. I guarantee it could get to be real exciting. But of course, it will be our little secret. No one else is to know. You have something that I want, and I'll have something that you want." Then William's voice turned ominous.

"I want you and Hawk to bring me that ruby, Sienna Russell. If you do, I just may tell a story to the police that you will like much better concerning what happened out there at the farmhouse." He paused. "But since I'm not a mean man, I thought I'd give you further incentive. Bring me the ruby within seven days and you just may see the Dawn again." He laughed at his own play on words. "One more thing . . ." Sienna switched off the machine and sat down beside it, the realization of what had taken place hitting her like a ton of bricks.

The tape-recorded message had pushed her to the brink, and her head felt as if it might explode. With her hands pressed against her temples, her mind began to replay the events, and she finally realized this chain would never end if she did not put a stop to it.

All her life Sienna had felt as if she had been chosen just to suffer. To suffer loss. To suffer want. To suffer need. It was only after she had become a grown woman, having managed to start a business of her own with insurance money inherited upon her parents' deaths, that she had begun to feel as if she were a real player in life. Until then she had felt only like a pawn. And now she felt as if that control was being taken away from her again. Sienna knew she had to face the dreadful whirlwind that had snatched her up, invading her life. But that also meant facing the fact that she had been born a Stonekeeper, and that her destiny involved fulfilling this role that threatened her very existence and now the life of the only friend she had ever known.

"So, you're not through with me yet, are you?" She spoke out loud to the powers that be, as she had done as a child. "Are you disappointed that I didn't lie down and die back then? Well, I've got news for you: I don't plan to do it any time soon," she determined through her rage and her fear.

But Sienna had no idea how she would go about finding the ruby. Would the legacy she had inherited endow her with special abilities? Or would she be forced to flounder about in the darkness of night, in a place she'd never been before?

The sound of the front door closing brought Sienna back to the present. Had William changed his mind and decided to come after her? She stood with her blood pumping wildly, her gaze searching the room for something to help defend herself. Quickly, she grabbed a small lamp from Dawn's dresser and braced herself with a powerful stance, her dark eyes riveted on the bedroom door.

The shadow of a man blanketed the entrance and Sienna drew back, ready to strike. But she halted in midair when she recognized him. Relief flooded her, weakening her knees.

"Hawk." This time the name sounded sacred.

"I like the way you said that." He raked her over with one glance. "You were ready to do some real harm, weren't you?"

Sienna ignored his question and posed her own.

"What are you doing here?"

"You left the front door open when you went inside, and when it stayed that way I decided to come in and see why."

"But how did you find me *here?*"

"Simple. I followed your bus into Atlanta. After that I watched you catch a cab, and I followed you here."

One of Hawk's dreadlocks had escaped the leather tie and it hung down provocatively from his temple along the side of his face. Sienna searched his features, trying to figure out why he was so diligent in his quest to follow her. As she stood in front of him she could feel his strength, along with something else . . . a cognition that was hard to describe.

"What is it that you want from me?" She searched his amber gaze. "I can't imagine what could drive you so. If you had wanted the stone

for money, you would have taken William's offer. But you refused it. Why are you being so
persistent?"

His eyes appeared to smolder as he watched
her, giving Sienna a glimpse of the intensity of
the force that compelled him. Suddenly, a part
of her wanted to hear him say it was simply she
whom he wanted, for she had no doubt the force
of his love would be a hundred times as great
as what she witnessed now. Sienna knew she had
never before been loved by or known a man like
Hawk, and the thought of being engulfed by
such a force was an intoxicating elixir.

But she dashed the thought away as soon as
it surfaced. She had known this man for less
than twenty-four hours. Sienna admonished herself, blaming her musings on her overwrought
state.

"I have a need to be" was Hawk's silky reply.

Sienna looked away, shaking her head. This
time when she returned his gaze, her eyes were
not clouded with confusion.

"All right. Last night you told me you had
the skill, expertise, and knowledge that I will
need in order to meet this thing head-on. At
the time I wasn't interested, but now I know I
have no other choice. William has my friend
Dawn"—Sienna pointed to the recorder. "This is
a person who would never do anything to hurt
anybody, and she is in danger because of me. He
has given me seven days to find the ruby and bring
it to him. I'll do whatever he says as long as he
sets her free."

Hawk stepped up to Sienna and took the
lamp, paying heed to her resolute features.

"Maybe you will be lucky, and we all will be

set free." His amber eyes became hooded as he spoke.

Time seemed to stand still as they stood, almost touching. Hawk's gaze trailed from her eyes, lingering on her mouth. Trying to escape the hot, liquidy sensation that was beginning to move inside her, Sienna looked away, hiding her eyes beneath her thick, curly lashes. The seconds seemed interminable as Hawk continued to stare at her face. Finally, unable to resist her natural inclination, she lifted her gaze to his smooth, brown, pink-hued lips. As Sienna tilted her head upward, her chaotic emotions churning within, Hawk placed a light but lingering kiss on her lips. Surprised yet pleased, her mouth yielded to the gentle motion that planted a seed for more passionate things to come.

"Why did you do that?" she questioned as a tingly feeling made itself known.

"It felt like the right thing to do."

"From what little I know about you, you don't seem like the kind of man who lets his feelings sway him. As a matter of fact, you seem to hide them quite well." Her words were breathy.

A glint filled Hawk's eyes as he arched a thick eyebrow. "It depends on what the feelings are, Sienna," he said, purring her name. "Some things are hard to ignore. Like the soft, inviting lips of a beautiful woman. One who is in distress, in need . . ." His hand traced a soft path around the side of her face.

Sienna trembled ever so slightly from his caress, but she was determined not to let him know how attracted to him she was.

"You spoke of your own need earlier, one that is apparently connected with the ruby and something else you refuse to talk about. With all of that going on, do you think you're capable of handling someone else's needs as well?"

"I'm capable of handling that and more." He spaced out the last three words meaningfully.

Sienna could feel the heat of emotion rising to her face and she stepped away, turning her back. Too much was happening too fast.

She heard Hawk place the lamp back on the dresser before he began to speak.

"The bracelet indicates the ruby will be found in the French Antilles on the island of Martinique."

Sienna turned, startled. It had never occurred to her that finding the ruby would mean traveling outside the United States.

"That means going to the Caribbean," she thought out loud.

Hawk nodded.

"While I was waiting for the bus last night, I decided to read Aunt Jessi's journal. I could tell she had begun writing in it when she moved back to Campbell. After all that had happened at the farmhouse I don't know what I expected, but there was nothing more than her daily reflections on working the farm. Of course, some of the pages could be missing," Sienna admitted. "Once in a while she would say how something reminded her of her experience in Egypt and another in South America, but that was all." Sienna sat down on the bed. "When I lived with her, she never mentioned that she had traveled outside the United States. As a matter of fact, I never realized she had ever traveled far from Campbell. Aunt Jessi was a very different kind of woman." Sienna became quiet as she reflected. "But there was something else. Something I thought was a little peculiar. It was a piece of paper that she had folded up and placed inside the journal. Listed in her handwriting were three gemstones: ruby, emerald, and diamond. Beside each one she had placed an equal sign and another word. *Passion* was written beside *ruby, greed* was beside *emerald,* and *allure* was beside *diamond.* Maybe that's what the stones represented to her," Sienna remarked, looking at Hawk again.

Hawk remained silent, and Sienna felt as if he were holding something back. Finally, he said, "The hieroglyphics on your bracelet spell out the same gems."

Sienna studied the bangle as she had on earlier occasions. Five lines of intricate markings circled the two-inch silver ornament. Each appeared to be carved by a different tool, although the symbols used were the same. For years the bracelet had remained in a drawer, Sienna having considered it more a keepsake than something to be worn every day. She had worn it to the funeral to honor Aunt Jessi. In the beginning she had wondered if there was any significance to the markings, but her curiosity had faded with time.

"And it also mentions Martinique?"

"Yes." His features were veiled. "You will find the ruby there."

"I never thought this would mean leaving the country. But the truth is, I haven't had much time to think at all. That could be a problem, you know. My leaving the States. The police will probably be looking for me."

"From what you've said, I'm pretty sure they

will want to question you. Maybe you should go to the police first. It's up to you. If you decide to go, you can count on me to go with you."

A surge of gratitude welled up within her as she looked at Hawk, but Sienna managed to keep her feelings under control. Over and over again he had offered his help, yet he refused to tell her why. Because of that, she couldn't help but remain skeptical of his motives. Yes, so far he had proven he would do her no harm, but as long as he kept his reasons a secret, Sienna didn't think she could really trust him.

"I had planned to do just that, but William made it clear on the tape that I mustn't tell anyone. He claimed he might clear my name once I've brought him the ruby." Sienna was speaking to Hawk, but she was trying to convince herself. "Right now what's most important is he's holding Dawn. Oh, wait a minute." She walked over to the tape player and switched it on again.

Hiss-ss-ss. "Don't try to take this tape to the police. Sunshine, here, will regret it."

Sienna cringed at William's threatening words, then she looked at Hawk. "I've made up my mind. The first thing I must do is help Dawn, and I'll worry about clearing my own name after I return. The way it stands now the police might decide to hold me if I go there, and I can't afford that." Sienna paced the room, her mind clicking. "What about this map that William keeps referring to? Is this bracelet the map?"

"It points the way," Hawk replied. "It tells us where the ruby can be found, so I would say yes, it is a kind of map. Perhaps that piece of paper you found in your aunt's journal is another clue." He ran his hand beneath his smooth shaven chin. "Once we reach the island of Martinique, we can start asking questions. Through my martial arts and other experiences, I've come to understand there is a flow that we are all a part of. It's quite obvious to me that if your mission as a Stonekeeper is as important as it appears to be, you will be guided to the right places and people. It will be up to you to recognize them."

Sienna attempted to understand the wisdom behind his words. Somewhere deep inside she knew that what he said was true. For so long she had denied anything existed outside of what she could see and feel. Now it was as if she were being prodded by the very force she had tried to deny because of her pain. Prodded in a way she could not ignore. It was a profound realization, and much too taxing considering everything else she had to face.

"But that's another thing. I don't have a visa or anything else that will allow me to enter the country. I'm sure they require some kind of document."

"They do," Hawk answered. "They ask for a passport, but I believe we can get around that. I've had dealings with the museum in Fort-de-France. It's called the *Musée Départementale de Martinique*. An old friend of mine still works there. With the museum's help, we can get you through customs."

"Are you sure?" The abilities that Hawk possessed were continuing to amaze her.

"Yes. This person and I go way back. With my friend's connections, it will be just a matter of a few phone calls." He walked over and picked up the receiver of a nearby phone. "If everything goes okay on that end and we can get a flight out, we can plan on leaving this afternoon."

"I can't go like this. I'll need some clothes." Once again, fear was making her hesitate. She continued to talk to calm her nerves. "But I don't think that I should go to my place to get them. The police could be looking for me there."

Sienna looked over at Dawn's closet, where a colorful knapsack hung on the door. The vibrant hues reminded her of her friend, of her zest for life and of the inspiration she never shied away from giving,

Once again Sienna mustered her determination. She turned to Hawk. "Go for it."

It didn't take long before all the arrangements were made. His call to the island had been well received, and Sienna had thrown a few of Dawn's clothes into the knapsack. She decided she could buy sandals and whatever other articles she might need once she arrived.

"If we hurry, we can catch the next American Airlines flight, which leaves in two and a half hours. I told Mickey that will be the flight we'll be taking. We'll make a couple of stopovers— one in Miami, another in San Juan—before we actually fly into Fort-de-France. Mickey will meet us in the main customs office, and we'll simply go from there."

Sienna realized she was swallowing hard. No one could have told her yesterday that she would be flying to Martinique with a man she had just met and who still remained an enigma. How quickly one's life could be turned inside out in a matter of hours, she thought.

She had never before been outside the States,

and now she was embarking on a mission that she had no idea how she would accomplish. All of a sudden Sienna's legs felt like water and she had to brace herself against the dresser in order not to fall. Luckily, Hawk's back was turned, and she was glad he did not see her in her moment of weakness.

For the first time since her parents' deaths Sienna's heart beseeched, without anger, the very source she had denied. Under her breath, her eyes closed, her lips formed a silent prayer. "I am willing to face whatever is in store for me if you will be there."

Hawk's deep voice reached out to her just as she opened her eyes.

"I called a cab. It should be here any minute. Are you ready?"

Sienna pushed away from her makeshift crutch, drawing herself up straight and tall. "I guess I'm as ready as I'm ever going to be."

With her consent, they headed for the door.

Five

The airplane circled for the last time, drawing closer to the island. Looking out the window, Sienna noted that Martinique resembled a large green leaf floating in an expanse of turquoise blue. Even from the air, she could tell it was very different from any place she had ever been. The island seemed to exude a kind of mystique, a place that possessed secrets.

The captain's voice over the loudspeaker announced their descent. Sienna gave the woman who sat beside her a slight smile as she timidly leaned toward the window, attempting to get a better view of the tropical island.

She listened to the roar of the flaps as they extended out of the plane's wings. Anxiety welled up inside her, mingling with anticipation. Now that she could see the island, it made what was happening to her seem that much more real.

All of a sudden she had the strangest feeling, a kind of déjà vu. It was if she had been catapulted into a dream, one that had commenced long before she was born. Somehow Sienna understood that what she was doing now was fulfilling her role.

Several rows ahead, Hawk's head rose above

his seat; because of their quick departure, they had not been assigned seats together. Actually, Sienna was glad. It had given her a little time to think about and adjust to their strange and developing relationship.

It was clear from the way he had been able to arrange their hasty trip to Martinique that Hawk was a man very capable of taking care of business, and if all the other talents he claimed to possess were true, he would prove to be invaluable. Sienna had to admit his presence comforted her, but she warned herself not to become too dependent on this man whom she knew so little about. Yes, she realized there was no way to ignore the fact that he had arranged for all her physical needs, and she appreciated it; still, she would not allow herself to become psychologically dependent on him.

Landing at the Lamentin International Airport was nothing like the hustle and bustle of Hartsfield, where planes waited their turn to touch down. Once they were on the ground and began to taxi up to the building, Sienna noticed their craft was the only one in sight.

She felt dog-tired as they entered the small airport, Hawk walking in silence beside her. Perhaps it was the combination of plane hopping and everything else that had occurred, but she longed for a place to lie her head down and truly rest, if only for a short while. As they approached the customs agents Hawk took the initiative, greeting them and speaking briefly in French. In reply a uniformed attendant pointed toward an office several yards away, before turning back to the next traveler in line.

"So amongst your many talents, you speak

French, too?" Sienna couldn't pass up the opportunity to bait him.

"Nothing more than your basics. I picked up
a few words in my travels. Just enough to get
around."

"Well, good. That's one thing I have that you
don't. I do pretty well when it comes to French.
One of the women who ran the orphanage, Mrs.
Arnette, had a mother who was French. I acquired a pretty good command of the language
from her."

"You lived in an orphanage?" Hawk's voice
was low as his amber eyes searched her tired
face.

"Yes. So you see, you're not the only one who
has secrets." Sienna gave him a beguiling smile
as he opened the office door, allowing her to
enter first.

"Hennessy Jackson."

Sienna's head was turned in Hawk's direction
when she heard the name, and when she faced
the speaker she was taken by surprise. An attractive, vivacious, dark-skinned woman with
shiny, dark eyes and full features, dressed in a
bright, colorful headdress and a suit, had her
arms stretched out in welcome.

"Mickey Audell" was Hawk's reply, then the
nearest thing to a smile Sienna had ever seen
on his staunch features crossed his face.

"You must give me a hug, *mon chou*. It's been
much too long," the woman enunciated, her accent giving the words an even more sensuous
lilt.

More eagerly than Sienna would expect, Hawk
wrapped Mickey in his strong embrace, nearly
sweeping her off the floor. Feeling as if she

were spying on a very private reunion, Sienna looked over at the customs officer who stood near a desk. Unlike her, he was oblivious to the couple, his mind seemingly focused on the mound of papers that lay in front of him.

Once the woman's enamored repeating of his name died down, Hawk extracted himself from her clinging arms and turned toward Sienna.

"Sienna Russell, this is Michelle Fournier, better known as Mickey. She is the curator at the museum here in Fort-de-France."

"Hello, Ms. Audell. Nice to meet you."

Sienna felt as if she were talking to herself, it was so hard for Mickey to pull her gaze away from Hawk's face.

With a kind of delayed reaction, Mickey finally said, "Ah, *bonjour,* Sienna. It is good to meet you as well. Of course, you are the reason we are in here, *vrai?*" She poured on a genuine smile, which added even more sparkle to her large eyes, if that were humanly possible.

Sienna could tell Mickey was reluctant to leave Hawk's side, but she did so out of necessity as she crossed the room to address the customs officer. After a small chat that was laced with familiarity, along with a little uneasiness on the customs officer's part, Mickey signed the paper he presented, then beckoned for Hawk and Sienna to do the same. After the paperwork was completed, and Mickey and the officer had said their goodbyes, the three of them headed out the door.

"In case you were wondering about the paper we just signed," Mickey explained, "it simply verified that you are in Martinique as my guests. I would even go so far as to call you business acquaintances who are expected to work with me on a few things at the museum." She gesticulated expressively. "I have done this before in the past, legitimately so, with visiting museum personnel."

"We appreciate your help." Hawk looked down at the willing female who remained by his side. "Now we have to get ourselves situated in a hotel. If Sienna feels anything like I do, I know she must be tired." He turned toward Sienna, and just as she had begun to nod her head in agreement, Mickey's lilting voice chimed in.

"Hotel? *C'est non.* No way have you finally come back to Martinique that I am going to see you here at the airport for a brief while, only to let you disappear in some hotel. I have plenty of room in my house for the both of you." She placed her hand on his arm. "I am doing quite well for myself, Hennessy. It's not like the days when we were still struggling students in graduate school."

"I don't know, Mickey. We're really pressed for time, and we've got our work cut out for us."

"Work. Work. That is my magic word. I know about that, if nothing else." Mickey allowed her head to tilt proudly. "But I still say since you are tired and I have plenty of beds, my home is open to the both of you. And as far as the work goes, you never know, I could be of help. This island is my home, and whatever the reason may be that you are here, I could prove to be quite useful."

Hawk looked at Mickey, then his amber gaze rested on Sienna, who raised her shoulders in a slight shrug as she stared back at him.

"I will be greatly offended, Hennessy Jackson,

if you do not take me up on my invitation,"
Mickey insisted, her voice taking on an emphatic
edge.

"All right, Mickey." His eyes became hooded.
"How can I refuse?"

"C'est bon." Mickey's blood-red pouty lips
turned up in a vibrant smile again. "We need
to get your luggage, and my car is parked out
on the road back this way"—she pointed delicately.

"What you see is all we have," Hawk informed
her.

Mickey looked at Hawk's leather carrier, then
at Sienna's colorful knapsack. Afterward, her
mascaraed eyes took in Sienna's rumpled jeans
and shirt, halting on her face and unkempt hair.

"Well, you must have been in a very big hurry
to come so . . . ill prepared." Sienna recognized
a mischievous glow in the depths of Mickey's
eyes.

With all that had happened to her, Sienna was
in no mood for female backbiting. Not even
from this woman who had extended her hospitality.

"Maybe if I had known the reception would
be so colorful"—she stared at the headpiece the
woman wore with her conservatively styled suit—"I
would have made arrangements to wear something
more appropriate."

Mickey released a gay-hearted laugh that Sienna was certain covered more snide emotions.

"You are talking about my *madras*"—she patted
the bolts of colorful material piled high atop her
head. "It is most definitely Martiniquan, and not
something that I normally wear. As a matter of
fact, I wore it for Hennessy's benefit."

Hawk's eyebrows shot up in a quizzical fashion.

"Have you forgotten, or maybe you never knew?" Mickey prodded him. "How long ago was it that you came here? Four or five years? And your stay was so short, you may not have known of this tradition." Her eyes glistened as she spoke. Mickey took Hawk's arm as they headed in the direction of the car.

"You can tell by the number of points on a woman's *madras* what her marital status is. If I were married, four points would let an interested party know that I'm still open to possibilities, three would simply state that I am a married woman, and two would say I'm engaged."

"But you only have one," Hawk commented as he looked down into her beaming face.

"I can tell you are still as smart as you used to be," Mickey teased. "One means I am available." She held his gaze.

Hawk rubbed the bottom of his chin with the back of his hand before replying, "I'll keep that in mind."

Sienna could barely hear Hawk's response, but hear it she did, and for some reason the whole exchange didn't sit too well with her. Intentionally, she began to walk a couple of steps behind, observing this woman who had obvious plans for the man beside her.

Sienna noticed how the royal-blue suit Mickey wore accentuated her bountiful hips, bust line, and waist, and she couldn't help but be aware of her own less-endowed form.

Since the days of her childhood, she had always been told she was pretty. It was the one thing in life on which she had been able to count. A smile given to a cafeteria worker at The Children's Sanctuary had always yielded a more generous portion of food, and as an adult Sienna had witnessed a certain kind of eagerness on the parts of both males and females to be in her presence. She had experienced a sense of power in the way she looked, and although she had never abused it, Sienna was glad it was there, for underneath it all lurked a distinct feeling of loss. For no matter how beautiful she appeared to the outside world, the loss of her parents at an early age, along with the accompanying feeling of abandonment, had left a tender scar.

The three of them climbed into a shiny black car parked on the outskirts of the airport, and once Mickey began to drive, they were instantly thrust into downtown Fort-de-France. They hadn't gone far before Sienna reacted like a child enthralled with unfamiliar sights, her face remaining perpetually fixed on the rear window. Needless to say, the island city was a far cry from Atlanta, Georgia, and a farther one still from Campbell, Alabama.

Mickey was adept at maneuvering their vehicle through the narrow streets lined with pastel buildings, all decorated with ornate wrought iron balconies. To Sienna the scene was like a live painting, illuminated by enchanting sunshine. The buildings gleamed a soft pink, green, and beige, while the people's skin tones were a multitude of shades clothed in a rainbow of vibrant colors.

Sienna had forgotten her uneasy feelings of moments ago, the magic of the island having totally swept away her real reason for being there.

"Sienna," Hawk called from the front, "have you ever been to the French Quarter in New Orleans?"

"No," she replied, still taking in the scenery. "The farthest I've ever been from Atlanta is Savannah, Georgia."

"Well, Fort-de-France is very much like the French Quarter, except that the Quarter is flat and Fort-de-France, as you can tell, is very hilly."

"Ahh. It is gorgeous." Her voice was a combination of pleasure and awe.

"So you like my island," Mickey surmised. "I forgot, how do you say it in the States . . . you ain't seen nothing yet? Wait 'til you see my place, Hennessy. It is French colonial traditional, like the buildings you see here, but it sits facing the Caribbean Sea."

They continued to travel eastward, and through the rear window Sienna could see businesses and houses clinging to the hillsides behind downtown Fort-de-France. As she settled back into her seat again, the landscape began to change. Sprawling suburbs began to sprinkle the area as the car climbed, leaving behind the more organized communities, yielding to an array of expensive homes nestled attractively against lush hills.

Finally, they entered a modest wrought iron gate that enclosed a driveway, sandwiched between tropical trees ranging from mango to coconut. Before long the controlled forest thinned into a wonderful garden. To Sienna, it was like the Garden of Eden. Flowers of all colors and sizes abounded.

Before she knew it, an involuntary gasp escaped her lips as she watched hummingbirds dip their tiny beaks into the fragrant centers of colorful hibiscus, their minute wings vibrating at an incredible speed. Although the air was filled with a flowing dichotomy of nature's sounds, Sienna could still feel a calmness in the balmy breeze, and she was absolutely amazed at the beauty she was blessed to behold.

Finally, the house appeared, a two-story beige building wrapped in a maze of wrought iron. It possessed a special distinctive air and the sight of it caught her by surprise, for up until then it had been hidden behind a thick ridge of trees.

"This is it," Mickey announced as they pulled up beside another much older vehicle nestled beneath a three-car arched carport. Moments later, Sienna was following Mickey and Hawk up a sidewalk lined with all kinds of flora, including a waxy, ancient-looking plant that Mickey called an anthurium.

"I thought I would bring you in through the front door. The house shows better that way," Mickey commented as she pressed against the thick wood portal.

Inside they were greeted by tiny rainbows of color, the offspring of an elaborate chandelier hanging in the foyer. From what Sienna could see, there was a feeling of airiness throughout, although the house itself was well furnished with something of cultural significance in every nook and cranny.

"Sylvie," Mickey called loudly, but she need not have done so, for a young girl appeared before the second syllable of her name was pronounced.

"Yes, Sylvie, would you please show *Mademoiselle* Russell to the third bedroom upstairs and put *Monsieur* Jackson in the second bedroom down here on the main floor." She turned to her guests. "I'm sure from what you've told me that you want to relax for a while, and I've got some phone calls to make. So just make yourself at home, and I'll tell Josephine to have dinner ready in a couple of hours," Mickey informed them, before bestowing a lingering smile on Hawk.

Following her mistress's instructions, Sylvie stepped forward to direct them as Mickey disappeared around the corner. She was a shapely young girl of about fifteen years, who wore her thick, coarse hair high on her head in a ponytail.

"Would you come this way, please," she said in a soft but clear voice as she walked toward a wide hallway lavishly decorated with Martiniquan art.

"This is *Mademoiselle* Audell's *chambre,*"—she pointed to the first door that they passed—"and this one will be yours, *monsieur.*" She pushed open a door several yards away, then stepped aside to allow Hawk to enter.

Unbeknownst to Sylvie, one of Sienna's eyebrows rose in mock surprise as she gave Hawk a pointed stare. But to her dismay he ignored the innuendo, perturbing Sienna all the more, for he was pretending not to notice how conveniently close Mickey had placed his bedroom to hers.

Stepping inside the room to have a look, Sienna had to admit it had been tastefully decorated in earthtones, with just the right amount of accents.

"I hope you find everything to be comfortable," the girl added in a heavily accented voice. "If you need anything, just pull the cord and I will answer as soon as I can."

Sienna sidled up to Hawk and spoke so that only he could hear. "I'm sure there must be another cord attached to Mickey's bedroom, since she is obviously into convenience." Before he could reply, she turned and walked back out into the hall without a second glance. As Sylvie closed the door behind them, Sienna could feel Hawk's burning gaze upon her back.

"This way, *mademoiselle,*" Sylvie directed as she started back up the hallway, her slim back ramrod straight, her hands folded neatly behind her. "We must climb the stairs in order to reach your room."

Sienna couldn't help but marvel at Sylvie's mature countenance, and she loved the way she spoke. Sienna realized that Sylvie was much more worldly than she recalled being at that age.

"So, Sylvie, are you a relative of Mickey's?"

"Mais non" was her quick negative reply. It was the first hint of spontaneous emotion Sienna had detected in the girl's voice.

"I simply live here with *Mademoiselle* Audell and her grandfather. I come from a large family, and it was in everyone's best interest when I moved here. *Mademoiselle* is making sure that I receive a proper education, and I am well taken care of. In return I do chores around the house . . . run errands or whatever else she may need."

"Oh, I see." Sienna became very pensive as

she followed the girl up the stairs. "In the United States, that kind of living arrangement isn't usually done."

"Is that so?" Sylvie stopped in front of one of the doors, genuinely surprised. "It is quite common in this part of the world—the Caribbean, I mean. I must admit I've heard some horror stories where children are taken in and abused, but overall the system has worked quite well for everyone involved." She appeared to try to take on an even more sophisticated look in light of Sienna's ignorance. "Those who have more are willing to share with those who are less fortunate. We understand that here." She turned the doorknob and stepped inside.

"This is your room, *mademoiselle*. Just like *Monsieur* Jackson, you have your own private bath. This is your cord"—she wiggled an elaborately twisted rope. "Just pull it whenever you need anything."

"*Merci,* Sylvie."

Sienna was pleased to see the girl's eyes light up just from a thank-you spoken in her native French. "I appreciate your showing me to my room, and thanks also for the mini lesson in Martiniquan culture."

Sienna watched a wide smile sweep across Sylvie's face, instantly changing her from a young girl who had a need to feel older than she actually was into simply a young girl.

She waited until Sylvie closed the door behind her, before she really surveyed the room. It was a tad smaller than Hawk's quarters, and the dominant colors were a rich blend of mauve and deep rose. A large, colorful rug graced the high-gloss wooden floor that ended at the bathroom, where an imported tile began. Sienna walked over to the window and became captivated by the view. Her bedroom, like the two below, was in the back of the building, set high on a hill that commanded a wondrous view of the Caribbean Sea.

A light knock interrupted her thoughts.

"Come in," Sienna called out as she turned around.

"Mademoiselle, here is the bathrobe and slippers *Mademoiselle* Audell told me to give you." Sylvie slid the packaged robe onto a small table beside the door. "I was also told to inform you that there are clothes in the closet that would probably fit you, if you care to look through them. *Mademoiselle* Audell has so many clothes, she no longer wears them all." The girl glanced down at the floor. "Plus, they are no longer her size." A sparkle filled her eyes when she looked up once again. "I will leave you alone now. You won't be disturbed again until dinnertime." With that, she closed the door quietly.

Well, I won't be wearing any of Mickey's discards, Sienna thought belligerently. Still, she found herself at the closet, pushing aside the sliding glass door. Of course, it had been quite obvious from the house and all that Mickey fared quite well financially, and the clothes Sienna saw hanging before her attested to the same.

Leaving the closet door ajar and feeling a little annoyed, Sienna crossed to the bed, where she had deposited Dawn's knapsack. She knew it wasn't like her to assume such a catty attitude, but Mickey had made her feelings quite plain from the start. She hadn't waited to find out if Sienna and Hawk had a special kind of relationship, because in her mind it did not matter.

Mickey had her own agenda, and although there was virtually nothing between her and Hawk, Sienna still resented her pushy attitude.

Deep in thought, Sienna picked up the knapsack and began to remove its contents. Just seeing the clothes was a jolt of reality, rekindling the real reason she was in Martinique. This was not a sunny vacation in the Caribbean. She was here because of William's threats and to ensure Dawn's safety.

She sank down on the bed with her elbows on her knees and her face in her hands. Despite the sunshine that flowed through the window, her heart was instantly heavy. Images of what Dawn might be facing assaulted her, then rapidly evolved into what might lie ahead in her own future. How quickly had her thoughts changed from frivolity to the issue of life and death.

Determined to keep her spirits high, Sienna laid out the few articles of clothing she had brought with her: a pair of jeans and two shirts, along with the suit she had worn to the funeral. A meager lot compared with the wardrobe that hung only a few yards away.

She had never been the kind of woman to buy impractical things. Even with the money she had inherited when she turned twenty-one, Sienna had never indulged herself by buying more than she actually needed. Perhaps it was the result of the frugal life she had lived in the orphanage, but she had saved as much of her inheritance as she could in order to open The Stonekeeper.

Sienna had always dreamed of having a business of her own. Someplace where she would be totally in control, making her own money. A place that no one could ever take away.

As she looked back now, opening The Stone-keeper had been a lifelong venture. Stones had always fascinated her, and ever since Mrs. Arnette first displayed her rock collection, she and the older woman had become fast friends at the orphanage. Soon Sienna learned that doing extra chores at The Sanctuary would earn her money to buy rocks, or maybe even an extraordinary stone brought back by Mrs. Arnette from one of her many excursions. When Mrs. Arnette passed away, she left her stone collection to Sienna; indeed, this collection was the first thing she put on special display at The Stonekeeper.

Sienna attempted to smooth out the deep wrinkles and creases in her suit, but it was in vain. She knew Mickey would probably be dressed in her finest, continuing her attempt to arouse Hawk. Not that it mattered in the least to her. After all, she had no special feelings for Hawk, she told herself.

But still he remained in her thoughts, for he was such a strange man, and Sienna knew she had never really been allowed to see him for who he was. The man she had met on the farm had been unnaturally cold, and initially, he had sparked a chord of fear within her. His energy had been like that of a caged tiger. A tiger who, if it ever got the opportunity to be free, would never be caged or controlled again. Yes, there had been moments when he had softened toward her, but they were like small cracks in his iron-clad veil, begrudgedly given as if he wanted no part of them.

No, Sienna concluded. All she wanted from Hawk were the things he had promised. His expertise and knowledge in helping her find the ruby.

From out of the blue, a shiver coursed through her as her mind conjured up the smooth softness of his lips. Shocked by the vividness of her memory, Sienna's hand shot to her mouth as if to shield it, and she shook her head in an effort to block out the incident. She could not deny she found him physically attractive. Any woman would, and with the pressure she was under there was no wonder she was so susceptible to his touch.

Sienna determined to do everything she could to keep him at a distance. He was not the kind of man to whom any woman should open her heart, for he would not be interested. In other things, yes, but not in her heart.

Sienna walked over to the closet and closed it firmly. She decided that whatever Mickey had planned for Hawk it did not matter, as long as it didn't interfere with their reason for being in Martinique.

She gathered up all the articles of clothing in her arms and laid them neatly across a chair, placing her clean jeans and a shirt on top. They would suffice for dinner. She would not parade around in Mickey's clothes for anyone's benefit, but most of all, Sienna told herself, she was not competing for Hawk's affection.

With her mind focused and her body exhausted, Sienna picked up the new robe and slippers and entered the bath. She would bathe and take a nap before dinner.

Six

"So, how do you like it?" Mickey asked gaily, her soup spoon balanced flamboyantly in her hand.

"It's spicy but quite delicious," Sienna answered truthfully. "What is it called?"

"It's a creole fish soup. It's quite popular here. But of course, no one makes it as good as Josephine does." Mickey's voice rose an octave as she turned toward the door from which Sylvie had been bobbing in and out.

"Sylvie, pour me some more champagne, *s'il vous plaît,* and *Mademoiselle* Russell and *Monsieur* Jackson as well. Oh"—she stopped as she looked at Sienna's glass that was nearly full—"You have not drank much at all. Don't you like the champagne?"

"Yes, it's fine. I'm just not much of a drinker, that's all."

"Shame on you, right, Hennessy? I think between the two of us, we have downed at least a bottle and a half, and the main course has not even been served yet."

In a gallant manner that was definitely exaggerated, Hawk held his empty glass out toward Mickey.

"As I recall, this was one of the areas that we both excelled in at graduate school, was it not?"

"Yes, but I wish we had excelled in other things." Mickey's voice dropped to a seductive low.

"Still the same old Mickey." Hawk awarded her with a wry smile.

Sienna looked back down at her soup. They hadn't been at the table for more than thirty minutes, and already Mickey had her seduction act in high gear. She looked up again and found Hawk's gaze resting on her. Sienna did not falter under his probing stare; instead, she returned it. She wanted him to know that, unlike Mickey, his masculine allure would be wasted on her. He and Mickey could play cat and mouse all night, but she was strictly here for business.

During the first few moments of the evening, just after the sun had set, Sienna noticed Hawk appeared to be on edge, and no matter how Mickey attempted to entice him into a conversation, his responses had been stilted. Then finally he downed a full glass of champagne in several gulps, placing the crystal on the table with a clink. Mickey had reacted with overzealous encouragement while Sienna had sat quietly, wondering what had brought on the obvious change. It was as if he were holding his own celebration . . . as if in some way he had beaten the odds.

Hawk lifted his glass as Sylvie filled it almost to the rim. He had not expected the Stonekeeper to be a young, attractive woman. Someone who would tug at emotions he had long denied.

His amber eyes studied the look of disapproval on Sienna's face. He wondered if it reflected her feelings for him. On every occasion she had submitted to his help only after she believed she had no other choice. Why did she find him unacceptable even after he had shown his trustworthiness? Could she feel the instability within him that lurked just beneath the surface?

Hawk recalled how her mouth had succumbed to his mere hours ago. Did she rebuke herself for allowing it? She was such a strong-willed, beautiful woman, he thought.

His eyes narrowed as he watched her, and despite his feelings of inadequacy, he longed to feel the softness of her lips again. But Sienna's apparent disdain caused him to want to rile her.

"So, Sienna, are you the only sober and chaste vessel here?" Hawk's highly suggestive question was not lost on Mickey. "That champagne flute has barely touched your lips," his deep voice continued to prod her.

"If you consider my not indulging as much as you chaste . . . well, so be it," Sienna replied, overly aware of Mickey's eagle eye on the two of them.

His gaze lowered to the wide view of cleavage above the knitted top Sienna wore. It had not occurred to her when she stuffed it inside the knapsack how much smaller Dawn was than she. The bright purple top clung to her frame, the scallops that surrounded the neckline stretching across the tops of her round breasts.

"Hennessy." The name was spoken almost too sharply to be considered polite. "How has life been treating you over the last five years?" Mickey commanded his attention.

"It's been interesting, Mickey." He twirled the champagne glass between his fingers. "I've been a lot of places, met a lot of people, and I've done okay financially. I can see you haven't done too badly yourself." Hawk looked around the large, immaculately decorated dining room. "Not bad for a young woman who claimed to come from meager beginnings and who had a yearning to know all there was about hiero-glyphics."

"So you both studied archaeology in grad school? Is that how you met?" Sienna inquired.

"Yes, we met in grad school, but Mickey was the one who was totally into archaeology, I just kind of dabbled a little."

"And what a dabbler you were." Mickey put her hand behind her head and leaned her face into her arm. "You might as well have been an archaeology major. You spent more time exam-ining artifacts than did some of the regular ar-chaeology students. And then one day you just up and disappeared. Poof"—her red lips re-mained in an exaggerated circle—"without a sin-gle word."

"Yeah." A mask descended over Hawk's fea-tures. "I had some heavy things go down around that time."

"You could have at least said *au revoir*, Hen-nessy," she continued to admonish him. "I didn't know what had happened to you, and I had no way of finding you. A year and a half went by before I heard from you again. And by then I was back here in my native country. The only reason you contacted me then was because of work." She leaned forward, her heavy bosom heaving underneath the thin material of her blouse. "You came and you went. But this time I won't let you get away from me so easily."

One corner of Hawk's full lips lifted in what was supposed to be a smile, but to Sienna it resembled a snarl.

"Be careful, Mickey, or you'll have us taking you seriously."

The swinging door opened once more, and Sylvie entered carrying a large steaming container. It was obvious she was laboring hard under the weight of it. She almost made it to the table but then she stumbled, spilling some of the hot liquid on the elaborate rug. Instantly, Sienna was out of her chair, taking the heavy container away from the girl and asking if she was okay.

"Oui. Oui. I'm fine, *mademoiselle,"* Sylvie responded, her large eyes full of trepidation.

"You should not be so clumsy, Sylvie," Mickey scolded her. *"Mon Dieu,* look at my rug. You get something to clean it up. Right now."

Sylvie nearly ran from the room in tears.

"The container was rather heavy even for me, Mickey. Maybe she shouldn't have been carrying it in the first place." Sienna could not hold her tongue. From personal experience, she knew there were some things children could do and others they could not.

"That's what I tell her all the time." An older man with grey hair and a mustache entered the room. "She's got enough money to do whatever she wants. But she's always getting children to do the work that only adults should do. But that's because they serve her purposes well. *Ce n'est pas vrai,* Michelle? Is that not right?" His red eyes became even cloudier. "I remember a time when my unique needs depended on my dear Michelle and her doings. But that was long ago." The old man's head dropped forward heavily and he weaved a bit on his feet, then his head popped up abruptly. "But you will discover that Michelle is very protective of what goes on around here."

Mickey's eyes nearly flashed fire as the man walked past them with the distinct smell of liquor emanating from him. Unceremoniously, he plopped down in a chair with no table setting.

"Papa George, I thought you were going to be out of town for the next few days. I did not expect you would be having dinner with us tonight." Her lips trembled with repressed emotion. "You see I did not have Sylvie set a place for you."

"You never have Sylvie set a place for me. But that's okay. I'm not offended. I'll just use this fancy little plate right here that you've set aside for your used utensils and such. That will be good enough for me." George sat up straight but he still appeared to slouch, because the shirt he wore hung on his lean frame at an angle.

Mickey nodded her head as if she were trying to maintain her control.

"Well, I want to introduce Papa George, my . . . grandfather."

George looked at her with a slight smirk on his face.

"Papa George, this is Sienna Russell and Hennessy Jackson."

"Hennessy Jackson. I vaguely remember Michelle mentioning you before. You were the one who attended that school with her in the United States, and you came here a few years ago."

"That's right," Hawk agreed.

"*Oui,* as I recall, Michelle had a special interest in you."

"Papa George," Mickey cut him off. "I don't need for you to tell them about my special interests. If I choose to, I will do that myself."

George ignored Mickey and leaned away from the table, aligning himself so that he could see Sylvie, who was busy cleaning the rug. "Ah, there she is. How is *ma fille* today?"

Sylvie acknowledged George with a timid smile, but she never stopped her scrubbing motion.

"When you are done there, little one, bring Uncle George a fork and a knife, so I can dive into this grilled shrimp." He threw his head back, his wide nostrils sniffing the air. "The sauce smells hot and garlicky. Just as I like it."

Mickey let go of a nervous laugh. "Good. I hope everyone likes it. Go ahead"—she motioned toward Sienna and Hawk. "Try it."

For a while the dinner proceeded under an awkward silence, although Sienna thoroughly enjoyed the food, which included rice, asparagus, and plantains. As they waited for Sylvie to serve dessert, Mickey decided to put on some music.

"Do you like soka?" she asked over her shoulder, dancing even before the music began. "It's one of my favorite sounds," Mickey continued, as if she really didn't expect an answer.

As the steady blend of Latin and Caribbean rhythms filled the air, the larger woman began to move subtly to the beats. Her movements were extremely sensuous, and Sienna couldn't help but wonder what Hawk thought of them. But once again she found his eyes riveted on her instead of on the enticing spectacle Mickey made.

"So, how do you like that music, Sienna?" he queried, his words only loud enough for her to hear. "You look like the type of woman who could really make some interesting moves if you put your mind to it." Hawk rubbed the rim of the champagne glass against his lips. "How about it? Do you think I'll be blessed with such a provocative sight before the night is over?"

His gaze was so intense, Sienna felt as if it were melting the clothes right off her, and despite herself, her heart began to beat a little faster.

"I didn't come all the way to Martinique just to entertain you, Hawk. I think you've forgotten the real reason we're here."

"No, that's just it. I'm more than a little aware of it. More aware than you would ever know." He took a couple of swallows of champagne. "Life is such an interesting adventure, Sienna, with unexpected twists and turns. There's no telling what might happen to either one of us even before tomorrow"—his gaze bore into her. "I think that we should take advantage of any and all pleasurable opportunities that we can."

"*Mon Dieu,* it's getting warm in here," Mickey commented loudly, and she began to undo the small buttons along the front of her large, thin top. After she finished, her well-endowed body was on display in an emerald-green body suit, and for the first time Sienna noticed the vibrant ruby that hung from her neck on a gold chain.

"Now, that's better," Mickey cooed, before picking up a bottle of vintage rum from the wet bar and making her way to the table.

"Care for some with a little pineapple juice?"

She leaned over to serve Hawk, flaunting her chocolate breasts and the ruby.

"Why not?" he answered, his eyes glued to Sienna's face.

Mickey's yielding smile almost turned rock hard, but she managed to continue her hostess duties, pouring Sienna a bit of the dark brew, then passing the pitcher of fresh juice.

"You forgot about me," George called from the end of the table, "but I can see why: I don't have a glass." There was mockery in his voice.

"From some of the things you said earlier, I believe you've already had more than enough to drink," Mickey admonished him.

George ignored her as he got up from the table, taking another flute from a magnificent case. Afterward, he walked over to Mickey and took the entire bottle before saying a perfunctory, *"Merci."*

"That's quite a lovely necklace you are wearing." Sienna stared at the gem that sparkled against Mickey's dark skin. "It is a ruby, isn't it?"

"Yes." She fingered the smooth stone. "It is one of my favorites."

"I guess there are all kinds of gems available here in the islands, and I've heard all kinds of stories." Sienna picked her words carefully. "I'm sure you have, too. So many people travel from faraway places just to purchase jewelry in the Caribbean."

"Mais oui, the islands are full of gems and full of stories. In both categories there are those you cannot trust, but there are others"—a strange look surfaced in Mickey's eyes—"that you might think are unbelievable, but they are the ones that are really true."

"I can think of a few stories myself," George commented before emptying his glass, his words a little slurred.

"Can you really?" Sienna looked nervously across the table at Hawk.

"Sure I can," George boasted. "We are rich in folklore here on the island of flowers. We have as many stories as there are flowers." He leaned forward, placing both hands on the table. "Pick a color. Any color. I bet we have a stor-ry." He wagged his finger in the air.

Sienna swallowed hard. "All right"—she turned and looked directly at George—"ruby red."

"Uh-oh, you are good. You are real good." George leaned his head against the high-backed chair. Then he looked at Sienna, a strange seriousness behind his red eyes. "Have I got a story for you." He paused. "Or maybe I should let Michelle tell it. From what I can remember, it is one of her favorites. Tell them, Michelle." His liquor-filled eyes tried to focus on her. "Tell them the story of the Passion Ruby."

Sienna's heart almost stopped beating at the mention of the name, her gaze locked with Hawk's. She couldn't believe the man. George had actually said *the Passion Ruby!* She tried hard not to show how strongly his words had affected her.

"The Passion Ruby." The words sounded breathless even to her own ears. "What a name for a story."

"*Mon Dieu,* Papa George"—Mickey fluttered her hand in front of her face—"no one wants to hear such fairy tales tonight. It's just a superstitious island story, that's all. I'm sure Sienna wouldn't be interested in hearing it."

"Oh, but I would." Sienna attempted to keep her voice even.

"You heard her, Michelle. The young woman wants to hear the story. Of course, I could tell them my version of it, starting with the letter that is connected with the stone, which you personally tested to find out how old it was."

Mickey sat stark still as George spoke.

It was Hawk who broke the silence.

"You actually have a letter that is associated with this legendary ruby?"

"*Oui,* it is purported to be associated with the stone, but no one has actually ever seen it." Mickey shifted her weight uncomfortably. "And once you hear the story, you will know there is no truth in it. It is too farfetched."

"At the moment, I'm willing to listen to anything. So try me, and let me be the judge of that."

"Since you insist . . ." She drew in a deep breath. "Let me see how well my memory serves me." Her eyes became riveted on Papa George. "It is said the stone was found outside of Paris, France, over two hundred years ago by four women who came to be known as the Fabulous Four. They came across it when they were very young women trespassing on private property. The story goes that during their explorations of a stream, they found an intricately carved jade box nearly buried at the edge. When they finally dug it up, it is said, they found two rubies inside, and there was also the letter."

Mickey became silent.

"Is that all?" Sienna looked from Mickey to

George. "That doesn't sound so hard to believe. How did it become a legend here in Martinique, and why the name the Passion Ruby?"

"As she said, two rubies were found. One was simply an ornament, but the other ruby was believed to possess unusual powers," George picked up the tale. "They say when the stones are used during an ancient orgiastic ritual, the person performing the rites is endowed with unimaginable passion, longevity, and prosperity. So it is called the Passion Ruby." He paused for a moment. "The story became known here in Martinique when the women erected a kind of temple to have their rituals. They say it was around 1789 when the French Revolution encouraged those of us of color to fight for our emancipation."

"But you say no one has ever really seen the stone," Sienna pressed the issue.

"No it has never been found," Mickey answered, while George picked his fingernails.

The serving door swung open again, and this time Sylvie entered with a tray of desserts.

"Ah, we are having one of my favorites tonight," Mickey sighed. "Guava tarts."

Sylvie had regained her composure and was able to serve the desserts with a practiced hand. Once she had served everyone, she turned to Mickey.

"Will that be all, *mademoiselle?*"

"*Oui,* Sylvie. Now go and help Josephine clean up the kitchen, and you will be finished for the night."

The young girl nodded her head before exiting the room.

The guava tarts went fast, except for Sienna's.

She was too deep in thought to eat the dark jelly-filled pastry. Sienna was certain the ruby that Mickey and George spoke of in the story was the one she had come to Martinique to find. Yet Mickey had said no one had ever seen it. Was the Passion Ruby simply a figment of someone's imagination? If that were true, what would she tell William that would appease him? He was dead set on owning the ruby her Aunt Jessi had probably spoken of during the last days of her life. He would not be willing to accept that the ruby was simply a legend. He had been convinced otherwise after seeing the emerald Janice claimed she had gotten from Aunt Jessi.

Sienna began to notice the effect the large quantities of champagne and rum were having on the people around her. More and more often Mickey's bejeweled hand reached out to touch Hawk's hand, arm, and face, while at the other end of the table George had fallen almost into a drunken stupor. Every once in a while his head would loll to the side and he would right it with a jerk. She and Hawk were the only two who appeared to be fairly sober. Like hers, his thoughts seemed to have turned inward, for he paid little attention to Mickey's advances.

"It was a wonderful dinner, Mickey," Sienna announced, "and I appreciate your hospitality, but from the way I feel I think it's time for me to go upstairs to bed. It's been a long day, and I believe we've got quite a bit ahead of us tomorrow." She moved her chair away from the table and stood up.

Sienna tried to ignore Hawk's amber gaze, which followed her every move. For a moment she felt awkward as his eyes slowly took in her

fitted sweater and tight jeans, then rose again
to her face.

"So you've decided to deny us the further
pleasure of your presence, Ms. Russell?" The
silky, taunting question hung in the air.

"If you're asking me if I'm leaving, yes, I am.
I believe I have had all I can take for one night."
The glib words rolled off her tongue before she
could stop them. "Good night, everyone."

Sienna was aware of Mickey's satisfied eyes
shining brightly. She turned and walked out of
The room, disconcerted by the jealousy that
boiled within her.

Seven

Sienna entered her bedroom and closed the door. In minutes she was out of her clothes and had donned, as a makeshift nightgown, the slip she'd worn under her suit.

She thought of the embarrassing words that had slipped out moments before. It wasn't like her to be so short of patience. She wondered if she felt more for Hawk than she had admitted to herself.

Sienna turned and looked at her reflection in a freestanding oval mirror, and was drawn closer to the glass as her gaze rested on the mark between her breasts. Slowly, she stroked the tiny, dark spot that she had naturally come to accept as a birthmark. With her finger, she traced the edges that clearly formed the shape of a crystal. Her thoughts became tinged with skepticism. Considering the weakness she had shown only moments before, she wondered, Am I really a Stonekeeper? If so, will I be able to live up to the appointed task when the time comes?

She released a long sigh as she climbed beneath the fragrant covers. Her body ached with a need for rest, and she closed her eyes as the soka sound floated up from the rooms below.

Sienna fell asleep quickly. Several hours later

she awoke to semidarkness. The moon was shining brightly through her balcony door, and the
house was silent. She tossed and turned for a
while, willing herself to go back to sleep, but
her mind remained busy no matter how she
tried to calm it.

Finally, she climbed out of bed, pushed the
lace curtains aside, and opened the balcony door.
The night breeze from the sea was invigorating,
and the sound of the waves and the occasional
cry of a sea gull added to the mood. Sienna
walked over to the rail and leaned against the
wrought iron balcony, as a more aggressive breeze
blew her hair from her face, causing her slip to
cling closer to her in a moist embrace.

"Did anybody ever tell you it's not safe to lean
so far out over a balcony rail?"

The silky male voice caught her by surprise
and she stood up with a jolt, her eyes searching
the darkness.

"And did they also tell you white slips are quite
transparent in the moonlight?" This time the
voice was closer, and Sienna recognized the familiar sound just as she heard footsteps approaching.

Hawk stepped onto the platform from the
stairway in the corner. He was shirtless, and his
dreadlocks hung loosely about his shoulders.
The belt he wore around his waist was unbuck-
led, and Sienna thought if it were not for his
well-shaped buttocks, his jeans could have easily
slid down to his feet.

"What are you doing out here?" she asked
lamely, aware of her state of undress but unwilling to run back into her bedroom.

"I could ask you the same thing," he said as

he came and stood beside her, then began to lean out over the rail facing the sea.

"I couldn't sleep, so I decided to come out here and get some fresh air and enjoy the view."

"Um-m-m" was his monosyllabic reply.

Sienna didn't know if she should lean against the rail again beside him or put some distance between them. Instead, she stood with her arms folded protectively in front of her.

Hawk glanced at her over his shoulder before looking back out at the sea. "Did I steal your place?"

"No. Not really" was her hushed response. "I just feel a little uncomfortable with you being here, that's all."

"Why?" He turned and faced her, his elbows resting on the rail.

Her thick, curly lashes covered her eyes for a moment. "You don't find this to be a bit unusual?"

"What? Being in the presence of a semi-nude, beautiful woman?" He continued to stare at her face. "No, I don't find it unusual at all."

Sienna shifted her weight uncomfortably.

"I would have thought from the energy that was flowing earlier in the dining room tonight, by now you would have had more than your share of feminine arousal."

A slight smile touched Hawk's chiseled lips.

"For as long as I've known Mickey, she has always been the proverbial flirt." He studied her cloaked features and wondered if, by chance, she might feel a bit jealous. Then he decided against it.

"It's never been my way to let a woman pick

me up, no matter what she may be offering. I do the picking."

At that moment he allowed his gaze to linger on her lips, before making a slow, deliberate assessment of her body beneath the thin material.

"Well, I don't know what kind of women you've dealt with before, but the way I handle things, whatever happens between me and a man, it has to be by mutual consent."

"That's the way I'm used to it as well. But I'm pretty sure the women I've dealt with recently weren't like you."

Sienna's dark eyes widened with confusion and curiosity. Was that supposed to be an insult or a compliment? Her slightly pointed chin tilted upward a notch, making her thick hair fan out around her shoulders. She used both hands to push the dark cloud off her face.

"The feeling is mutual," she retorted, in case it was a veiled insult. "I can assure you I have never dealt with anyone like you."

Still, her curiosity was overwhelming.

"What kind of woman am I, may I ask?"

His gaze registered the intended barb, yet it continued to smolder with a more compelling emotion.

"The kind who wants a man to love her mind, her soul, and her body." His words were soft and silky, like a caress.

"I don't know very many women who don't want that."

"Me either. That's why, since I have come to know better, I've kept my . . . what should I call it . . . activities to a limited few. From the very beginning I know what they expect from me, and they know what I expect in return."

He rose and stood in front of her, then reached out and touched the tiny bow of her slip that fell between her breasts, his gaze focusing on the mark between them.

Sienna caught his hand and removed it.

"So, are you saying you expect me to have sex with you in order for you to help me?" She could feel her adrenaline flowing at the thought of it, but the question had to be asked.

Hawk noticed how fast her breasts had begun to rise and fall. It was obvious how she felt, and his eyes narrowed into slits as he answered her.

"The kind of arrangements I was talking about were strictly professional from their side and a matter of necessity from mine." He let the words sink in. "No, I don't expect you to go to bed with me, Sienna, unless you want to. It's just that it's been a helluva long time since I've been in continuous contact with someone like you." His hand came up again and he entangled his fingers in the ends of her hair. "It feels as if I've never before met anyone like you."

Sienna felt as if she were being hypnotized by his eyes, which looked so steadily into her own. Before she knew it, his hand had found its way up the back of her neck and had begun to massage her. As he did so, Hawk stepped closer, and she could smell the masculine scent of him, could feel the heat emanating from his body. In one smooth, strong stroke, he pulled her against him and they stood there, their bodies flush. As soon as she felt as if she could drown in his eyes, he leaned her face against his upper chest, then slowly wrapped his arms around her. A little voice cried out a warning to stop, if she did not want things to go any further, but Sienna ignored it because she felt so warm and protected in his embrace.

They stood there, bathing in the moonlight, his hands massaging her back, his head lying on top of hers.

"God, you feel so good." Agony reverberated in his voice, and it made Sienna stiffen against him. Hawk pulled away from her just enough to look down into her eyes. "I'm not just talking about your body, Sienna. I can feel your very soul. It must have been wonderful to view life the way you have. I can tell you have been hurt, and for a very long time you have depended on no one but yourself. Yet in the midst of all that, you still remain kind and giving, believing in the good of your fellow man." He spoke with his lips in her hair. "Do you realize how precious a gem that is? Some of us may have had that kind of peace just for a moment out of a lifetime."

Sienna maneuvered her head so she could see his face. She could feel the sincerity in his words, could feel his desire for what he described. But he was like a wolf baying at the moon, fascinated by its existence but never able to really touch it.

"How do you know anything about me, Hawk?" She pulled away from him and walked back toward the rail. "What do you really know? You've touched on some things that I could say are true, but they could be true for just about anyone." Sienna turned to face him. "I think in saying what you feel about me, you are simply examining yourself. There's something that haunts you, Hawk . . . that makes you see me the way you do. I am far from some pure, perfect vessel"—she shook her head dramatically—

"that you can get near, and the goodness rubs off like a charm. I've got my problems like everybody else. You should be the last person to whom I have to explain that."

"No, you may not be perfect, Sienna Russell"—he walked over and put his hands on her face—"but there is something special enough in you that out of all the human beings walking on this earth, you were born as the last Stonekeeper. A soul so trusted by Mother Earth herself that she would entrust the job to you of returning to her bosom her most beautiful and powerful gems. That's damn special"—he stared into her eyes with a fiery intensity as his mouth slowly descended toward hers—"and probably the closest that a man like me will ever come to heaven."

Hawk's mouth captured hers in a rapturous hold. Once he started to kiss her, his lips moved across her yielding ones in a sensuous, exploratory fashion, as if he were sampling the rarest of fruits, one so sweet and tender that another just like it might never ripen again.

Sienna had never experienced such intensity tempered almost with reverence. A honey sweetness began to seep through her limbs as his hands left her face and his arms brought her to him once again. Finally, his mouth left hers and commenced a blazing trail over to her ear, then down the side of her neck. A moan escaped her lips as she murmured, "How can someone so dark and troubled give so much pleasure?"

Hawk froze instantly at her words, and before Sienna realized it he had stepped away, leaving her senses reeling.

"So you see me as dark and troubled, huh?"

Sienna blinked several times as she tried to

calm the pleasurable feelings his kisses had evoked. Through the haze of passion, she could see his face had turned stony, and his words, although soft, were full of bitterness.

"No. I mean, yes. I know something is troubling you."

"So, what did you think? That I would be cruel and harsh? That my desires would be abnormal? That a man like me wouldn't know anything other than that?"

Sienna just stood, shaking her head.

"I don't know what I thought."

"That's right. You just keep that in mind." His eyes became hooded. "You don't know."

With that, Hawk turned his back on her and disappeared in the dark.

For a while she just stood there, staring at the place where he had been. She had never in her life met a stranger man. One moment he was kissing her, the next he was as distant as a human being could be. But Sienna knew that wasn't where the danger lay. With a heated glance he could make her pulse beat faster, and with a single touch he created shivers up and down her spine. It was frightening because her mind was afraid to trust him, yet her body was following a path of its own.

Sienna walked back into the bedroom and closed the balcony door behind her. She was shivering, but it wasn't because she was cold. Those few moments with Hawk had rocked her to the core. She did not want to be attracted to him. She could not afford it. Deep embedded memories warned her it was a sure path to pain and loss.

As she climbed into bed, she feared her relationship with him was entering a phase she had neither expected nor wanted. There was something about him that magnetized her, like a child being hypnotized by a flame. She knew that from this moment on she would have to be extra careful, or her overwhelming physical attraction to Hawk might cause her to get burned.

Eight

Hawk's muscles relaxed into the pose, his eyes closed as he faced the rising sun. He made a concerted effort to block out the sounds of the animals and the insects as his tongue pressed gently against the roof of his mouth. Finally, he began to slip into the alpha state.

From where he stood the sound of the waves crashing against the seashore was a constant beat inside him, but he continued to relax his body, soaking in energy from the sun and the earth.

This was a time he had come to love, a daily ritual of *hsing-i,* when he became one with the very elements around him. Here he was more than just a man at the whims of the powers that be. Here he was a flowing part of the universe, accepted and welcomed.

Hawk eased into his second stance and thoughts of his childhood entered his mind, memories that were heavily laced with images of his mother. Rossie had been such a strong influence in his life, always there pushing in whatever direction she felt was best. She was gentle yet strong, a rock in her convictions, and was determined to prove the theory that a single mother could successfully raise a male child. As he looked back, in truth, before she died she had accomplished her goal.

He was only sixteen when it happened, and if it hadn't been for Mr. Williams, his martial arts instructor, and his wife, Hawk might not have made it through. From the day he moved in with them until he went to college, then to grad school, he never gave them a moment's trouble. It was during his last year in grad school that everything changed.

Hawk drew in a deep breath, focusing on it as the symbol of life, but his mind remained more active than he wanted. Today the calm that usually accompanied his morning ritual evaded him. He frowned, his eyes still closed. Was there no place he could find peace?

He could feel the anxiousness inside him. For five years he had waited for this time. A time when he would meet the Stonekeeper, whom he had heard about during his worldwide search. A being so connected with the pureness of nature and the earth that that person had been born entrusted with the task of recording the history of mankind inside precious gems. But what interested him most was he had also heard that during the Stonekeeper's ultimate moment of power, she enabled those in her presence to see themselves as they truly were, thereby opening a door for change, if desired, or bringing peace when change was not possible.

For so long he had wondered if such a person actually existed, or if the Stonekeeper were just a hope-filled illusion. Hawk's handsome features grimaced. Yet every time he went through the agonizing pain of the transformation, it was clear to him that if he could experience such an abomination, anything was possible.

And now he had found the Stonekeeper: Sienna Russell.

Feeling his ritual that morning was a waste, Hawk performed his last salutation to the sun, bowing deeply. Last night he had told Sienna the truth when he said she was nothing like the women in his life. Because of the hand fate had dealt him, he had totally shied away from relationships, and his sexual exploits mainly involved women who made their living pleasuring men. It was an expensive way to ease his needs, because his taste required women who would never consider peddling themselves on the street. Fine hotels were their places of preference, and through the years he had selected his favorites, having learned a lot in the process.

Yet, when he thought about it, all that time he had never envisioned the human being who would embody the legacy of the Stonekeeper. Hawk had been consumed by one thing: the Stonekeeper's capability of helping to set him free. Now that he had met her, a warm, beautiful woman within whose eyes fear and fire could shine equally as bright, he had encountered another kind of danger, for he knew she could reach his heart, something he had forever denied having.

Hawk picked up a rock and threw it, as the muscle worked in the back of his jaw. He had no right to have thoughts about any woman, especially one like Sienna Russell. Inside he cursed his life as he knew it. What woman would tolerate, let alone accept, a man like him in her life? A man who was damned. He could not assure her of any kind of future. Hawk's amber eyes clouded over with memories. Maybe years ago he could have. But not now. He was uncertain of the possible far-reaching effects of the thing that haunted him. Would it be over tomorrow? Or would it manifest itself in ways that he had not yet experienced? Ways that could be dangerous for him, but most of all for someone who had the unfortunate position of being close to him.

Because of his predicament, Hawk had tucked away his most tender part . . . the part that allowed him to truly give of himself to a woman. Sadly, he had buried it a long time ago. He could never expect a woman to accept him when he could not fully accept himself.

Sienna took several swallows of the mandarin juice as she watched Hawk in the garden. He was like a work of art, his body movements so graceful, his tiny dreadlocks flying in the wind. In all her life she had never seen anyone move like that. He was like a large hawk in flight, awesome to behold. She wondered where he had learned his ways, for the men she knew seemed to be so impatient. Yet the man she watched now was beyond space and time, and it had to have taken years to become so masterful.

"Ooh, isn't he beautiful?" Mickey's voice, still thick with sleep, cooed as she entered the room. Instantly, Sienna stiffened at the woman's statement. Yes, she thought he was beautiful, but she did not see the need to express it to anyone. She was beginning to feel Mickey had a knack for taking over, and sister-girl was well on the road to rubbing her the wrong way.

Although Sienna was up and dressed for the day, she wasn't quite herself. It had been hard to go back to sleep after Hawk left, and she was in no mood for Mickey's lascivious attitude.

Without turning around, Sienna greeted her. "Good morning, Mickey."

"It is a great morning." The implication was clear. "Too bad you decided to go to bed so early last night. Things were just really getting hot when you left."

"The heat was one of the reasons I left," Sienna replied, turning to look in her direction.

Although Mickey was clothed in a floor-length housecoat of the richest midnight blue, Sienna observed she had put on a full face of makeup and her hair was styled to a tee. It made her wonder if Mickey was afraid to allow anyone to see her natural features.

"I thought that Hennessy might be having breakfast this morning." She picked up a piece of pineapple from the table that was supplied with fresh fruits and bread.

"I was wondering what had gotten you out of bed so early on a Sunday morning," George remarked as he entered the room.

This time Mickey didn't try to hide her fangs. "The question is, how are you even coherent this morning? This is a rarity."

"You see how much respect she has for her . . . grandfather, don't you, Sienna?"

Sienna looked from George, whose hair was not combed, to Mickey, who was giving him the evil eye. The friction between them was palpable.

"Well, at least you've gotten rid of that sickeningly sweet act you were putting on last night.

I think it made me more ill than all the rum I consumed."

"Sometimes you tend to forget, so I'm warning you, George, don't go too far," Mickey threatened, their eyes locking in combat.

She turned to Sienna, donning a fixed smile, and somehow she appeared to be much older than she had the day before.

"I bet Hennessy hasn't had the opportunity to tell you, so I might as well: We'll be going to the museum today. I'm going to dig up that letter on the Passion Ruby for him to see. You might feel a little out of your league there, so I'm sure you'll find plenty to do around here while we're gone." Before Sienna could reply, Mickey walked out.

"She speaks so high and mighty." George pulled a flask from his pocket and poured the contents into a glass of cane syrup, then threw in a slice of lime. "She's always threatening me, but one day her foul deeds are going to catch up with her. I wait for the day when she meets her match." He shook his head and took a long swallow of the *ti punch*. "Until then . . . I wonder what role you and Mr. Jackson, out there, have in her latest scheme. It's been a long, long time since we've had overnight guests in this house. But when I think about it, she's had a yearning for that man for a long time, something that's quite unnatural for her, an obsession almost." He leaned up against the rail and placed his knee on it.

"Exactly how long have they known each other?" Sienna asked, provoked by his candid remarks.

"I'd say at least six years. She had tried a few

times to get him out here on the island while they were in school together. Lucky for him he never made one of those trips." George put his hand over his abdomen, as if it might be in pain.

"Michelle was crazy angry when he left school without telling her. She came home and had us all walking around here on eggshells. She never realized I knew why she was carrying on so. Alisha, a young woman who came to live with us, like Sylvie, told me everything." Suddenly, his elderly face turned youthful, a softness surfacing in his vein-filled eyes, before he frowned and took another swig.

"It must have hurt her a lot, and they must have been very close at the time." Sienna felt her stomach tighten at the thought, so she sat down, grabbed a plate, and began to fill it with fruit. "But it doesn't make sense for him to leave the university without saying goodbye."

"You have to know Michelle to understand why she acts the way she does. It's not necessary for a man to be interested in her, because love has nothing to do with it. When she feels the time is right, ch-chump"—he made the noise and snapped his hand closed like a person catching a fly—"then she strikes. I think she had been baiting him along up until then. But I must admit the way she spoke of him was different from the way she spoke of most men." He put the empty glass on the table. "As far as his leaving goes, Alisha said Michelle felt it had something to do with some artifacts they had found. At the time, Alisha and I both couldn't make sense of it. But she said Michelle told her they were at the point where they were about to break some kind of code. She never saw him after that—that is, not until he popped up here in Martinique working on some project a year and a half later."

"I sure would like to know more about that. Maybe it has something to do with why he is the way he is," Sienna thought out loud, and when she realized she'd spoken, she caught George looking strangely at her. "I'm just curious, that's all," she rushed on. "You see, we're working on a project together," she said, skirting the issue. "Maybe I could speak to Alisha. She might be able to shed some more light on the situation."

"Alisha can't talk to you or anyone about nothing." Suddenly, he seemed more close-mouthed than before, a deep sadness darkening his gaze. "She shouldn't have had anything to do with me." He started toward the door. "You be careful around here. There's all kinds of things that go on in these islands, and I'm not talking about *chanbois,* or voodoo, as you foreigners call it. You just be careful."

Sienna sat and ate her fruit in silence, thinking about the things George had told her. If he only knew her reason for being in Martinique, he'd understand that the islands weren't the only place where extraordinary things happened to ordinary people.

"Bon matin, mademoiselle," Sylvie greeted her as she stepped out onto the veranda. "I hope you slept well."

"It wasn't too bad. Thank you." Sienna gave the girl a slight smile as she looked at the flower she wore in her hair.

"Mr. Jackson told me to tell you you will be going to the museum today." Her brown eyes sparkled. "So I thought I'd wait to give you a few more minutes' sleep, but I find you out here, dressed and ready for the day."

"Well, I'm glad you found me."

"He told me to tell you you all will be leaving in about an hour and a half."

Sienna nodded, considering what Mickey's reaction would be when she discovered Hawk had invited her to come along.

"Thanks, Sylvie."

The girl nearly skipped away before she turned abruptly.

"Do you like my flower?"

"It's gorgeous."

"Mr. Jackson gave it to me." She smiled brightly. "He said it reminded him of me. A flower almost in full bloom."

"And he was right," Sienna assured her.

She watched Sylvie depart with a satisfied look on her face.

Having a little time to kill, Sienna spent the next hour exploring the large garden they'd passed through on their way up to the house. As she walked she pondered all the things that had happened since they arrived. She finally concluded, considering Mickey's attitude toward her, that she would not spend another night under her roof. Hawk could do what he wanted, but she would not remain there. Sienna had enough on her mind not to be further burdened by a catty female. She was also anxious about beginning her search for the ruby. It was like performing a balancing act. All of this was so new to her. Hawk. Martinique. Mickey. It seemed like a dream, but she only had to think of what had occurred, and she knew this was reality. William's

threats were real; Dawn's kidnapping was the
most potent proof of that.

Two large butterflies swooped by her in a fluttering chase. Although their movements were
chaotic, they managed to dip and dive between
the plants and trees almost effortlessly, never
striking a single one. Sienna remembered how
Aunt Jessi used to say there were messages in
nature, but a person had to be open and aware.
For some reason the butterflies reminded Sienna of herself and Hawk—unsure of their
movements, but nevertheless caught in an ageless
dance. She watched until the fluttering patches
disappeared into the blue sky, safe from any ob-
stacles, suddenly free to soar as high as their wings
could carry them.

Was she to understand that only with Hawk's
help would she be successful? That their paths
were intertwined, and one could not fly free
without the other? The words "Follow your first
mind, child; it won't lead you wrong" echoed
in her head. Once again they were Aunt Jessi's
words, and Sienna wondered if they had helped
her in her early days when she was carrying out
the legacy of a Stonekeeper.

Sienna started back down the path toward the
house. She was a little nervous about the day
ahead, and more specifically about coming face
to face with Hawk. She knew she had wounded
him before he left her the previous night, although that had not been her intention.

Despite her struggle not to allow it, hurting
him bothered her. She did not want to care about
Hawk's feelings, not to the extent that he was
almost constantly on her mind. He was adamant
about not telling her why he was interested in

the ruby. Sienna would not allow herself to forget that, because it meant she couldn't trust him.

As she climbed the stairs to the house, the front door opened. It was Hawk cleanly shaven, with his clothes freshly washed from the day before.

"Good morning," Sienna said as she clasped her hands together in front of her.

"Mornin'," Hawk replied, his face a controlled mask.

"Look, about last night . . . I didn't mean to say anything to upset you." She found herself apologizing.

His amber eyes rested on her in a steady gaze. "It doesn't matter."

Sienna didn't quite understand what he meant by that. What didn't matter? All the things they had said last night? The kiss they had shared? Or whatever was developing between them?

She stuck her hands in the pockets of her blue jeans, causing them to tighten around her slim, round hips. Sienna could detect the invisible wall he had decided to erect between them, and she wasn't sure how she felt about it. For a moment their eyes locked, before she looked down at her feet, exposing the long, curvy back of her neck. That morning she had pulled all her hair together in a large rubber band, creating a billowy Afro pouf.

"Oh, here you are," Mickey exclaimed as she opened the front door, where Hawk blocked her view of the steps in front of him.

"I was just thinking about an interesting place where we can have lunch after we do our research. It's called *Le LaFayette*. It is a *salon* on the second floor of a hotel that has been totally"—

Hawk shifted his position, affording Mickey a view of Sienna—"renovated."

"That sounds interesting," Hawk replied.

"Are we ready?" He looked at Sienna, then at Mickey.

"So, you changed your mind and decided to go after all?" Mickey's eyes glittered like smoky topazes as she spoke.

Sienna didn't hesitate with her reply. "Sure, I decided to go after I was invited."

Mickey's thick lips turned into a smirk instead of a smile, before she walked down the stairs, heading for the car.

Nine

The trip back into town was pretty much a silent one, and Sienna welcomed it. She didn't
think she could stand the syrupy words Mickey
directed at Hawk and the sugar-coated daggers
she reserved for her. When they arrived at the
museum, Mickey introduced them to a couple of
staff members. Their reception was quite reserved, and Sienna didn't know if it was her and
Hawk's presence that evoked their timidity or if
it was Mickey.

Moments later Mickey sequestered them in a
back room filled with both cataloged artifacts
and some that were assembled in a less orderly
fashion.

Sienna made it her business to stay out of the
way as Mickey searched for the letter. As time
passed she began to browse around, but she
never touched a thing. Hawk, on the other
hand, had become engrossed in a thick set of
onionskin papers.

"I've found it," Mickey finally announced, as
she gently pulled the letter out of a box full of
documents.

Sienna was anxious to see the letter, which
was protected in a clear, plasticlike substance,

but Mickey positioned herself so that only Hawk could see it.

"As you can see, Hennessy, I surface-cleaned it, did any kind of archival mending that was necessary"—she pointed to a couple of spots that appeared more worn than the rest—"and deacidifying it wasn't very difficult at all," she continued.

Hawk nodded his head, acknowledging her, but like Sienna he was more interested in the contents of the document than in Mickey's archival preservation techniques.

"It's written in French," he proclaimed as he made room for Sienna.

"I recognize a few words," Sienna remarked before Mickey took the thin polyester film that encapsulated the letter from Hawk's hand.

"Let me translate what it says," Mickey began.

"In my feeble way I am giving this gift back to its original owner, the earth. For this stone has been the source of much pain and pleasure. If found by some brave soul, I am leaving the wherewithal to draw its power, but remember in the end justice can only be found with the Stonekeeper . . . whom or which, *I* have not had the fortune to find."

Sienna's brown eyes enlarged slightly and her heart began to beat erratically. Up until now the whole concept of a Stonekeeper had been just that . . . a concept, even with everything that had happened. Yes, she had dreamed about it and Hawk had spoken of it, but she had never seen any concrete proof that someone called a Stonekeeper actually existed. Until now.

Hawk's voice was low and steady.

"From your test, how old is the letter?"

"About three hundred years old."

"And this was the only paper that was found?" Hawk continued. "The writer says he left some instructions with the stone."

"*Oui,* this was the only paper that came into our possession." Mickey looked back down at the letter. "Like I told you before, no one has ever seen the stone or the instructions this letter talks about."

"May I see it?" Sienna asked.

After a moment's hesitation, Mickey gave her the document.

Sienna brushed her hand over the slick, plasticlike film as she stared at the tiny scratchy writing it protected underneath. Could what was written here be true? And was she the Stonekeeper to whom the letter referred? No matter what, it was still hard for her to believe.

As a child, when Sienna lost her parents, she did the most practical thing she could think of: separate herself from a God whom she believed saw justice in pain and suffering. Now as an adult, not only was she being forced to take a second look at what she had chosen to be reality, but she was also being shown possible proof that she was a key player in a game that seemed to be fashioned by a higher power. If it hadn't been for Hawk's grim expression, she would have laughed aloud at the irony of it. Sienna knew what he was thinking. They were running against a clock, and the letter had not yielded a single clue as to how to go about finding the ruby.

"So now, after I have come here and dug
through stacks of documents to show you
this"—Mickey extended the letter toward Hawk—
"do you mind telling me why this is important to
you? I know you don't believe it." She placed her
hands on her ample hips. "At least tell me why
it's important, since you won't tell me the specifics
as to why the two of you have come to Martinique."

Hawk placed his hands on the woman's arms.

"Mickey, you know I appreciate all that you
have done for us, but I simply can't tell you why.
It could be dangerous for all of us."

"Dangerous . . . uh-oh, that's a heavy word"—
then Mickey looked at his hands upon her—"but I
think I will just keep on helping you. You never
know, it might lead to other things that I'll find
more satisfying."

On their way to *Le LaFayette*, Mickey was full
of chatter. It was almost as if their melancholy
mood was the cause of her joy. She even attempted to engage Sienna in a civil conversation,
as she pointed out landmarks and other trivial
things over the constant sound of blaring horns
and *zouk* music. In the end, Mickey pulled up in
front of a charming building, informing them
the restaurant was no more than a block away.

Strains of a guitar floated on the balmy breeze
as they started down the sidewalk, and Sienna
could see a small crowd forming several yards
away. As they drew nearer, a man in a white
jacket and turned-up hat could be seen performing inside the circle of tourists and natives.
His fingers appeared to have a knowledge of
their own as he strummed the guitar, belting
out an old island tune. The man's teeth were a

vibrant white as he smiled and sang, his foot tapping out the beat on the ground.

In the beginning Mickey tried to circumvent the enthusiastic audience, but as the crowd grew thicker, they found it more convenient to stop and listen. When the song was over, Sienna, like many others, stepped forward to drop money inside a waiting, open guitar case. As she reached out the silver bangle shone in the sunlight, and before she knew it the old man had taken hold of her hand to give the bracelet a closer examination.

"This is quite beautiful, you know?" His smile included his eyes, which were unusually bright for a man his age.

"Thank you. It's rather special. It was a gift from my great-aunt, and it is the reason why I am here in Martinique."

"Oh, I see." He rocked back and forth. "It is very special, then. It would be even more beautiful if it had been set with special stones. A ruby maybe?"

Sienna's mouth dropped open in response to the elderly man's remark.

"We should pity those who cannot see the beauty. For they cannot see the forest for the trees, even though it is the forest that they look for." He let go of Sienna's hand and she backed away, still stunned by his words.

"What's wrong with you, girl?" Mickey remarked when she saw Sienna's anemic face upon her return.

Still shocked by the old man's uncanny insight, Sienna replied, "That man . . . he said some—"

"Who? Josei?" She motioned back toward the performer with her head. "Aah, he thinks he's some kind of seer. Pay him a dollar, he will tell you anything."

Hawk's face seemed to stiffen at Mickey's remark and Sienna turned around to look at the old man again, but he paid her no attention as he continued to say goodbye to his paying audience.

They entered *Le LaFayette* and were instantly surrounded by clusters of greenery vibrantly displayed against a background of white latticework. A large selection of colorful Haitian paintings adorned the walls, creating an atmosphere of fine dining.

They were seated at a table near the window, and as the meal progressed Sienna found that the food was as excellent as the setting. Mickey was the focus of attention, with her endless talk, but Sienna didn't mind in the least, for the performer's words continued to gnaw at her. Was it just a coincidence that he had mentioned a ruby? Or could what he said possibly be the clue for which they had been waiting?

Mickey's accented voice droned on in the background as Sienna laid pieces of shrimp in the hot oil, frying them in preparation for fondue sauces ranging from spicy to sweet. Although her thoughts focused mainly on the old man's words, she was acutely aware that Hawk had not looked at her once since they had left the house earlier that morning. Sienna knew his change in attitude was the result of how they had parted the night before, and even though she hated to admit it, she found his standoffishness unsettling.

Mickey's chatter came to an abrupt halt as she began to wave to another woman across the room.

"It's *Madame* Santana," she informed them. "She is a loyal beneficiary of the museum. Will you excuse me? I think I should go and speak to her." Mickey rose from her seat, leaving Sienna and Hawk alone.

Sienna noticed how many of the patrons at *Le LaFayette* watched Mickey's movements. Some of them stared openly, while others whispered amongst themselves.

For a brief moment, from beneath her lashes, Sienna focused on Hawk's profile. The jagged edges were exceedingly masculine, and with his dreadlocks drawn back in a ponytail, they appeared that much more powerful. She noticed how he seemed to concentrate more than necessary on the grilled lobster he had ordered, thereby touching a soft spot in Sienna's heart.

Suddenly, she felt an urge to reach out and touch the tiny, soft curls that had formed around his hairline, to caress his face and plant a kiss at the corner of his rigid mouth. Startled by the direction her thoughts had taken, Sienna sat back in her chair, popped a succulent shrimp in her mouth, and began to chew pensively.

"Hawk"—she was glad to be able to call his name—"do you get the feeling that somehow we're being led to just the right people and the right places?" Her eyes were dark, seeking pools.

His wary gaze rested on her face a moment before he answered.

"Yes, I do. But I told you, when we were back in Atlanta, that it would be that way. I've seen it happen before. You only have to be open to it. You have to be aware." His gold-tinted eyes stared into hers. "But it could go either way. Negative or positive. Yet it all amounts to our

being given the opportunity to learn something."
He paused. "Take a series of accidents, for in-
stance. That would be perceived as negative. Still,
you cannot deny you are in a particular kind of
flow." Hawk looked down at the food on his
plate. "Sometimes it takes something drastic and
unpleasant to wake us up . . . to put us on a different path."

Sienna's smooth brow furrowed. "Like all the
things that forced me to come to Martinique?"

Hawk nodded his head slowly.

"Maybe that was the only way you could possibly open yourself to your legacy." His eyes
were full of wisdom as he continued. "Think of
meeting someone for the first time and things
click so well you feel as if you've known the person all your life. There's so much chemistry between you, you can almost touch it." His words
were a compelling whisper. "Then it would be
seen as something good, something wonderful."
Hawk's gaze dropped abruptly to the table. "At
least by most people's standards it would."

His features became very staunch, and Sienna
watched his jaw muscles tighten before he took
several more bites of lobster.

"Well, I think we are definitely in a positive
flow now." She thought about the performer's
words and the charged electricity between her
and Hawk.

"Yes, I would say we are." Hawk spoke without looking in her direction. "Mickey and
George told us the story of the Passion Ruby,
then, on top of that, Mickey had a letter verify-
ing the stone's existence." He chewed and swallowed several times as Sienna nodded her
agreement. "I would say we're on the right path,

but we need something more. Something that would point us in a more specific direction."

"Well, I believe we have it."

This time when Hawk turned to her, his eyes narrowed with speculation.

"What are you talking about?"

"The old man . . . the performer . . ." Sienna leaned closer, her face nearly touching his. "He said some things to me, and I believe he told me where we should go."

"Exactly what did he say?"

"First he commented on how beautiful the bracelet was, and then he made a statement about a ruby." Her eyes turned bright with excitement. "But the last thing he said—and I've repeated it over and over again in my mind so that I wouldn't forget—was, 'We should pity those who cannot see the beauty. For they cannot see the forest for the trees, even though it is the forest that they look for.' "

As she spoke Hawk's eyes also began to change as he watched the excitement that played across Sienna's beautiful features. Her face was so close to his that if she moved, even the slightest, their lips would have touched. Sienna watched his amber eyes turn a smoky green, and she could feel the change in direction of his thoughts. Her spine began to tingle and her face suddenly felt cool, as if she wanted him to touch it.

"So don't you see"—she licked her lips because they had suddenly become dry—"it is the forest that we should be looking for."

Sienna's words seemed to break the spell between them. Almost reluctantly, Hawk sat back in his chair.

"The forest . . ." He repeated the words just as Mickey reclaimed her seat.

"Did I hear you say *forest?*" Her eyes cut a path between the two of them. "From the way you were huddled together, I expected to hear something much more intimate than that," she chided. "So what is this talk about a forest? Did I miss something important?"

"I'm not quite sure." Hawk rubbed the back of his hand against his chin. "You've come back just at the right time." He grabbed her hand. "Tell me, are there any forests on the island that are especially well known for their beauty? Some that may have a certain claim to fame?"

For a moment it appeared as if Mickey's mind were racing, and Sienna wasn't too sure all her thoughts were conjuring up the answer to Hawk's question.

"Of course, we have forests here. This is a tropical island, *mon chou.* Almost the total northern section of Martinique is tropical rain forest, and the infamous active volcano, *Mont Pelée,* is there. In three minutes it wiped out the entire town of St. Pierre around ninety years ago. Is that famous enough for you?" She smiled a syrupy smile.

"I think that just might be," Hawk replied as he looked at Sienna, who was more than aware that he still held Mickey's hand.

"Might be what?" Mickey threw up her arms in exaggerated ire. "I'm beginning to feel like a box of tissue around here. You're only sweet to me when you need something or when you want to use me. But it seems no matter what I do, you won't let me in on anything." She assumed what was becoming a familiar pout.

Sienna was amazed at all the different faces Mickey wore according to her mood. The woman who sat before them now appeared to be totally wounded because she felt she was being misused. But Sienna could not imagine the Mickey who had spoken so coldly earlier that day having any such emotions. She wondered if Hawk were aware of the contradictions in Mickey's personality, or if his feelings for her blinded him.

"I'm not trying to use you, Mickey." Hawk's tone reflected his sincerity. "What I am saying is, that forest may be the place that Sienna and I are looking for."

"My, my . . ." Mickey settled back in her seat and looked at the two of them. "Leave you two alone for a second and you sure work fast. I hadn't been gone a good ten minutes and you've come up with this. You know I'm the one who likes to make all the discoveries, Hennessy."

Hawk allowed her innuendo to pass. Already his mind was plotting a new plan of action.

Suddenly, Sienna noticed a thin, dark-skinned man making a beeline for their table. As he approached she recognized him as one of the staff members from the museum.

"Excusez-moi, s'il vous plaît." He made his apologies, then presented a folded piece of paper. "This message was delivered this morning for your guest, Ms. Russell. I would have given it to you when you were at the museum earlier, but I assumed Henri had done so." He gave a stunned Sienna the paper. "The gentleman who came by was very nice and he apologized for using the museum as a message center, but he said it was the only place he knew where to contact you."

"Merci," Sienna managed to reply, and she attempted to hide her frightened reaction.

"What did the man look like who delivered the note?" Hawk asked, his voice low and silky.

"He was a man with a bald head, a large scar, and a pair of earrings in his ears."

Sienna and Hawk looked at one another. They knew the man whom the staff member had described was Spike.

"Please excuse me again," he repeated, before turning and walking away.

Sienna could feel both sets of eyes upon her, and she wondered if her anxiety showed. How had William tracked her to Martinique? Instantly, a light sheen of perspiration broke out around her brow as she unfolded the note.

Wanted you to know we arrived ok. I'll stay in touch with you. By the way, the Dawn is still beautiful in Atlanta. Bill

"Is everything okay?" Hawk asked.

"Sure. Sure. Everything is fine." She folded up the note and placed it in her pocket.

Mickey sat for a moment watching Sienna in silence, before she asked gaily, "Now, where were we? *Mais oui,* we were talking about the rain forest."

"That's right." Hawk surveyed the restaurant in a casual manner, but his eyes were on the alert. "I've heard of Mount Pelée. It's in the northwestern part of the country. How far is it from Fort-de-France?"

"About sixty miles. But what you have to understand is a twenty-mile mountain drive here in Martinique is quite different from even driving in hilly areas in the States. If you are thinking about traveling into the rain forest near *Mont Pelée,* you would want to do it carefully. It can be unbelievably beautiful up there in the evening and during the night." Mickey smiled suggestively at Hawk. "Why don't you stay at my house one more night . . . have a good dinner and a good night's sleep? I've got some business that will probably take up the first half of the day tomorrow, but after that I am totally free and I can be your private guide on this trip. Sounds good, *oui?*"

Sienna didn't wait for Hawk to answer, having already made up her mind.

"Mickey, like I told you before, I really appreciate all that you've done for us, but I don't feel we can afford to waste one more night." The note from William was making her acutely aware not only that he knew where she was, but also that he or Spike might even be watching.

"Sienna's right. We've got to get going. If you take us back to the house, it won't take us long to get our things, and we can rent a car before the night sets in," Hawk backed her up.

Sienna could tell Mickey wasn't very pleased with the turn of events, so she was surprised when she agreed without a fuss.

"If you insist. I'll take you back, and I'll drop you off at the car rental agency on my way back into town. But you must promise to come back through Fort-de-France before you leave the island," she insisted as she fingered the ruby around her neck.

Hawk looked at Sienna, who gave a slight nod. "It's a deal," he replied.

Ten

"I just got a good return on an investment, boss." Spike slumped in the wooden chair, then flipped a coin up in the air. "I paid a few francs to some locals to keep their eyes open, and sure enough I just found out Hawk and that woman rented a car a couple of hours ago. I told them to keep an eye out for my cousins," he smiled broadly. "They said they headed west on Route N2." Spike slapped the coin down on the table, more than pleased with himself.

"Is that right?" William commented as he removed a slice of pineapple and one of lime from the rim of his glass. "Are you sure it was them?"

"Sure I'm sure, or I wouldn't be telling you." Spike leaned back in his chair, until William gave him that look he'd seen before. Quickly, he adjusted his attitude, hunching his thick shoulders forward as he rested his elbows on the table. "Well, according to the description they gave me, I'm pretty sure it was them."

"That's better." William tapped his straw against the tumbler before turning the greenish drink up to his mouth.

"It'll do you good to remember what happened to Carl. I don't like for anybody to cross me. And I don't like for people to get out of their places." He paused to let his words sink in.

"I am the mind behind this operation. You haven't been making any decisions before now, and I don't want you to start."

Spike just stared at the smaller man beside him. He had worked for William for over a year, and there were two things he had come to know. First, although the man was smart and appeared to be a class act, beneath all the glitter and glamour was a truly cruel human being. He could think of things to get back at a person or to hurt him that the average man would never think of. Revenge was something that Spike understood, but there were times when William went beyond what he considered to be sufficient payback. Times when he was fanatical. All in all Spike had decided that William wanted to play God, wanted to use people like chess pieces in a game. Reward them when he was pleased, punish them when he was not. It was during those times that Spike feared him most. The second thing was, William had a weakness for women.

Spike looked down at his large, folded hands. No, he never wanted to be on the receiving end of William's schemes, and with all that he knew about William, Spike realized he would never be out of his clutches until one of them was dead.

"So, the next time you decide to pay someone to do anything that involves me," William continued, "you ask me first."

"I hear ya." Spike's thick features creased with grave concern.

Suddenly, William slapped him on the back.

"That's okay, man. Lighten up," he chuckled. "You are now in a one-of-a-kind place. The island of Martinique, where the flowers are beautiful and so are the women." William winked at a woman across the room.

A slow smile began to spread across Spike's face as he looked at the table of women that had captured his boss's attention. William never had any trouble catchin', Spike thought, as the most attractive woman threw his boss another smile. It was all in the way he looked and carried himself. Smooth caramel skin, precisely cut wavy hair, and a smile of which any orthodontist would be proud. Spike, on the other hand, wasn't so lucky. Yeah, most women found his body attractive because he was big and muscular, but that attraction usually stopped when they saw his face. Spike frowned at the thought of it.

He had been in plenty of fights when he was growing up, using fists to knives, and they had left their mark. One, in particular, was a large, fearsome scar straight down the middle of his mug.

"So, how do you like those babes over there, Spike?" William asked as he wiped his mouth with a paper napkin.

"They all look good to me," he replied as he licked his lower lip. It had been a while since he had a woman. For him, they were hard to come by.

"I don't know about all that," William said between deceptively stiff lips, "but there's one or two that I kinda like. What do you say I invite them over here for a drink? We can wine them and dine them a bit. You know, big shots from the States and all that, and I think before the evening's over, we just might get lucky." He pulled out a stack of francs and piled them in the middle of the table.

"You know, I feel kind of funny about having such a good time without Carl, even with every- thing that went down between us."

"Well, don't. Carl's not your concern, he's mine. I think he got the wrong impression when I took him on as a partner in the law firm, you know? Because I don't play. So he's got to prove himself to me again, and that's what he's doing by staying up in Atlanta and keeping an eye on the woman."

"Yeah, that's another thing. What are we gonna do about Hawk and that Russell broad? Aren't we gonna follow them?"

"No, I don't see the need to. I've already maneuvered them into going and finding the ruby for me. And the note clearly stated that we're here in Fort-de-France waiting for them. So when they find the gem they'll be back, and we'll be waiting for them, ready and able to claim the treasure." He finished off the last contents of the glass. "Don't you know me by now, Spike? If I can get around doing the work by having someone else do it, that suits me fine. Just like I had the woman Dawn call the telephone company and say some long distance phone calls had been made on her phone that she didn't want to be responsible for. Just like that"—he snapped his finger—"we were able to find out where Hawk and Ms. Russell were headed. And we had the added luxury of finding out they had contacted somebody at the main mu- seum over here." He ran his hands through his wavy hair. "You see, Spike, some of us are born with more than our fair share of this"—William's index finger tapped against his temple. "And we let it work for us, man, in more ways than one."

William beckoned for the waitress to return to the table.

"You see those lovely ladies over there?" He made certain the women saw him asking about them. "Would you tell them we'd love for them to join us for drinks."

"All three of them?"

"Yes, all three." William looked at Spike.

"Sure, I will. It's your moan-ee. But let me warn you. You must be careful dealing with some of the women here. There are stories that would turn your hair white instantly. I would hate for that to happen to a good-lookin' man like you." The waitress smiled at William as he paid for the drinks they'd just consumed.

"Save some for my tip," the woman flirted.

"Don't worry, baby, I've got you covered."

The waitress walked over to the table where the women sat and delivered the message. Moments later, all three of them joined William and Spike, and introductions were made. They were on their second round of drinks when the most attractive of the women was summoned to the bar to take a phone call. When she returned, Spike noticed her eyes seemed to shine brighter and she appeared to be a little nervous.

"How's it going, sweetheart?" William leaned over to watch her fold her long, shapely legs underneath the table.

"*C'est bon*. It's fine," she replied, although from time to time she kept looking through the large plate glass window.

"So, what type of plans do you ladies have tonight? Are you busy? Or do you have time to hang out with us?"

"I've got time for anything you want," the attractive, dark brown-skinned woman called Germaine replied.

One of her girlfriends looked at her, surprised, while the other one's features became cloaked in subtle understanding.

"As long as you are here in Martinique," she smiled at William charmingly, "you can count on me to show you a good time. Your wish is my command."

"I think it's about time for me to be goin'," the second woman remarked, obviously displeased at the aggressive stance her friend was taking. "How about you?" she asked the third female named Claudette.

Claudette's gaze locked briefly with Germaine's, before she looked at the money piled in front of her. Next, she gave Spike a good going-over, starting with his scarred face, then on to his muscular body. Her decision made, she said, "I think I'll be staying."

"Suit yourself, then." The second woman grabbed her bag and walked out in a huff.

William's unexpected laughter broke the silence that had descended within the group. In seconds, Germaine's sensuous laugh joined his.

"What did I tell you, Spike?" William pushed another island drink toward his friend as he grabbed the rim of Germaine's chair and pulled it up beside his. "There's not another place in the world I'd rather be than Martinique."

* * *

"How do you think William found out we we're in Martinique?" Sienna asked Hawk as the road began to climb sharply.

He did not answer her immediately, devoting his attention instead to the hairpin turns, his face a mask of concentration.

"I guess there are a number of ways, from planting a tape recorder to tracing the calls that I made. If I had been thinking more clearly, I would have waited until we left to make them."

"I guess it really doesn't matter. He probably would have found out no matter what." She shrugged her shoulders.

Deep in thought Sienna looked to the east, where the Caribbean Sea was spread out like an undulating sheet of brilliant blue silk. She had never seen a more beautiful place in her life, and she wished the circumstances of her visit here were different. They continued down the road, where a green mountain loomed in the distance. Its sloping sides were sprinkled with red-roofed white houses, reminding Sienna of a Christmas tree decorated with red and white ornaments.

Sienna and Hawk remained silent as the sun started its descent out of the sky. The country-side continued to yield romantic treasures as they passed another fishing village adorned with pastel-colored houses. Down in the water colorful boats danced to the beat of the sea, bobbing within its grasp like a tree branch in the wind. Sienna watched the scenery pass by, her thoughts in constant flux, ebbing and flowing from the situation she found herself in to the man beside her. Suddenly, a sign that indicated the nearness of St. Pierre swooshed by.

"I think we should take the advice Mickey and

the guy at the rental office gave us," she announced. "They told us to stop in St. Pierre and settle down for the evening. After that the map indicates the road will start to climb very sharply, and I don't think we need to try our hand at it tonight."

Once again she had noticed a change in Hawk's attitude as it began to turn dark. He appeared to be more tense, and his silence seemed to hold a concentrated energy. From time to time he would touch the side of his face in a nervous fashion and check his reflection in the rearview mirror. When Hawk didn't respond to her statement Sienna became quiet, and she decided to wait until the first buildings came into sight before pressing the issue again. It wasn't very long before they began to drive down what appeared to be the main road in St. Pierre.

"There is a restaurant where we can stop"— she pointed to a place that was humming with people. "Perhaps we can get something to eat there and find out where we can find a decent place to sleep."

Hawk still did not verbally respond, but he pulled up in a parking space no more than a block away. With all the pressure Sienna was under, his silence was becoming unbearable and she could feel her resentment rising. She had no idea what plagued him. She only knew she was experiencing a great deal of stress, too.

"Look, Hawk . . ." She turned around in her seat and faced him as he turned off the car. "Right now this is an awfully hard time for me as well, and I would feel so much better if we could at least get back to where we really talked to one another."

"Leave it alone, Sienna. You don't know what you'd be getting into." The eyes that pierced hers were those of a stranger.

"It couldn't be anything worse than what we're dealing with right now," she pressed. "We've got criminals following us, and Lord knows what they will do to us once we give them the ruby. On top of that I'm being framed for attempted murder, and as you said, they'll probably make you my accomplice."

"Believe me, there are some things that are even worse than that," he replied in a hollow voice.

"You make it sound as if you turn into a were-wolf or something," she teased him. "But if I remember that story correctly, you need a full moon for that."

Hawk simply turned away from her and climbed out of the car.

Sienna was shocked by his abruptness. Despite herself, the thought kept running through her mind that after all they'd been through together, when it came right down to it she still could not trust him. In truth, she knew virtually nothing about him, what made him tick, and most of all why he had put his own life in danger to accompany her to Martinique.

As she climbed out of the car a catchy *zouk* rhythm permeated the area, which was filled with customers standing outside the establishment. Sienna was captivated by the music, and it was obvious she was not the only one. The fast-paced sound was so contagious that every once in a while someone would break out in spontaneous dance.

Soon she realized that *La Vogue St. Pierre Hotel*

housed a restaurant and a barroom, and it was
the latter that appeared to function as a local
hangout. Once they found the restaurant they
were seated in an instant, and their orders were
taken just as quickly. They both ordered a simple fare of creole food, consuming their meal
in virtual silence.

"What about a drink, mum?" The smiling
waiter came back to the table. "We always want
our customers to leave here satisfied."

Sienna looked around the room at the variety
of glasses topped with tropical fruits. She was
tired of Hawk's sullenness and she longed for
a reprieve from her own thoughts.

"Yes, I think I will have a drink," she announced, sitting back in the seat and crossing
her legs. "Do you have anything like a hurricane? I've heard that's a very potent drink."

"Hurricane?" the waiter repeated, puzzled.

"Yes, hurricane. It's a very strong drink," she
overemphasized, as if that would make him understand.

"You want strong, I'll make you strong." His
cheekbones rose with his facial movements.

She gave him the okay sign.

"And would you care for another beer, sir?"

Hawk nodded his head.

"Good. I'll be right back." The waiter smiled
and walked away.

Sienna began to move ever so slightly to the
music, which could still be heard. She refused
to focus on Hawk, who she knew by now had
begun to watch her. Her life had become crazy
enough, and she would not allow whatever dark,
dank secret Hawk possessed to push her over
the edge. She needed to feel free of the pres-

sures that had plagued her during the last seventy-two hours. She didn't care what Hawk thought of her.

Sienna began to rub her temples, but it did little to relieve the tension. With adept fingers, she removed the rubber band that had held her hair. That simple motion alone sent relaxing waves down her neck and through her shoulders. Sighing, she combed through the stubborn locks with stiff, outspread fingers. Satisfied, she patted her hair into some semblance of order as she waited for her drink to arrive.

"Strong. You got it," the waiter proclaimed as he set the glass in front of her.

Sienna immediately popped the large green grape into her mouth, before taking a bite of the pineapple slice. Moments later, she was gulping down the orangish-red drink that was sweet as well as tangy.

"I think you'd better take it easy on that drink," Hawk warned her. "You might regret it if you drink it too fast."

"I don't need you to tell me that." Sienna looked up at him, her eyes ablaze. It was so easy for him to tell her what to do, yet it was so hard for him to talk about himself.

By the time the glass was half empty, Sienna was starting to feel a healthy buzz, but that was what she had expected. She knew consuming the potent liquid at a rapid pace would bring on the effects much quicker.

The music had changed to a saucy merengue and Sienna felt the overwhelming urge to dance. On purpose, she finished her drink with a loud gurgling sound through the straw, then shimmied her shoulders to match the static beat.

"I think I'll have another one of those," Sienna announced to no one in particular, then looked at Hawk, daring him to challenge her.

He narrowed his eyes and slid down farther in his seat, and her response was to mimic his actions.

This time a woman appeared and set down what Sienna assumed was a refill in front of her.

"Wow. I'm impressed," she smiled at the new waitress. "All you have to do is say what you want around here, and it simply appears." She waved her hand, as if she were performing magic.

A secretive smile touched the woman's lips before she began to walk away.

"Hey, you forgot to ask him if he wanted another beer." Sienna turned abruptly to remind the waitress, but she was surprised to find the woman no longer in sight. Raising both eyebrows and shrugging her shoulders, she looked innocently across at Hawk. "I guess they'll get you later."

As she was concluding her prediction, the original waiter reappeared.

"I thought by now you would be ready for a second drink, but you haven't touched the first."

"No, you are wrong," she sang, wagging her finger. "Not only did I finish that one, but one of the other waitresses was watching me and brought me a fresh drink."

"Other waitresses? We don't have any females working tonight," he informed her.

"You must. She brought me this drink."

First the waiter looked confused, then because of the dimness of the lighting, he leaned forward for a closer look.

"Mon Dieu!" he exclaimed, his eyes wide. "You did not drink any of that?"

Now it was Sienna's turn to be confused. "No," she replied, shaking her head.

"Don't. Don't even touch it." His accent had thickened with his excitement. "That drink is garnished with the fruit from the *mancenille* tree. If you just touch it, or if it gets wet and the liquid falls onto your skin, it causes painful blisters that leave a horrible scar."

"Say what?" Sienna looked down at the little green fruit that she had assumed was another grape. But now as she gave it a closer examination, its looks were more akin to an apple.

"It is true," the waiter insisted. "All over the island there are warning signs posted on the trees by the Forestry Commission. I cannot imagine what would happen to your insides if you drank this."

A cold chill went down Sienna's spine as several customers at the table next to them began to whisper. Slowly, her frightened gaze rose to Hawk's face, where she saw deep concern etched into the harsh lines. But what alarmed her most was that she could see he, too, believed someone had tried to kill her.

"I don't know who is behind this, Sienna, but from this moment on, I'll be your official taster if I have to be." The sound of his voice was like steel.

As quickly as the fear rose within her, confusion replaced it. Through the fog of her first drink, she tried to think clearly. Never before had anyone made an attempt on her life. Even when Spike had thrown her on the bed, she knew his intent had been other than murder.

So why was William trying to get rid of her now? Before she had found and delivered the ruby!

Sienna looked around at the people in the crowded restaurant, their images beginning to waver as her adrenaline surged. How dare someone try to murder her!

Before she knew it she was on her feet, with her hands placed firmly on her hips. Hawk's consoling words seemed to come from a distance.

"Take it easy, baby. If I can help it, I'm not going to let anyone get close enough to you to try and harm you ever again."

But Sienna's anger had reached a boiling point.

"Whoever tried to do this, you better watch out," she threatened loudly, weaving on her feet. "It's going to take a lot more than some stupid fruit from some tree to get rid of me."

The last thing Sienna remembered was Hawk lunging toward her. Then all went dark.

Eleven

Hawk placed Sienna on the bed. Immediately, her hair covered her face, and her arms and legs spread out at awkward angles. At first he had tried to secure a room in the hotel where they had eaten, but he was quickly informed there were no vacancies. He wondered if he had been told the truth or if the proprietor had decided it would be a bad risk to give them a room. Luckily, a young boy who saw him carrying Sienna from the building told him his parents ran a place similar to a bed and breakfast. When he arrived they only had one room available, but at that moment it did not matter. He paid the cost and was given the key.

Hawk looked down at Sienna's unconscious form, noting that she was breathing heavily. Perhaps it was a combination of her fainting and the alcohol. His handsome features mirrored his concern, and he determined his main objective was to make her comfortable. As he looked at her he decided the T-shirt was okay, as it would not block her circulation, but the tight-fitting jeans were another situation entirely.

Throughout the day he had been more than a little aware of how closely the denim molded to her hips, and it took all the reserve he had to put the thought in the back of his mind. Now again the jeans filled his thoughts, but this time for a different reason.

The small silver button was hard to unfasten, but once accomplished he began to loosen the waistband. Hawk noticed a deep crease around Sienna's waist. The skin there was a brownish-red from the tight clothing, and he decided the best thing to do would be to remove the jeans entirely.

At that moment Sienna's head began to loll against the cover and she mumbled incoherently. With deep concern, Hawk watched her flushed face as he knelt down at her feet and began to study how to take off her elaborately strapped sandals.

As time passed he soon found getting rid of her shoes was the easiest job yet, for the removal of her jeans was an awesome task. Small beads of perspiration sprinkled his brow as he continued to tug and pull at the denim, which was like a second skin.

"Damn. How in the world did she get into these things?" he swore.

Finally, he worked his large hands inside the waistband and gave one mighty tug. Sienna's hips rose and fell accordingly, and the pants gave way, exposing her profusely covered womanhood to his surprised gaze.

"Well, I'll be damned." His amber eyes narrowed as he continued with the job at hand.

He could feel the heat from her body, and her outer thighs and legs felt like silk against the back of his hand. Despite himself, in a reluctant way, he attempted to hurry through the enticing chore. And when it was done Hawk breathed a sigh of relief, gently pulling down Sienna's T-shirt to hide the most captivating part of her wares. Afterward, he drew the thin sheet up around her and sat down beside the bed in the only chair in the room.

Hawk stared into the flame of an oil lamp as his mind rehashed the scene inside the restaurant. It was plain someone had attempted to kill her, and a deadly glint entered his eyes at the thought. Had Sienna actually swallowed the fiery brew, the tender tissues of her mouth and throat would have blistered easily, blocking off the passageways and causing asphyxiation.

A gentle, balmy breeze touched his face and he turned toward the window from which it came. The soft mosquito netting appeared to breathe in and out, reminding him of the woman who lay no more than three feet away.

His life had become so entangled with hers, more than he had ever expected. Hawk believed he needed her as the Stonekeeper, with whatever mysterious, innate powers she possessed. Yet, until the appointed hour, he realized neither he nor she would actually know what those powers were. He had no choice but to trust that all the words he had canted in ignorance that fateful day were true—not only the part he suffered from now, but also the part that promised that for him too justice could be found with the Stonekeeper.

For a moment Hawk thought his ears were deceiving him as he heard the familiar chords of a song floating through the window on the night breeze. As he strained to listen the volume grew louder, and he surmised it was a tape being played by a boarder in a neighboring room.

The tune took him way back to younger days, but at the same time the lyrics were appropriate to what he was experiencing now. The mellow Isley Brothers tune, "Voyage to Atlantis," filled his very soul, and the song he sang was deep within his throat as well as his heart.

"misty lady, set my spirit free."

As Hawk sang he closed his eyes and he ached deep inside. It had been so hard to keep his secret these past five years. Hard and lonely, for he felt he could never tell anyone. None of the academicians he dealt with professionally would ever believe this kind of thing existed, let alone see Hennessy Jackson, the museum exhibition designer, being a part of it. And the women . . . He had made sure their relationship was of the nature that it wouldn't matter. Now Sienna had been placed in his life. Not just Sienna the Stonekeeper, but Sienna the woman.

He recognized the exact moment in the restaurant when she realized someone had tried to kill her. At first he saw fear in her beautiful dark eyes, but it was a matter of seconds before it turned to confusion and then to anger. His lips turned up at the corners in a rare smile as he visualized her weaving and standing, letting it be known she wouldn't be easy to eliminate.

Slowly, Hawk's head turned toward the bed and he opened his eyes. Sienna was lying there watching him, her eyes still dreamy with the first moments of consciousness.

"So you decided to come back?" His voice was husky, for she had caught him at a rare moment when his guard was down and his reactions pure.

"Yes. I guess I did." She closed her eyes for a moment. "What happened back there? All I remember is someone tried to poison me, I guess, and suddenly this rush of adrenaline just went straight to my head as I stood up. I had to let them know I hadn't come this far just to croak on some damn drink." She smiled weakly. "I don't remember if I got to say what I wanted to say."

"You said it all right"—he remained relaxed in the chair—"right before you crumpled into my arms. Most people probably thought you had had too many of whatever you were drinking. I think it was a combination of the drink and the shock."

Sienna closed her eyes. She could feel the sting of tears behind her eyelids. She didn't want Hawk to see her cry. She could tell he was proud of whatever she had done, and she didn't want to spoil it.

She shifted uneasily beneath the sheet, and Sienna could feel the smooth material touching her legs and thighs. Suddenly, the realization hit her that she was no longer wearing her jeans. Her gaze flew back to his face, her eyes bright with unshed tears and astonishment.

"You looked as if you needed a bit more breathing room," he responded, knowing the direction her thoughts had taken.

For a moment they just stared at each other, then overwhelming embarrassment dawned on Sienna's features and she looked away.

Music continued to drift in through the window, causing Hawk to emit a low, forceful oath as he recognized the newest tune their musical neighbors were playing.

"What's wrong?" Sienna asked, glad to steer the conversation away from where it had been.

"It's that song, 'Groove With You,' by the Isley Brothers." His eyes softened. "Ah, but I forget. You're probably too young to remember it. That's back in the days when music was music. Hasn't been anything like it since."

"What do you mean, back in the days?" She turned, snuggling under the blanket. "I remember that song. I don't know the exact time when it came out, but I remember this older girl named Vernecia in the orphanage, who owned an eight-track tape player. Most of us used to be jealous of her because of it, even though she was always willing to play requests if you asked her." Sienna smiled and smoothed her hair away from her face. "She played the Isley Brothers all the time. But the truth is—and maybe if you weren't so over-the-hill you'd know," she teased—"the Isley Brothers are considered to be real sweet right now."

"Sweet?"

"Yeah, sweet. That means ba-ad in young folk talk."

"Is that right?" His eyes smoldered.

"That's right." Sienna closed her eyes once again, blocking out what she saw within his gaze and trying to rid herself of how she was beginning to feel.

"It was kind of you to wait here with me until I came to. I know you must be tired," she continued. "Go ahead and lie down and rest now. I'll be all right."

"Are you sure?" A mischievous gleam entered Hawk's eyes.

"Yeah, I'm sure."

Hawk rose from the chair, walked around to the foot of the bed, which was opposite the door, and stopped. Then he continued around to the other side of the bed and sat down.

"What are you doing?" Sienna sat up abruptly.

"Taking your advice." He pulled his shirt over his head and bent down to remove his shoes.

"I meant in your room." She eyed him suspiciously.

"This is my room." He began removing his pants. "They only had one room left. And you scared the folks over at the hotel so they turned us out." He removed the leather that held back his dreadlocks, before climbing beneath the sheet.

"Look, I don't know about this." Sienna remained sitting. "It's a little too close for me."

"I won't bite if you won't"—his voice was low and silky, then he turned and looked up at her—"but I'll sleep underneath the blanket, putting the sheet between us, if that will make you feel safer."

"It's not that I don't feel safe, Hawk," she replied, exasperated. "It's just that"—Sienna looked down into his eyes which were full of mirth—"you know what I mean!"

"Okay. I can see you can't trust yourself," he chided, as he got on top of the sheet and pulled the blanket up over him.

Hawk lay on his back, acting as if he had closed his eyes. He could see Sienna looking indecisively about her, and then her attention rested on the tight jeans that lay across the chair. Finally, she slid back beneath the sheet, making sure there was the largest possible space between them in the full-size bed.

Hawk was very aware of her as they lay in silence. He wanted to reach out and touch her, to draw her near, but she had made it clear that was not what she wanted. So he willed himself to lie still as he waited for sleep to overtake him. Finally, he dozed off, the strains of Sade's voice mixing with the night sounds.

Sienna was dreaming. She was trying to snuggle closer to the warmth and protection that made itself available to her, but she was being kept from it. She was being held back by the invisible arms of those who wanted to harm her, which made her yearn even more for the love and protection that was within arm's reach. Desperately, she struggled against her restraints, until she finally broke free. It was a hard-won victory, but her reward was just as great, for she was captured in a warm embrace by someone who loved her and cared about her welfare.

Sienna's bountiful lips stretched into a satisfied smile as she draped her arms around the smooth hardness. It felt so good and strong, and she knew no harm would come to her there. Still, in that place where dreams are tangible and wakefulness is an illusion, her curly lashes began to flutter open. But as she stared into the darkness, she realized she could see no farther than a few inches in front of her face. Then full consciousness claimed her. Her nostrils filled with the soft scent of sandalwood, and she knew the sleek hardness she felt was nobody's dream.

Totally awake, Sienna realized she was lying with her face in the crook of Hawk's neck, her arms draped possessively about him. She could feel the even rise and fall of his chest, his breathing smooth. Just for a second she thought to remove herself, that it was not right to be there. This was not her man, and they had spoken no words of commitment. In fact, this man remained virtually a stranger, despite all the things they had experienced together.

Sienna had lain in a man's arms before, but it had never felt like this. Without trying, she could feel the intricate definition of his lithe body, and she knew this was the closest she had ever come to such male perfection. "God," she mouthed into the moonlit darkness, "how could any one man be so magnificent?"

Afraid she might awaken him, yet wanting to take full advantage of the moment, Sienna lay as still as possible, then carefully slid her hand down his arm, marveling at the way the sinew and muscle rose and declined. She closed her eyes as she clandestinely explored his body, her hand becoming bolder with its discoveries, following the shape of his chest and the wavy definition of his abdominals. Yet she did not dare put her hand where her thoughts had begun to wander.

Suddenly, an overwhelming shiver coursed through her at the very thought of him—his eyes like sparkling amber, his body like carved sandstone, his kiss a haunting fire. Only now, without his knowledge but with him, oh, so close, could she let herself acknowledge the emotions and sensations he created within her. They were very real, and they frightened her.

Sienna yearned to look at his face as he slept. She envisioned his handsome features in sweet repose without the harshness he cloaked around him. She wondered what it would feel like to trace his eyebrows, his nose, his lips.

The moments passed, and Sienna could stand the temptation no longer. Gently, she lifted her head so her eyes could feast on his sleeping features. What she saw touched her heart, and her breath nearly caught in her throat. He was just as she had expected and more, for now with his face in a state of repose the years had also been swept away, and before her, she could imagine, lay the sweet and simple boy, Hennessy Jackson.

Sienna was not ready to let Hawk know how she felt about him. It was only at this moment that she had allowed herself to acknowledge the truth. She cared about him in a way she could not explain. It was deeper than the physical, more expansive than what she had come to know love to be. Then the thought hit her that maybe she was *in* love with him, something she had never been before.

Ever so softly Sienna raised her hand and began to trace the shape of his eyes and nose, her finger mere inches from his face. When she finally arrived at his mouth she traced it slowly, then closed her eyes, silently puckering up to plant an imaginary kiss. It was almost as if she could feel his lips upon hers, the warmth and the sweet pressure.

Sienna allowed her mouth to relax, reveling in the exquisite vividness of her imagination, when the silky feel of Hawk's tongue worked its way between her lips, his arms pulling her gently down toward him. Her eyes flew open, only to look straight into his, which were smoky with desire and something else that tugged at Sienna's insides.

All of a sudden she felt like melted wax, and she allowed him to deepen the kiss as he molded

her body to his own. The welding of their
mouths seem to draw her in, until she was no
longer the Sienna she knew herself to be. She
had transformed into a floating manifestation
of sweetness, tingling from head to foot, all of
her completely aware of the honeyed sensation.

She could tell she was not alone in her pleasure, for suddenly Hawk's body quaked with a
violent tremor as a groan rumbled deep in his
throat. His arms tightened about her, and in a
series of quick motions he kicked himself free
of the blanket and rolled over, pulling her beneath him. It was his weight that brought home
the full reality of their situation. She was no
longer dreaming, and their seminude states
were real. If she planned to turn back, the moment would be now and not later.

It was as if Hawk could read her mind, for
he released her from the kiss and began to stare
down into her face.

"I want you, Sienna. I've wanted you from the
very moment I saw you standing with that lamp
in your hand, ready to defend yourself, no matter the size of the enemy." His dreadlocks cas-
caded down around them, creating an intimate
shield. "You don't know much about me, but
there are some things I'm just not ready to reveal. But this I can say: I've never killed a man.
I'm not a liar, I'm not a cheat," he spoke with
his mouth excruciatingly close to hers, "and my
money has always come by honest means.

"At this point I can't promise you a future of
happiness, for neither one of us knows what our
future brings. But what I can promise you, Sienna Russell"—his amber gaze explored every
inch of her face—"is that you will never find a man

who will cherish you more than I do at this moment and who will love you the way I can."

Sienna had had promises made to her before, but none that touched her the way his sincere words did. Right away she knew her answer. She wanted this man as she had never wanted any man before.

"Oh, Hawk . . ." Her hands went up behind his head, and she drew him back down toward her. This time, with her eyes fixed upon his, she touched his lips with her own, then slowly closed them as she immersed herself in the kiss, drawing Hawk in with her. When they stopped to catch their breaths, Hawk placed both of his hands on her face, then brought an index finger up to his lips. "Wait," he said softly.

He got up off the bed and removed the rest of his clothing, then slowly drew back the sheet that had covered the lower half of Sienna's frame. Once again he climbed upon the bed, this time straddling her thighs with his knees. Hawk began to pull her T-shirt upward, until Sienna was persuaded to lift her arms, allowing him to draw the soft material over her head.

He sat back on his haunches as he dropped the shirt by the side of the bed.

"My, my, my, look what we have here," Hawk declared, drinking in the length of her with his thirsty gaze. "Sienna Russell, you are absolutely breathtaking."

Her heart was so full she could barely speak. So she didn't. Instead, she took pleasure in watching his every move.

His body formed a perfect V shape, enhanced by muscle and a subtle grace. For a moment he just sat back and looked at her, his head held perfectly straight, his eyes cast downward. Sienna watched him lift his arms as if he were about to conduct an orchestra, then he leaned closer, gently placing his outstretched palms against the sides of her neck. He allowed his hands to work their way down, as if he were molding her body out of delicate clay. Tenderly, they flowed over her silky skin, exalting in the very feel of her. When his hands reached her breasts he kneaded them sensually, awakening the nipples with the centers of his palms, causing them to become erect and hard.

At that moment he looked into her eyes. "This is wonderful brown sugar," he enunciated each word just loud enough for her to hear.

Sienna felt as if she were drowning in his praise and she continued to soak up the longing that was evident in his eyes. No one had ever made her feel so beautiful, so unique. She longed to touch him, to tell him her thoughts, but again he took his index finger, this time placing it against her mouth.

"Sh-sh, not yet, baby. I want to explore every inch of you. I want to know everything there is to know."

His hands continued their downward exploration, curving in with her waist, moving outward, tracing the lines of her round hips. Sienna saw him suddenly remove his hands, and she observed his breathing deepen. To her amazement he put his fingertips against his lightly puckered lips, then gently placed them on the curly, triangle between her legs.

Hawk stroked her with his palm and then with the back of his hand, a purring sound emanating outward. Sienna's breath caught in her

throat as she heard him whisper, not so much
for her ears, but to himself, "The world would
be nothing without a woman like you."

His fingers began to explore her further,
causing her to close her eyes in pleasure. With
gentle, knowing movements Hawk caressed
every part of her, until he caused her desire to
flow. In moments Sienna's hips responded to
his strokes, eagerly meeting the benefactor of
their delight.

Without removing his hand, Hawk lay down
beside her once more, placing his mouth close
to her ear. Over and over again he murmured
the most beautiful things, until her head swam
with his words and her body ached for his pene-
tration. Suddenly, he seemed to be everywhere,
planting kissing on her mouth, her neck, her
shoulders, her breasts.

"There's so much I want to do to you, Sienna,
but tonight there is one thing mainly on my
mind. I want to make you mine in a way that
only a man can."

By now every breath Sienna drew was a moan
of pleasure. No one had ever made her feel so
desirable, so wanted. The things Hawk's hands
and mouth were doing to her were unbelievable,
but it was the things he said that catapulted the
experience into another realm. Sienna writhed
and undulated with the fire that raged inside
her. She needed it to be quenched, and she
tugged at his arms and his waist, urgently pulling him toward her.

"Oh, God, Hawk, what are you doing to me?"
she pleaded in raspy tones. "Come to me now,
Hawk. Come to me now."

"I am going to come to you, sugar. I am on my way."

He settled himself between her thighs as he wrapped his arms tightly about her.

"This is where you come to know the Hawk, baby," he whispered as he flicked her ear with his tongue. "Come fly with me now, Sienna, and we'll soar together to a place we have never been. We belong together, you and me. I can feel it in every part of me, and no matter what might happen, I don't want you to ever forget that." His words were hot and moist against her ear. "Long ago before we were born, you promised to be mine, and I'm collecting on that promise, Sienna Russell. Do you hear me? I'm here to claim what's mine."

He entered her with one smooth stroke, and immediately she felt a delectable fullness. With a knowledge that was as natural as breathing, their bodies locked together. Hawk's fervor was intense and he pulled her up toward him, causing Sienna to arch her back. As the minutes passed their pace accelerated, until they were in a frenzy of movements and words. As they climbed to the heights of their passion the things Hawk said egged them on, evolving from words of love to statements of pure sexual abandon.

"Oh, baby, I can see that peak now! Can you see it, Sienna? Can you feel it?" His words were breathy and strained.

"Yes, Hawk. I feel it. I'm there with you, baby. I . . . am . . . there!"

It was an explosion of monumental magnitude, and for a moment Sienna lost all sense of time and space. All she knew was the height of the sensations that coursed through her now were new and overwhelming, and she wanted them to last forever. They continued to hold onto each other long after their passion was spent. It was strange, because now words were not necessary. They kissed, snuggling close, wondering what tomorrow would bring. For there was no doubt in Hawk's or Sienna's mind that they had sealed their fate together in the most powerful way possible for a woman and a man.

Twelve

"Look at this!" Sienna exclaimed as she hiked the knapsack farther up on her shoulder. "Can you believe it?"

Hawk was only a few paces behind her, and his eyes narrowed as they took in the two flat tires.

"Well, do you think they made it clear enough?" She threw her arms up in the air as she walked around the car, only to find all four tires were flat. "Somebody really doesn't want us to go any further."

"Yeah, I'd say you are right." Hawk looked up and down the street, which was virtually empty except for a few street vendors setting up their wares.

"Who in the hell do you think is doing this stuff?" The tone of her voice expressed her exasperation. "It doesn't make any sense for it to be William. Whoever this is, they don't want us to find the ruby. And after last night's episode, I don't think there is anything they won't do to stop us!"

"Uh-huh." He nodded his head in agreement. "You're in rare form this morning, Sienna, but I must admit you were in rarer form last night."

Her heart did an instant flip-flop as she turned and smiled at him. Not a toothy smile, but the smile of a woman well satisfied. Even so, Sienna was unsure of what to do about her budding emotions and the relationship evolving between them.

"Well, you weren't too bad yourself, Mr. Jackson."

"Is that right?"

"Mm-hmm," she agreed, as a flash of heat encased her.

He walked up beside her and placed his arms around her waist. "I'm going to let you in on a secret."

Her eyes looked expectantly up into his face and she wondered if he were about to reveal whatever it was that haunted him.

"There's quite a variety, and plenty more where that came from."

"Ohh, you . . ." She poked him playfully in the shoulder, trying not to show her disappointment. "I thought you had something to really tell me."

Sienna watched as the color of his eyes deepened, and that familiar hooded look came over his features. "I told you, baby, there are some things I cannot tell you."

Sienna looked down at his chest, which was at eye level, and she tried to control her reaction. He *had* told her, but somehow she had expected that after last night he would see things differently.

She could feel a gnawing ache in the pit of her stomach. Sienna realized the only thing that had changed was that she had given herself to this man, and as a result her love for him had grown deeper. As long as she had been able to deny her feelings, a part of her had resided at a safe distance. But after last night, that was no longer possible.

"Hey-ey . . ." Hawk placed his finger beneath her chin, lifting her face up to meet his again. "Baby, believe me. This is not something that you want to know." He searched her eyes deeply. "It's something that when the time comes, I pray will work itself out. Until then, I'm going to have to keep it to myself.

"But right now I'd say we've got some decisions to make." He took another glance down the street. "Let's see if they have a place around here that will rent us another vehicle."

Minutes later, Hawk and Sienna entered a small shop that had a sign outside advertising car and motorbike rentals.

"Bon matin. I am Smita, may I help you?" An almond-complexioned, thin woman greeted them.

"Yes, you can," Hawk answered. "We were wondering if you had any cars available to rent."

"No. I'm sorry. You have come at a busy, busy time." She spoke with her hands. "A large group of students are exploring the rain forest. That's why all the rooms were just about taken last night, and the same goes for rental cars."

"So that explains the Isley Brothers," Sienna commented, looking at Hawk.

"Quoi? What?" the woman asked, confused.

"Never mind," Hawk informed her, shaking his hand. "We'll try someplace else."

The woman came around the counter eagerly.

"I don't believe it would do you any good. It is much the same throughout town. But come, come, come," she beckoned to them. "I believe

I have something that you can use. Is it just the two of you?"

"Yes," they both replied.

She smiled broadly, her dark brown eyes shining. "I can help you then."

They followed the woman through a back door and out into a clearing. Not a single car was in sight, and Sienna's brows folded together in confusion.

"Here it is," the woman called from a few steps behind them. "It is a motorcycle. A good size one, too." She shook her head encouragingly.

Sienna eyed the machine with uneasy speculation. She had never before ridden a motorcycle, never having had the desire. But already Hawk was beside the bike, pulling it away from the wall against which it leaned.

"There is absolutely nothing wrong with it," the woman advised them. "The only thing is, it is missing the kickstand. I will rent it to you for a good price."

Images of the curves they'd encountered traveling from Fort-de-France to St. Pierre surfaced in Sienna's mind, and the thought of riding on a motorcycle, virtually unprotected, brought on an eerie feeling.

"Hawk, do you know anything about motorcycles?" She didn't like the daredevil gleam that had entered his eyes.

"A little bit," he replied as he climbed aboard, balancing the machine between his legs.

"How little?" she pressed.

"I know enough for us to get where we're going." He flashed her a wink, and before she could respond, he told the woman they'd take it.

Money exchanged hands, and the pleased female informed them the bike had to be back in two days.

"We'll have it back before then," Hawk assured her, then he turned to Sienna. "Climb aboard."

"I have never ridden one of these things before." She approached him warily. "And I want to know before I climb on this bike with you that you know what you're doing."

"Would I put my newly found brown sugar in jeopardy?" Hawk feigned offense at her question.

"I hope not," Sienna retorted as she assessed the small space on the seat behind him.

"No, I wouldn't," he reassured her as he started the bike with a loud rumble, causing Sienna to jump. "So put your bag and mine back in that compartment, and we'll be on our way."

Sienna did as she was instructed, then took a deep breath and mounted the bike. Automatically, she did what she'd seen so many bikers do, wrapping her arms around Hawk's waist.

"You ready to head to *Le Morne Rouge?*" he shouted above the motor's noise.

"I'm as ready as I'm going to get."

Before she had the last word out of her mouth, the motorcycle shot forward, causing her to close her eyes tightly and to hold on to his waist for dear life.

With sheer precision, Hawk swung into the street and headed up the road. In a matter of minutes, they were outside of the town and making their way against the hot tropical wind. At first the air felt as if it would burn her throat and her lungs, so Sienna hid her face in Hawk's back, squeezing him all the tighter.

"What's going on back there?" she barely heard him ask above the wind and the motor.

"The air is so hot I can hardly breathe." She tipped her face upward, shouting toward his ear.

"Well, if you think you've got it bad, try breathing while your woman's squeezing the life out of you," he chided her.

Embarrassed, Sienna loosened her grip as she gulped the hot, moist air. He had called her his woman and she pressed herself even closer to his back, unable to stop smiling from sheer joy.

Earlier that morning, when they had awakened in each other's arms, smiling, they'd shared an undeniable feeling of awe. There wasn't a trace of darkness behind which to hide. Nothing existed but the stark nakedness of their feelings and their bodies.

As they had silently watched one another after monosyllabic greetings, they'd shared admiring, tender touches of approval, along with lingering kisses that communicated their special feelings. After a while Sienna could feel her passion begin to flow and could see evidence of Hawk's mounting passion as well. But they honored it by savoring the intense feeling, holding each other close with promises of what the coming night would bring.

Sienna and Hawk had ridden for a couple of miles, driving deeper into the tropical rain forest. On both sides of them trees blanketed the landscape, along with a multitude of flowers and a bewildering variety of rich vegetation. Once Sienna became accustomed to breathing the hot air, she was amazed at how she could actually taste the flowers on the wind in this area, which was so alive and magical.

Few words passed between them as they continued to ride, as it was quite difficult to hear above the wind and the roar of the motor. Still Sienna rode behind him, strangely content, watching the forest flash by in an array of shades of green. Practically all of her life she had lived in Georgia, with an abundance of trees, but she had never seen such vibrancy as this. It was as if man had not dampened the spirit of Mother Earth in Martinique. In her natural state she exhibited the apex of her beauty, producing colors and sounds in the most powerful way.

Sienna began to close her eyes and hum to herself, her voice matching the vibration of the motorcycle beneath her. She envisioned a time when all of this was over, when they had found the ruby and disposed of it, and she and Hawk were able to be together under normal circumstances. It was almost hard to imagine a normal life with Hawk, for he seemed so much bigger than the kind of life she had known.

Sienna opened her eyes momentarily as they leaned into a curve, but when she saw the deep ravine that dropped off from the road mere yards away she wished she had kept her eyes closed. All of a sudden she heard the roar of a engine behind them, and she looked back to see a dark car approaching at a terrifying speed.

Hawk, too, had become aware of the vehicle and he turned the gauges at the end of the handlebars to accelerate, hopefully putting more distance between them. But as they sped up, navigating the dangerous curves, so did the other vehicle, until Sienna was beginning to feel as if they were being frightened or even worse.

"Maybe you should pull over on the opposite

side of the road and allow them to pass us," she
screamed above the wind.

"I don't think they're interested in passing us,
Sienna. I have a feeling they've got something
else in mind. I'm going to try my best to outma-
neuver them."

Hawk leaned into the wind, giving the motorcycle even more power. Sienna glued herself to
his back as he weaved the bike in and out, showing skill that proved he knew more than a little
about biking. Repeatedly, the car nearly came
alongside them, where it could have easily
forced them off into the ravine, but Hawk managed to keep them at bay.

"Hold on tight, baby. I've got to do this. And
I've got to do it now!"

With a move of smarts, dexterity, and sheer
guts, Hawk took a chance when he saw an on-
coming car. Giving the motorcycle all it was
worth, in an instant he crossed in front of the
vehicle, speeding onto a walking path that led
deeper into the forest.

"Oh, my God, we're going to get hit," Sienna
screamed as she buried her face in Hawk's
broad back.

The frightened driver swerved to miss them,
and in so doing caused the car in pursuit to
abruptly steer toward the ravine, where it went
over in a recurring crashing sound of metal hitting the earth. Sienna's scream filled the air as
they continued into the forest, dodging trees and
bumping over fallen trunks and humongous
roots.

Finally, they came to a skidding halt up
against a tree in the midst of a group of frightened, bewildered hikers. One of them, a young

man sporting a university T-shirt and the strong scent of beer on his breath, remarked, "It doesn't take all that to join our group. Just pay me with a six-pack from back home, and you can take my place on the rest of the tour."

The hissing sound of air seeping out of a tire rent the air, and for the second time that day Hawk and Sienna found themselves without a vehicle.

With her arms feeling like taut rubber bands, Sienna disengaged herself from Hawk and studied the hikers who stood before them. The group consisted of three women and five men. All of them looked like tourists.

"Where are you headed?" Hawk asked as he assisted Sienna in climbing off the bike. When her feet touched the ground, her head began to ache and her knees wobbled.

A young East Indian man stepped forward, and as he began to speak it was obvious he had been hired as a guide.

"We just started out at *Le Morne Rouge*"—he pointed in a southeasterly direction—"and we're headed for *Mont Pelée*. If you wish to join us, the charge will be sixty francs per person."

Sienna saw Hawk look at the guide, then back at the motorcycle. In her mind there was no decision to be made. There was safety in numbers, and with the way their luck was going they were going to need all the help they could get.

Thirteen

Sienna had never felt so much a part of nature in her entire life. She felt as if she were an extension of the earth and she knew what it really meant to be alive. Inhaling deeply, she realized the weight of the air had changed; it had become lighter as they slowly climbed the side of Mount Pelée, the volcano.

Hawk walked ahead with the guide, and every once in a while he would turn to make sure of her progress. It seemed to Sienna that as the day moved ahead, so did the anxiousness inside him. She could see it in his eyes and in the tenseness of his gait. She wondered if it was the result of what had happened on the road, or if it was the manifestation of the secret he so jealously kept.

She looked up above her at the tiny patches of sky that sprinkled the tree-filled forest. It was a magnificent world of light and dark, of scents and smells, of life in its purest form. Beams of sunlight pierced the trees, only to appear that much brighter because of the shadows that lurked beneath the dense vegetation. The contrast reminded her of Hawk, for Sienna continued to bathe in the light of tenderness he had shown her over the last twenty-four hours. She believed there was no way anyone who could give such love could be the vessel of anything evil. Whatever it was he felt about himself, it was shame and maybe even fear that showed so heavily in his eyes.

Sienna reached out and touched the large trunk of a mahogany tree. She could smell the wood mixed with the scent of bamboo growing nearby. She almost felt guilty about the exhilarating feeling the forest was evoking. It was as if it had become a part of her and she a part of it.

"We're going to be stopping at a clearing within the next five to ten minutes," the guide named Raja turned and informed them. "For those of you who want to continue farther into the interior to *Ciel de Marbre,* another guide will be waiting for you there. The remainder of the group will go on with me to *Ajoupa-Bouillon,* where we will stop for food before going on to *Basse-Pointe.* "

Minutes later another guide was waiting just as Raja had promised, but he was not alone. A small round-faced boy with shaggy bangs was also there. Sienna smiled at the child as they approached, and his eyes appeared to brighten at her presence.

For the majority of their hike she and Hawk stayed apart, but it was not of her choosing. He had consistently kept distance between them, staying ahead with the guide or sometimes even walking alone.

Feeling a need to be near him, Sienna let her eyes scan the group and she found him standing alone by a tree. She went to join him, as the two guides exchanged information and the hikers discussed their plans.

"Where do you think we should go from here?" Sienna inquired, gently touching his arm.

"I'm not sure." He turned a troubled gaze upon her.

His eyes were brighter than normal, the amber almost a piercing gold. The sight of them took her by surprise.

"Are you okay?" Sienna asked, placing her hand against his forehead, then moving it to his jaw and the side of his neck.

With the speed of a cobra, his grip cutting into her flesh, Hawk grabbed her hand, thrusting it away.

"Don't touch me."

Sienna was stunned by his actions and hurt by the fury she saw on his face and heard in his voice.

"Don't touch you?" she repeated with disbelief. For a moment she was speechless, but her confusion quickly turned to anger.

"What in the hell do you mean?" she demanded.

She could see he was trying to take control of his raging feelings, for his temple beat visibly and his face nearly trembled. Sienna observed a barrage of emotions flash through his eyes, but in the end the words he spoke were devastating.

"You're going to have to keep your distance from me, Sienna. Just stay away."

She watched him walk away, putting distance between himself and the group, and her eyes clouded over, forecasting an onslaught of tears. What possessed him to say such things to her? Knowing how badly she needed him . . . how badly she had come to believe they needed one another.

The change Sienna saw in Hawk was too great to fathom. It hit her like a shot out of the dark. Stunned, she leaned against the tree, placing the side of her face on the rugged bark.

She didn't have the strength to question him any further. She didn't have the will. For the past seventy-two hours her life had evolved into a roller coaster, with unexpected twists and turns. And for the first time last night she felt as if she had broken through. The lovemaking she and Hawk shared had taken her to new heights, and she had come to hope that no matter what was in store for her as a Stonekeeper, perhaps she had found someone in her life who would always be there. Someone she could love who would eventually love her in return. She had thought perhaps that was the purpose of it all. For her, Sienna Russell, to be given someone who would never leave her. A final sign from the powers that be that she had been forgiven for forsaking them.

Sienna didn't realize how far she had stepped out on the emotional limb with Hawk until it was unexpectantly pulled from beneath her.

As she continued to lean against the tree, she could feel a persistent nudging against her hand, which lay limply by her side. With teardrops nestled in the corners of her eyes, Sienna looked down to see the small boy, trying to press something into her hand. His dark eyes appeared soothingly clear, drawing her into their calming waters. Feeling compelled, Sienna opened her hand to allow him access, and with the gentlest of motions he placed a smooth green stone inside. Delicately, his small fingers curled her hand up around it, until it was hidden within her closed palm.

With hurried steps, the guide who had accompanied the child crossed the clearing in their direction and began to speak rapidly in a language Sienna did not understand. Then in stilted English, he apologized to her.

"I sorry, it is not like the boy to bother anyone. It no happen again."

"Oh, no," she refuted him. "He came to give me a gift." She stretched out her hand to show the rock.

The man looked at the stone, the little boy, then back at Sienna.

"It is very special that the boy has give you especially this stone. I have known him to carry it always. Many people in the village where he comes believe he was born with a special sight," he continued hesitantly, unsure of how Sienna would receive him. "Day after day he sits with his grandmother, who is a wise woman. She is a healer. She is in village of *Ciel de Marbre*. The stone is sign for you to go to old woman," he encouraged. "As guide I have studied the world and I have come to know signs, both natural and outside of natural. He is young, but his knowing is true. Follow his sign." He bowed slightly before grabbing the child by the hand and walking away.

The guide and the boy returned to the center of the clearing, where Raja and the hikers waited. Inspired both by the guide's words and the boy's kindness, Sienna had made up her mind. She would go with the guide and the boy to the village of which he spoke. Perhaps there she would be told where to find the Passion Ruby.

With her chin tilted upward to bolster her confidence, Sienna looked at Hawk, who paced the clearing on the outskirts. At the precise moment that she laid eyes on him he turned abruptly, causing their gazes to meet. His uncanny timing startled her and she stopped in her tracks. But before she could make another move he reversed his steps, disappearing into the rain forest.

Sienna looked about her, distressed, wondering if anyone else had witnessed the odd occurrence. Only the guides and the young boy seemed to have noticed Hawk's actions, the hikers apparently oblivious.

After sharing words with Raja, the guide and the boy walked toward her. Intermittently, his eyes searched the forest where Hawk had disappeared.

"So, will you be continuing up the volcano," he inquired, "or will you head to *Ciel de Marbre?*"

Sienna looked down at the stone she held in her hand, then over at the boy.

"I want to go to the village," she resolved, but her thoughts and her heart were with Hawk in the forest.

"Ma'am . . ." The guide spoke again.

"Yes?"

"Do not worry about your friend." Sienna's worried gaze returned to his face. "I have seen his kind before. He is like an animal of the forest. His senses are heightened. He is being guided by a higher force, even if he does not know it. He will not be led astray."

Sienna nodded bleakly, grateful for his words of encouragement.

"It is time to go now," the guide informed her, his steady gaze focused on her face as the boy stood quietly several feet away.

Sienna looked over at the hikers who were gathering around the other guide, Raja.

"Are we the only ones?"

"Yes. It is as it should be," he said, his eyes filling with a strange light. "The others are continuing on the road to the cities."

They waved goodbye and started down a narrow path. Like a zombie she followed in the guide's footsteps, the boy's hand in hers, her thoughts a massive clutter. Why had the boy given her the stone? What would she find at *Ciel de Marbre?* But most of all, her thoughts kept returning to Hawk. Why had he gone into the rain forest? What were the higher forces that the guide claimed had directed him? And at her heaviest moment she would ask: Why had he forsaken her? But no sooner did the thought enter her mind than she heard the distinct sound of footsteps, and Sienna felt a presence hovering around her. Somehow she knew it was Hawk, although not once did he show his face. Sienna came to believe it was his way of assuring her he was still there.

She had no idea how long they walked, but by the time they reached the village it was almost dark. The trees had thinned out to almost an orderly fashion, and the flowers began to appear in decorative patterns, as if placed there by man's hand. Finally, the narrow path became paved with stone, eventually widening into an entire road.

Sienna couldn't believe her eyes as she gazed at the sight before her. Large white buildings of Hindu design lined the streets. Some of the architecture was unbelievably august, but even the most humble structures were amazing to behold. But the strangest thing of all was that there wasn't a single building outside of those that lined the street. The structures formed an angular, upside-down U, with the most magnificent edifice at the center.

"My God! This is like another world," Sienna cried as she walked in a circle, surveying the unexpected scene.

"I'm sure it appears that way to you. But for those who live here, the outside world is another world."

"What does *Ciel de Marbre* mean?" she asked in awe.

"It means 'Sky of Marble.' All the buildings here are made of white marble, and it has been that way for as long as the people's memory have served them. Their records, both written and oral, attest to the same."

They walked down the unusually clean, quiet street. It was so quiet, in fact, that Sienna thought she could hear the echo of her own footsteps.

"Where is everyone?"

"They are in their homes."

"Everyone?" she questioned.

"Yes, everyone."

There was an odd sense of calmness, almost a solemnity, to the place. It was difficult for Sienna to believe that this extraordinary village existed nestled deep within the rain forest. If she hadn't seen it with her own eyes, she would have thought she was dreaming.

Sienna was overwhelmed by curiosity. One question after another popped into her mind. Another question was on the tip of her tongue when the guide cut her off, making his intentions clear.

"I am taking you to the woman's house. I will tell her about the boy giving you the stone, and she will know what to do from there. It will be up to her to tell you all you need to know."

Minutes later they came to a medium-sized building with a domed center. On the face of the dome was a circular window made from what appeared to be multicolored glass cut into pie-shaped slices. But as they got closer, Sienna could see that the windowpanes were actually made of thin pieces of stones ranging from purple amethyst to yellow citrine.

The guide knocked on the door, but his tapping was so light Sienna was sure it was impossible for anyone in a building that size to hear him. Immediately, however, almost as if by magic, the door swung silently open and they were welcomed inside.

Sienna noticed that like the outside, the interior was also white, with countless numbers of candles and sconces providing illumination. At first she thought the huge hall was empty, until she caught a glimpse of someone she assumed was a young woman, walking rapidly ahead of them, then quickly disappearing inside an alcove to their far right.

"We are to follow her," the guide commented as he headed in the woman's direction.

"Well, I tell you if I was back home, she wouldn't be considered your most hospitable hostess." Sienna tried to bring some humor to the unworldly situation. "No hello. Nothing. We didn't even see her face. And she's practically making us find our own way."

The guide did not acknowledge her remark, which only magnified the bizarre stillness of the house, the nerve-racking sloshing of Sienna's sandals the only sound to be heard. Not being able to stand it any longer, she hurriedly propped herself up against a wall to remove the shoes, as the guide and the boy turned the corner and disappeared as well.

Sienna continued down the large, empty hall alone, her feet padding softly against the warm marble. When she came to the spot where the others had disappeared, she found an arched opening, with the height a perfect fit for a four-foot-tall child. She was shocked by this newest development and she leaned forward, hunching her shoulders together in order to fit through.

As Sienna unfolded her body to its fullest height, she was surprised to find herself in a triangular-shaped room. Young females of all shapes and sizes sat against the wall in the lotus position, theirs legs crossed one upon another, their palms placed together in a prayerlike fashion, gracefully centered on their chests.

A multitude of eyes rested calmly on her as she surveyed the room, finally settling on the guide and the boy, who stood quietly beside a magnificent woman wrapped in garlands of lotuses, who sat at the head of the isosceles-shaped area.

Like most of the women around her, she was tiny in stature, but there was something about her presence that emanated a grandness far exceeding her physical being. She seemed to shine like the jewels that they all wore in abundance, but this woman herself was the most precious jewel of all.

"Come here, Sienna Russell." Her voice filled the room in bell-like tones.

Stiffly, Sienna began to approach her as the guide and the boy left the room through a side door. She didn't know why, but despite the woman's loving demeanor, she began to feel fear bubbling up inside her.

So much had happened to her over the last few days that it was enough to send anyone over the edge, and as Sienna came and stood in front of the woman, she began to question her own sanity. Was she really in this place? Were these people real, or were they the result of her warped imagination?

The guide had said he was taking her to the boy's grandmother, whom he sat with every day. But the woman Sienna saw before her was so young and beautiful that she couldn't imagine her having a child, let alone a grandchild.

"I understand that the boy has presented you with a stone. May I see it?" She stretched out her tiny hand.

Sienna placed the green stone inside her palm and she watched as the woman stroked it lovingly, then held it up to the light of a nearby candle, where it gleamed a scintillating delicate green.

"It is beautiful jade," she announced as she continued to examine the stone. "The boy has given it to you to give you clarity, courage, and wisdom." Her large, kohl-outlined almond eyes rested on Sienna's face. "With this stone, which is so nurturing, you will be able to manifest those particular things in your life. Things you will need in great abundance as the last Stonekeeper. You will need them in order to reclaim the Passion Ruby and return it to her rightful owner, Mother Earth."

"You know about the legacy of the Stone-keeper?"

"Yes. They have been in existence for the last five hundred years. You are the last Stonekeeper before what is called the end times."

"But I don't understand." Sienna balled up her fist in front of her. "Why am I the last Stonekeeper? And what is my purpose?"

"You made a promise before you were born. All human beings do," she answered calmly. "You come to this side of life willingly, to learn the lessons that you can only learn being a physical being. You, Sienna, promised to fulfill the job of the last Stonekeeper."

"But how can I fulfill a mission that I don't understand?" she stressed, trying to make the woman comprehend her.

"I will tell you this: The Stonekeeper's purpose is to store the stories and events of humankind inside special gems. This is necessary so that future generations can access the information, and learn from man's mistakes and his triumphs.

"You are on a quest to find the Passion Ruby. In your most recent recorded history, it was one of the main jewels in The Peacock Throne, built by the Shah Jahan. The events in his life and many others are recorded within the ruby, placed there by Stonekeepers like yourself. The only responsibility of the Stonekeepers before you was to record the events inside the gems. You are the last Stonekeeper. Your task is twofold: record the events and return the stone to Mother Earth."

"But how will I know where to find it? And what will I do about the man William? He is holding Dawn. He will kill her if I don't give him the ruby."

"The people who are caught up in the power of the ruby are also fulfilling a role. They are the reincarnations of the ones who have encountered the Passion Ruby before. Their destinies are not fixed; it is a time of opportunity for them, as it is for all living humans. Their sole purpose is to live each life acting out the highs and lows of human nature, a mirror of mankind as a whole.

"What you are doing, Sienna Russell, is for the future of mankind. Do you think any human being will have the ability to stop what the Creator has put into motion? Simply follow the signs as they are given to you. Always remain open and aware. You will be protected, Sienna. Your mission is vital to the whole."

The woman had begun to close her eyes, as all the women in the room were beginning to do. Sienna could tell she was being dismissed, but she was not yet ready to go.

"But what about Hawk?" she blurted out, causing the woman's eyes to open abruptly.

Her voice rang with the tinkle of distant chimes.

"The man Hawk is tied to the gemstones as well. But you and he have a special bond. He is your twin flame," she declared. Then her eyes closed, and the room was perfectly still.

Sienna wanted to ask more questions: What did she mean when she said that Hawk was her twin flame? And what was the secret that haunted him? But the guide appeared at the back doorway alone, beckoning for her to follow him. Reluctantly, she obeyed his instructions and they returned, through a passageway, to the quiet streets.

Fourteen

"Uh-uh-uh." Sienna heard the deep-throated moan, and she wondered who it was that was in such pain. As she turned her head to seek the source of the sound, a throbbing spasm exploded inside her skull.

"She's awake, Pria! Come quickly," Raja called.

Again Sienna attempted to see what all the commotion was about and she tried to pull herself up on her side, but immediately she found herself flat on her back.

"No, no, no. You must not do that." A grim-faced woman hovered over her. "You are just coming back to us, and you must not move around."

"I'm what? Did something happen?" Sienna looked at the woman, then over at Raja. "Where is the guide and the boy?"

The two people looked at one another curiously, and then the middle-aged woman began to shake her head.

"I don't know who you're talking about," the woman confessed, her dark eyes confused. "Do you know what she is saying?" She turned to Raja, who was approaching the bed.

"I was your guide, Ms. Russell. Remember?

You and the man came crashing into the forest where I was conducting a tour. When the motorcycle stopped, you hit your head against a tree. At first you appeared to be okay, but then you collapsed. You've been unconscious ever since."

Sienna put her hand up to her forehead.

"But wasn't there another man? A guide and a young boy? They took me to a village called *Ciel de Marbre*. The guide told me it was located between some village which is hard for me to remember and another called *Basse-Pointe*."

The woman's hand flew up to her mouth, and she began to mutter in a language Sienna did not understand. Raja's eyes became enlarged, and he began to stutter.

"Th-th-there was once a village called *Ciel de Marbre,* located deep within the forest between *Ajoupa-Bouillon* and *Basse-Pointe,* but that was a thousand years ago. I have heard people say the vegetation is so thick there now that you can hardly see the remaining ruins of the buildings. But one of our legends say that when *Ciel de Marbre* was at its peak, it was one of the most magnificent villages on earth. All the buildings were made of—"

"White marble," Sienna interrupted him. "And they were all built on one continuous U-shaped street." Her eyes took on a faraway look. "There was a woman there, a very beautiful woman, who wore garlands of lotuses and who lived in a building with a circular, colorful window."

"*Dieu,* God," Pria exclaimed. "She speaks of the House of Chakras. And of the Goddess Lakshmi. But how do you know such things?"

"I was there," Sienna replied. "Or at least I thought I was." She looked down at her quivering hands. "She told me why I was a Stonekeeper and that I would be protected. And she spoke of Hawk." Sienna lifted her overly bright eyes back up to their astonished faces. "Have you seen him?"

"Are you talking about the man who rode the motorcycle with you?"

"Yes, that's Hawk. Have you seen him?"

"He is a strange one." Raja looked at her warily. "He would not let anyone else touch you. He insisted on carrying you by himself all the way to the place where I knew we could get transportation. And that is how you came here to Pria's house."

"But where is he now?" Sienna insisted.

"I do not know." Raja shook his head emphatically.

"When he brought you in here and laid you on the bed," Pria interjected, "his eyes looked like they were on fire. I asked him if he had been hurt, but he wouldn't answer me. He demanded to know if I was capable of taking care of you. When Raja told him you were in the best hands within miles, he left the house without saying another word."

Hawk was cold to the bone, although he was dripping with perspiration. His shirt stuck to his body, along with dirt and debris from the corner in which he crouched. Suddenly, his body jerked with another racking pain and he covered his face with his dust-smeared hands, touching the atrocity into which he had turned.

He had known that this time would be upon him after the accident, that the thing he dreaded most in his life was at hand. But Sienna had been injured and he had to make sure she would receive proper care, even if it was to his own detriment.

His body started to quake as a fit of nerves seized him, and he slung his head back against the wooden wall. Slowly, Hawk dragged his hands down from his face and he quivered, this time not from cold but with self-pity, for he could feel the horrible ridges and potholes of the blistering rash, and he knew from experience the unsightly figure he made.

He had not had time to find a safe place to hide, for he had held off the change for as long as he could. But the minute the familiar pains had begun to boil in his belly, he knew he had to take cover fast.

Suddenly, he could hear the sound of a dog sniffing, scratching, and whimpering at the door, and Hawk stared into the semidarkness, feeling like a cornered animal. When the deep barks began to ring out he wanted to run, but the pains were so strong they immobilized him.

"What be it, *chien?*" a male voice asked. "What is it, heh? You think something's in there?"

He could hear slow footsteps shuffling up to the shed, then the sound of someone fumbling with the handle. As a shaft of moonlight spilled into the room, Hawk tried to press his body farther into the corner, the nighttime tropical air mixed with his sweat causing him to shiver all the more.

With the instincts of a canine, the dog immediately ran to the corner, where he cowered, and

began to growl and bare his teeth. In his anger
at his predicament, Hawk's eyes glared and he
bared his teeth as well. It felt good to vent the
restlessness inside him that way. It mirrored the
volatile emotions he was trying so hard to control. For a moment the dog's barking stopped,
then he continued on, backing up several paces
as he pranced.

"What be going on, boy?" an old-sounding
voice asked. "What have you found? Who's out
here?" the man demanded as he saw Hawk's
feet. He began to hit the bottom of Hawk's shoe
with a carved wooden stick.

For a moment Hawk was silent, but he knew
that he had been caught. Reluctantly, he answered the man's question.

"They call me Hawk. I'm a stranger to these
parts." He continued to press his face into the
shadows, finding solace in the fact that it was
still hidden in darkness.

"You would be considered a stranger in most
places judging from the way you are acting,"
the man commented calmly. "Who are you hiding from, young man? Are you in trouble with
the authorities?"

Despite himself, Hawk managed an ironic
laugh.

"No. At least not the ones you're talking
about."

"Don't assume too much . . . Hawk. I am
aware of many authorities, both human and
otherwise. Even those here on earth who think
they are the true authorities . . . their powers
are limited. As a matter of fact, I was told I
would have a special guest today."

"Told by whom?" Hawk was surprised at the turn in the conversation.

"By those who are everywhere: the animals. To some people they are virtually invisible because they mean very little. But to those who are open they are very valuable. Sacred."

Hawk sat quietly listening to the old man's strange words. He wondered if by chance he had come across the village idiot. But somehow he felt this was not the case.

"No, I am not insane," the man answered, as if he could read his thoughts. "Most of villagers consider me a wise man, a healer. So whatever your situation may be, Hawk, believe me, I have seen better and I have seen worse. Come up to the house. . . ." He turned and began to head toward the door. "We have things to talk about. Things to share. Come, *chien,*" he commanded, and Hawk could hear the old man's footsteps departing, accompanied by the tapping of the dog's paws on the wooden floor.

Stunned by the conversation, Hawk eased his pain-racked body upward, leveraging it against the wall. For years he had suffered alone with his secret. With no one he could tell. No one to help him understand. But there was something in the old man's voice that led Hawk to believe the things he said were true.

Hawk pulled himself together, and he was glad to find the pain had already started to subside. Slowly, he followed the old man out of the shed and into the yard.

"Have a seat, Hawk," the man invited when they entered the house, without looking in his direction. "Care for a cup of coffee? Or a drink of water?"

"No," Hawk replied as he sat down at a table and began to examine the room.

The entire space was like a tribute to the animals of the forest. There were live animals and images of animals everywhere. Perfectly preserved specimens were perched high on shelves, while paintings of them in their natural habitats adorned the walls. One corner was filled with wonderful wood carvings in various sizes, while another displayed hand-painted clay sculptures.

"As you can see, I am a lover of animals," he said, shuffling around near the stove and putting on a pot of boiling water. "I've been all around the world, and I've come to believe it be the animals that have remained truest to their purpose on this earth. If you listen to them, they have much to say. I believe in them, so they in turn believe in me."

A medium-sized brown bird with yellow spots began to move around nervously in its wooden cage. For the first time Hawk noticed one of its wings had been bandaged. Then it dawned on him that the majority of the caged animals wore bandages or splints of some kind.

"They come to me when they be hurt." The man walked over to the cage to soothe the bird, his thin but surprisingly muscular body quite visible because of his style of clothing.

He wore a vest made of porcupine quills and hollow bone, along with a tattered pair of shorts. There wasn't a single hair on his body, but the hair on his head was a thick silver grey. It hung loosely, reaching below his shoulders.

"The animals honor me by allowing me to help them," he explained, returning to the stove and adding herbs to the boiling water. "It be their gift to me and mine to them."

Hawk continued to watch the elderly man, remaining silent and tense.

"I believe we are all given gifts of some kind," he continued, pouring himself some tea, then making his way over to the table, where he sat down slowly, raising his gaze to Hawk's face. "Some of them we may not know about or understand. Those be the treasures . . ." he paused, looking deeply into Hawk's eyes, "because they have to be unearthed. They be all the more precious to us as a result of that."

Hawk waited for the look of repulsion that he was sure would come, but the man calmly looked away, taking several timid sips of tea.

"So, am I to believe that this is a gift?" Hawk's voice was full of incredulity as he pointed to the massive rash that covered the entire right side of his face and neck.

This time when the man focused his gaze he made a close inspection of the growth, causing Hawk to feel uncomfortable under his unwavering stare. After a few moments' examination, with a look that Hawk could call no other than one of wisdom, he said, "It is no ordinary occurrence, this outbreak of yours, so it must be a gift. Tell me, how did you come to have it?"

Hawk eyed the man suspiciously, for he had held his silence so long he wasn't sure he could talk about this part of his life. Then almost before he knew it, the story began to spill forth. His words were like water behind a cracked dam: Once the fissure had been made, tons of it rushed forward.

"I was in my last year of graduate school,

where I had been a student of fine arts, but my interests reached further than my major. I delved in many things, but I specifically had a love for old things. Buildings. Rocks. Maps . . ." He traced a crack in the wooden table with his finger. "So I began to spend a lot of time in the science complex, particularly the area where the archaeology students hung out. That's where I met Michelle Fournier. She lives here in Martinique. . . ." Hawk leaned forward, gently rubbing his face.

"It seemed no matter when I visited the area where artifacts and other interesting discoveries were kept, Mickey would always be there. You see, I was still going through a hard time. I had married early and my wife had recently died in a car accident. So I was glad for Mickey's company and we became good friends. We could talk about anything—our lives, our aspirations—and it was because of Mickey that I still realized I had hopes for the future.

"Eventually, we ended up finding out that we both had a love of hieroglyphics." His amber eyes took on a faraway look. "I had messed around and learned quite a bit on my own, but Mickey was an excellent student with a vast amount of knowledge. But you wouldn't have suspected it from the way she presented herself. She wasn't your average studious student, if you know what I mean."

Hawk looked at his surroundings, then across the table at his companion, and for a moment he doubted that any of this would make sense to him. But he was encouraged by a constant nodding of the man's grey head, so he decided to continue.

"One day, just thrown in a box with a bunch of rocks, we discovered two small quartz crystals. At first I thought they weren't anything special, but I could tell Mickey had a totally different feeling about them. It was as if she had unearthed this great find. . . ." He paused before continuing. "When she took them over to the window where the sun was shining through, I could see there were writings on the stones. We were both extremely excited and, like children, we vowed to keep 'the find' as our own secret until we deciphered the hieroglyphics. Then we planned to tell the university and claim all the fame for ourselves. . . ." His lips turned into a wry smile.

"We worked on deciphering those characters for weeks, then Mickey was called to an emergency here in Martinique and she had to return back home. She said she would only be gone a few days, and that I was to wait for her so that we could make the discovery together. . . ." His gaze sobered as he looked at the old man. "Well, I didn't wait. I just couldn't. I knew we were on the brink of discovery, and it was like a fire in my blood.

"That evening I worked for hours, trying to understand the two characters that were keeping us from breaking through. Then it happened. . . ." His eyes grew bright. "All of a sudden I understood. I was so excited, I couldn't believe it. I took a piece of paper and began to write down what I believed the message was. I remember when I had completed it I felt a little apprehensive, because the message was so strange. Now I realize it was a kind of incantation."

"What did it say?" the man prodded him.

Hawk's gaze clouded over as he recalled the words that to this day he had never forgotten.

"It said: 'Take not these crystals into your hands lightly, for they hold the power of sight. Cast them away from you if you cannot bear this worldly burden. Hold them near to your heart if you claim it as your own. But remember in the end, justice can only be found with the Stonekeeper,'" he concluded, with his eyes closed. "I was ecstatic that I was able to decipher the message. I remember I danced around as I memorized the words, then playfully held them against my chest. But as I repeated the phrases again I felt as if some kind of electricity struck me, and I doubled over from the intensity of it, throwing the crystals against the wall. Then all of a sudden my face and neck felt as if they were on fire. And I just sat there in the middle of the floor, wondering what in the hell was happening to me. I remained there for maybe three to five minutes before I tried to stand. I was able to make my way into the bathroom, and when I turned on the light, that was the first time I saw this"—Hawk gestured toward his face. "I don't know how long I stared at myself in the mirror, but after an undetermined amount of time, the rash began to disappear right before my very eyes."

"Be that all?"

"No. A few moments later the voices began. . . ." He balled up his fist on the table. "They went on for days. I thought I was losing my mind. I knew things that were going on far away and things that were going to happen in the future. That's when I left school and practically went into hiding. I couldn't tell any of my intellectual friends I was having psychic visions. They would have been the first ones to say I had gone insane." Hawk got up and began to walk around the room.

More creases appeared in the old man's forehead before he spoke. "Did the voices stop with time?"

"Yes, they did. And for months I was free of it all. Then it came back. At first the rash would disappear as soon as it came, with no pain, and the voices would be loud and clear, lasting for a matter of hours. But as the months went by, each time the rash returned, it would be accompanied by an acceleration in pain while the sound of the voices grew softer. . . ." Hawk looked at the old man, his eyes tormented. "Now, when the rash comes, it is more extensive. It will gradually fade throughout the night, but it won't disappear entirely until the morning. But there is also an intense restlessness inside me during these attacks, almost like a festering anger. I'm afraid one day if it continues to increase, I will not be able to control it."

"And the voices?"

"I can barely hear them."

"I see. . . ." The man drained his cup, pausing before he spoke again. "How be it you were given an animal's name? The name of Hawk?"

"My real name is Hennessy Jackson. The boys in the neighborhood where I grew up gave it to me. . . ." He ran his hands along the smooth lines of a carved wooden mongoose. "They said I reminded them of a bird of prey. The color of my eyes, my legs . . ." He gave a semi-chuckle. "At the time I was deep into karate. I

liked to show off, kicking and spinning. The
guys thought I was tough, and I was glad. . . ."
He sat back down. "I have been on the martial
arts path for a long time. I didn't like fighting
back then, and I don't like it now. But I'll do
what I have to do to protect myself"—he looked
down at the table as he thought of Sienna—"and
those whom I love."

"So you think you be given that name by
chance?"

Hawk stared at him before answering. "It's
obvious that you don't think so."

"No, I do not."

The man walked over to the wall and removed
a fan made of large bird feathers from a nail.

"As you may know, the hawk be a bird of prey.
He can be merciless with his targets. Why?" He
ran his large hands over the feathers. "Because
of his eyesight, and because of his ability to move
well, move quick. Like the eagle he be special in
the bird kingdom. Some people believe if you
dream of a hawk, you dream of a person with
the gift of vision who uses his powers without
mercy," he explained, returning the object to its
original place. "In your case, Hawk, it be almost
the opposite. You be given the gift of sight, but
you have refused to use it. So it being used mer-
cilessly against you in the form of these attacks."

The old man waited for Hawk's response.
When there was none, he continued.

"It be my guess that by now you have determined what the voices were."

"I have an idea, yes."

"Why did you choose to ignore them?"

"Why?" Hawk shook his head back and forth,
then ran his hands over his dreadlocks.

"You have to understand where I come from. I grew up in the United States as a Black boy in the ghetto, with my mother as my only parent. The odds of my getting out and 'making something of myself,' "—he made quotation marks in the air—"were stacked against me. So when my mother died when I was sixteen, I vowed that all the sacrifices she made for me would not be in vain. I'd finish high school. I'd go to college. I'd do something with my life. Well, lo and behold, I did more than that. I ended up in graduate school, one of the leading students in my class. I had deeply maneuvered my way into mainstream America, and I had intellectual friends both White and Black. I had beaten the odds," he said triumphantly. "So when this 'thing' happened to me, it turned my life upside down. There was no way I was going to share my secret with anyone, for I would immediately have been discredited. All my mother's dreams and all that I had worked for would have been for nothing. . . ." Hawk sliced his hand decisively through the air.

"So I did what most self-righteous scholars do when they come across something that doesn't fit into their neat little packages: I ignored it. I simply pretended it didn't exist. Voices and all. I was able to do that pretty easily until about a year ago. Then the pain and the rashes seemed to increase, and I knew I had to find a way to rid myself of this abomination," Hawk gritted his teeth.

"What you consider to be an abomination could be a gift from God."

"Or a gift from his unsavory counterpart," Hawk retorted.

"They be simply two parts of the whole," the man replied. "You cannot know how wonderful the light be unless you are aware of the dark. There be order to all things, Hawk. It be up to you to decide which one will be your master."

"I'm not into masters anymore." Hawk looked at him pointedly. "What did you say your name was?"

"I didn't say. My name be K'in."

The two men sat in silence.

"Are you sure you wouldn't care for some tea? Or water?" K'in asked him calmly.

"I could use a glass of water."

K'in walked over to the corner where the carvings were displayed and picked up a cup with a bird-shaped handle. He filled the container with water, then brought it to Hawk.

"So, how do you plan to get rid of what you call the 'abomination'?" K'in asked as he sat back down.

"I believe I am finally on my way." Hawk looked over the ridge of his cup before placing it on the table. "I told you about the incantation that was carved into the crystal. If you remember, the last line referred to someone called a Stonekeeper. . . ." His voice turned low and silky as he continued. "For the last year, I followed whatever trail I could that would lead me to that person. I traveled nearly halfway around the world and then, in the end, through a strange chain of events, I found her in Campbell, Alabama. . . ." His amber gaze softened. "She is the only hope I have. . . ." He paused. "And you say there is divine order in this world." His tone was full of irony. "She is a beautiful young woman who has become

saddled with something she can hardly understand."

"Like yourself, I believe you be giving her less
credit than she be due. . . ." K'in walked over to
the front door, opened it, and began looking up
at the sky. "With all the order that be evident
here on earth and in the heavens, could it not
be possible that you two people be exactly where
you supposed to be?" He glanced at Hawk over
his shoulder. "I can hear in your voice that you
care for her. This be good. For you be like a
wounded animal who simply licks his wounds to
heal a mighty sore. I think this woman that you
speak of can help you heal . . . if you let her."

"Obviously, she can." Hawk's words became
tight. "I told you, she is the Stonekeeper."

"As a Stonekeeper, she can only heal one part
of you." K'in came and stood beside him. "As
a woman, I believe, she can heal all of you. It
be all a part of the whole. . . ." He placed his
hand on Hawk's shoulder. "Tell her the things
that you have told me. It is clear she be very
special. She will understand your pain, and she
will accept you for what you be."

Silently, Hawk traced the rash that marred his
features, before he stiffened his back and finally
said, "How can I expect her to accept me when
I don't know the extent of what this will do to
me or what it means? Have I seen the worst of
it? Or with time will the transformation involve
more volatile emotions on my part?" His amber
eyes burned with uncertainty. "Even with her
help as a Stonekeeper, I may find out my destiny
involves a life that is not fitting for any woman.
The forces that control this"—he pointed to the
rash—"may come up with other ways to make me

dance to their tune," he ventured, looking back down at the table.

In silence, K'in walked over and picked up a wood carving that was in progress. With precise strokes, he began to whittle at the rich mahogany.

"I remember you say you practice martial arts."

"Yes. Every morning I go through a ritual of *hsing-i*. It is the only place that I find peace. . . ." Hawk paused, recalling how he had felt making love to Sienna and the peace he'd found afterward while they lay in each other's arms. "At least it used to be."

"I believe the time will come when you will turn inward the wisdom that has flowed in your life. And your Hawklike vision will be as keen for yourself as it be for others. Until then, you will continue to walk the road of self-doubt. I hope it does not stay lonely and full of pain for too long, and that your search for peace will be a short one."

For a moment Hawk was silent.

"I had harbored hopes that part of the answer I needed would be found in the rain forest. . . ." He outlined the bird's features on the cup with his hand. "We had been led to believe it would."

K'in pursed his lips in a pensive manner.

"The search I talk about, Hawk, is inside you, ready for you to take at anytime. You speak of something physical. I take it, it is very important to you?"

"It is important to both of us," Hawk spoke passionately. "The Stonekeeper and me."

"What be this thing that you seek?"

"It is called the Passion Ruby, and at this point it is not clear if it is fact or fiction. We believed it would be found in the rain forest, but up to now there has been no evidence of it. . . ." He paused. "There are many things that lead me to believe it is as real as this cup I hold in my hand, but from what I've been told, no one has ever seen it."

"I believe there are those who have seen it, for it be real," K'in announced.

Hawk's amber eyes narrowed as he leaned toward the older man. "Have you seen it?"

"No, I have not. But I know what it be capable of doing, and I have seen the effects of its power both good and bad," he informed him. "It seems to contain the total power of the *kundalini,* a powerful place in our bodies where passion be stored. It infuses the one who is seeking its power with overwhelming sexual vigor, but at the same time if used unwisely or unkindly, it can drain the very life source from the body of the giver," K'in warned.

"We were led to believe the ruby would be found in the forest," Hawk persisted. "Is that true?"

"Yes," K'in replied. "But it will not be found in the rain forest here in northern Martinique. From what I understand, it be kept in a place near the *Savanes des Pétrifications,* or what you would call the petrified forest. It be at the southernmost tip of the island."

"The Petrified Forest . . ." Hawk mulled over the words.

He could feel his excitement growing as a sense of satisfaction coursed through him. He would be able to guide Sienna in the proper direction and he was grateful for that.

"Thank you, K'in. I will never forget your kindness or your wisdom."

The old man nodded his head in acknowledgment.

"I wish I could have mended you, Hawk, like I have healed so many injured animals that have appeared at my door. But I can see your path to healing be a special journey, and parts of the healing be the journey itself. Take care and listen to your heart, for it will be your heart and not your head that may save you in the end."

Fifteen

Sienna pulled the thin netted shawl up around her shoulders, wrapping it tightly about her. She knew it did little to keep her warm, for it wasn't warmth that she needed. She needed comfort and security, and the feeling that she found wrapped in Hawk's arms. The tiny cover did little to provide that.

She looked at the star-filled sky as she walked to the edge of the path leading from Pria's house. The sounds of the insects and the nocturnal animals of the forest were voluminous, while the tiny dirt street lined with houses was quiet and dark. She wondered where all the villagers had gone, or if it was customary for them to retire early.

Several hours had passed since Sienna regained consciousness, and she had not heard a word from Hawk. From what she remembered, he knew nothing about this part of the country and she was worried about his safety.

Sienna heard a door open and close behind her, and in moments Pria appeared by her side holding an oil lamp.

"What are you doing out here? I think you should still be lying down, at least until the morning."

"I'm too nervous for that," Sienna confessed. "It is way past dark, and I have not heard from Hawk. I'm worried about him."

"I understand. . . ." Pria put her arms about her shoulders. "But I still think you should come inside. I'll make you some tea. I think that will soothe you."

Pria began to lead her back to the house, when suddenly Sienna noticed flames rise up in a distant field.

"Pria! Look! There's a fire!"

Pria's features took on a clandestine look before she hurriedly turned away. "Don't concern yourself about that. You just come inside with me and you'll be fine."

"But there's a fire out there," Sienna insisted. "Aren't you afraid for the forest?"

"It is not the kind of fire that you think." She folded her worn hands in front of her stomach. "It will be out in the morning. They will see to that."

"They who?"

"Those who are participating in the ritual."

"Is that where everyone has gone?" Sienna looked at the dark street.

"Mostly everyone. But as you can see, I am here with you. And this is where I shall stay," Pria said adamantly.

"Please, don't stay away on my account. You can go any time you want. As a matter of fact, I wouldn't mind going. I believe the walk would do me good."

"Your being here has nothing to do with my not participating in that"—she flung her head back toward the fire. "I don't know why the people here still believe in such things. They are old ways.

Ways that are best forgotten . . ." She led Sienna through the front door.

"I wonder about that, Pria. . . ." Sienna glanced at the fire one last time. "When I think of the mess the world is in now, I wonder if the ways of people who lived closer to the earth, honoring her in the old ways, weren't better than what we are experiencing now."

Pria looked at Sienna, as if her injury might have affected her thinking, before she left to make the promised tea.

The matted herbs in the bottom of the cup had turned cold, and Pria snored softly in a rocking chair not far away. Upon the woman's insistence, Sienna had lain down, but a restful sleep had failed to come. As she listened to the familiar night sounds, she heard a droning drift in through the window, like the recorded sound of thousands of bees being played in slow motion.

Sienna went outside, where the sound was much clearer. She realized it was coming from the direction where the fire had been, but now the flames were gone. She thought of the ritual Pria had mentioned, and she told herself it was none of her affair. But curiosity soon got the best of her, and Sienna found herself heading toward the activity.

The closer she got, the more distinct the whirring sound became, and she could also hear a rhythmic clacking accompanying it. In a way the combination was comforting, and Sienna began to mimic the noise deep within her throat. She had only covered a short distance when she reached a spot that enabled her to see where the noise was coming from.

Beyond the trees the villagers had formed two

parallel lines, standing two- to three-deep, each group facing one another. Sienna was surprised to discover that the droning was a combination of their voices joined in a repetitive, melodious flow.

She remained as quiet as she could as she strategically maneuvered herself to get a better view. Moments later, as she crouched behind a fern, Sienna beheld an awesome sight.

The scene appeared surrealistic, because most of the villagers' faces were aglow. Their rich brown features shone, not from the moonlight, but from the reflection of a bed of red-hot coals that burned between them. Their eyes were closed as they sang, some of the men and boys striking together what appeared to be sticks to create the clacking effect.

At one end of the bed of coals sat a woman with an inert child held loosely in her arms. Sienna could tell from her posture that she was tired, yet she rocked back and forth, chanting, her own voice blending with that of the others. For untold minutes they remained that way, against a backdrop of midnight-blue sky, until Sienna felt the scene was frozen in time.

Finally, she observed a group of male villagers forming a line. They gathered together at the opposite end of the pit as the melodious chanting began to rise.

The first man was tall and thin, and he began to sway from side to side like a reed in the wind. As the chanting rose to its highest pitch, he placed his bare feet upon the coals and began to walk. He sang as he progressed, his eyes closed tightly, and before he reached the opposite side another man joined him upon the blistering bed, then another.

Upon exiting the coals, the first man laid a hand on the sick child's head, chanting for a moment before moving on, the next man taking his place. This went on until every villager in line had navigated the inferno, a short, stocky man dressed in shorts and an unusual-looking vest bringing up the rear.

The sound of someone in the brush behind her startled Sienna, and she turned to see Raja, who knelt down beside her.

"You should not be here, Ms. Russell. You should be back at the house."

"I couldn't sleep, Raja." She turned back to the marvel in the field. "What are they doing?"

"The girl has been in a coma for three days. The mother does not want to send her away to the hospital in the city, so they are performing the walk of the faithful. They prove their faith in God by walking on the hot coals. If their faith is strong enough to withstand that, then their faith is strong enough to help heal the child," he answered, his eyes mysteriously bright.

Sienna watched as the man with the flowing grey hair completed his walk, then stood with both hands placed upon the child's head. He remained there longer than the others, raising his voice loudly to the sky.

"Why are you all so secretive about this? In a way Pria even denounced it, as if she were ashamed of the ritual."

"Times have changed and are still changing," Raja replied, "just as they are in your country. Things like this that have been done for many, many years are frowned upon. They are considered pagan, evil, against God. But we are a God-loving people, Sienna." His gaze asked for understanding. "We don't want to be looked upon as anything other than that. It is our faith in God—whatever we may call him—that enables us to walk the coals, but it is not the way of modern religion. We want to be accepted, so we practice what is acceptable and we hide the old ways that have worked for us in the past."

Sienna thought about what Raja was saying, and she knew that he spoke the truth.

"Over the last few days, I have been forced to call upon a kind of faith. Something that, through the years, I had tried to pretend I didn't need. Seeing your walk of faith has encouraged me. . . ." She put her hand on his arm. "I know now, no matter what happens, I'll have to keep going, having faith that everything will be all right in the end. You have helped me to understand that faith in and of itself is the key."

Sienna gave a wistful smile and looked back at the villagers. She watched the last man help the woman with the child still cuddled in her embrace to rise. The woman began to walk away, her back to the pit, when slowly the girl lifted a thin, limp arm to her face.

A zealous shout rose out of the crowd as one of the villagers witnessed the movement, and at that moment all eyes focused on the woman and the girl, who began to wipe her eyes. Several more shouts rang out amongst the villagers, followed by many others repeating the same words.

"The girl moved!" Sienna cried. "I saw her. She moved!"

"Yes, she did, didn't she?" Raja's smile was ecstatic.

"What are they saying?" Sienna asked, not wanting to miss a thing.

"They are shouting praises to God for healing the child and are calling for a celebration."

The orderly gathering of villagers quickly turned into a boisterous crowd, all heading back toward the houses. A group of children began to run ahead, skipping and shouting, obviously happy to expend the energy that had been curtailed during the more solemn ritual moments before. Sienna and Raja broke through the trees, joining the animated group, as females and males alike patted each other on the shoulder, congratulating themselves for a job well done.

Before long many of the people gathered beneath what Sienna considered an oversized gazebo, other portions of the crowd flowing into the dirt street. A small group of the musicians united with guitars, along with an assortment of drums and flutes, and began to play an interesting mixture of music.

Under the bright glare of torches and oil lamps, for the first time Sienna actually noticed the mixture of faces that were present. Most of the people were clearly of East Indian descent, but there were many whose features were a blend of African, European, and Indian. The music was a reflection of the mixed heritages, a flowing European rhythm with the tingle of India and a decisive African beat.

Sooner than Sienna thought possible, a large container of a potent punch was provided, along with cups that the women brought out of their homes. It was clear the beverage was alcoholic in nature, for only the adults were allowed to partake of the brew. Sienna noticed how only one round of the punch was served before the vat was taken away, but after tasting the tangy drink she was sure one serving would be much more than she could handle.

Some of the people began to dance, and if there were no willing males, the females danced with each other. Sienna watched as a select group of young women began to execute a routine, and the jubilant crowd gathered to watch. Although she tried to get a closer look, she was caught amongst the spectators on the gazebo and was forced to sit on one of the railings in order to see.

The girls, who were dressed in western style, smiled and performed. Their dance was a combination of feet shuffling, hips swaying, and elongated arm movements. They were good at what they did, and the crowd cheered them on with sporadic shouts of enthusiasm.

At one point they took their sensuous motions out to the audience, singling out different males to be honored with a personal performance. Sienna noticed how some of the men would quickly move aside, while others stood their ground. One determined female led a man away under a gale of laughter, causing Sienna to surmise the men who remained were single and available.

The most stately of the dancers maneuvered her way through the crowd and onto the outskirts, where she made her choice. From Sienna's vantage point it was hard for her to see, but judging by the cries of excitement that arose from the villagers, she was certain they made an interesting pair.

At the finale of her exhibition the girl began to twirl, her long hair forming a black ribbon around her. As the music swelled to a crashing crescendo, marked by the thundering beats of the drums, she flung herself back into the man's arms and he caught her willingly, holding on to her for a moment before letting her go.

Everyone cheered, including Sienna, until the man stepped forward from under the shadow of a large tree. She was shocked to see it was Hawk, who glanced surreptitiously about him before disappearing once again into the forest.

Sixteen

"I don't know how you managed to sleep through it, Pria. Practically the entire village was there. The Walk of Faith was performed, and moments later little Shilpa awakened from her coma," Raja told her excitedly.

Pria looked at him from beneath heavy brows, her lips twisted to the side in disbelief.

"It is the truth. I swear it." Raja held up his hand. "Ask Sienna. She saw it. She was there."

Sienna was aware of the exchange going on between them, but her mind was on more immediate things. She could see Hawk coming toward the house, and he was not alone. At his side was the dancer from the night before, and Sienna couldn't help but wonder if they had spent the night together.

The dancer's mood was extremely playful as she bounded in front of him, turning abruptly to stop him in his tracks. Sienna could not hear what they were saying, but the young woman's body language was quite clear as she removed a large white blossom from her hair and presented it to Hawk.

"I told you to stay in bed at least for the night, Sienna," Pria admonished her as she began to wipe off the table. "The night air is not good for anyone. It puts strange thoughts into people's heads. . . ." Pria looked at Raja. "They end up doing things they would not normally do."

As she watched the young woman go her own way, Sienna wondered if the night had worked its magic on Hawk and the girl.

"Sienna . . ." Raja touched her arm. "Would you tell her what you saw last night? Tell her the old ways do still work, and that we don't have to cast them aside like a worn-out blanket. Tell her it is okay to embrace both the new and the old, so our people won't lose the knowledge of themselves in these modern times."

With her heart beating wildly, Sienna calmly complied with Raja's request.

"I saw the Walk of Faith, Pria. And I saw the girl recover only minutes afterward."

A knock sounded on the door, and a relieved Pria hurried to answer it. When she opened the door Hawk stepped inside, causing an uncomfortable silence to descend upon the room.

Sienna pretended to busy herself making up the cot where she had slept. Raja mumbled a quick greeting before leaving, and Pria disappeared in the back.

"Hello, Sienna."

She turned and looked at him, then looked away.

"Morning."

"How do you feel?"

"I'm just fine." She crossed over to the sink and rinsed the used herbs out of the cup. "But I believe if you really wanted to know, you would have checked on me before this morning."

"I did want to know," he said quietly. "And

I had my ways of making sure that you were okay."

"But coming to see me didn't happen to be one of them?" Sienna could feel her anger growing.

Hawk didn't answer.

She turned her back on him and looked out the window. Involuntarily, Sienna began to tremble, so full of hurt and disappointment was she. Then she heard Hawk crossing the floor behind her. She went stock still. Softly, he placed his hands on her forearms and, with a gentle stroking motion, rubbed his palms down the length of her arms, then back again.

"Where were you, Hawk?" she heard herself ask, although she had promised herself she would not.

"Don't ask me that, baby." He laid his face on top of her head.

Her body tightened at his answer and she turned to face him.

"But I am asking you, Hawk. Where were you last night?" Her brown eyes bore into his.

His eyes became hooded and his face turned into a hardened mask.

"I can't tell you that."

"You can't tell me, or you won't?" she pressed, as her stomach turned flip-flops inside.

His voice was soft and low when he answered. "It doesn't matter which one it is, Sienna." His amber gaze rested on her tortured face. "The answer is still the same."

"Okay. So that's how it's going to be." She walked away from him and sat down in a chair. "I saw that girl dancing in front of you at the celebration. And I saw you with her again this morning. Is she the reason you can't tell me where you were?"

"No" was his solemn response.

Sienna could tell her line of questioning was going to get her nowhere.

"Well, I guess the truth is, you don't owe me an explanation. . . ." She forced her gaze to be steady. "I know one night together is not a commitment. I don't know how I allowed things to get so out of hand with us. But I can tell you I don't like how I feel at all, and I have no plans to continue feeling this way."

"Sienna . . ." Hawk called her name softly as he attempted to interrupt her.

"No, Hawk," she stopped him. "If you can't tell me where you were last night out here in the wilds of Martinique, I don't know how in the world I could ever trust you in Campbell, Alabama, let alone Atlanta, Georgia." Sienna threw her hands up in the air before she began to pace. "That's another mistake I've made, having thoughts of dealing with you beyond this island. Somehow, I've gotten all mixed up." She closed her eyes as she spoke, her voice turning to a whisper. "And I can't afford to give what energy I have left to this thing between us. . . ." She looked at him, her eyes too bright and shiny. "We came here together for a particular reason. You were to help me find the ruby. No more and no less. I think it's best that we keep our relationship focused on that."

Their gazes locked across the room—Sienna's eyes hopeful that he would ease her conscience, Hawk's full of resolution.

"All right," he finally agreed, his features like carved rock.

He knew she wanted more, but that would only reestablish the unexpected path their relationship had taken. The curse was his problem, and he would deal with it alone. He had no idea what his future might bring. She had enough to contend with without his troubles, and he loved her too much to add to her burdens.

"I'm going to see about getting us a ride back to Fort-de-France. We've got some new plans that involve leaving right away for southern Martinique," he said slowly. "I understand a petrified forest is down there, and I'm pretty sure that's where we'll find the ruby." Hawk turned away and started walking toward the door, but just before he stepped through it, he looked back.

"I never meant to hurt you, Sienna. That's the last thing in the world I'd want to do." Having said that, he walked out onto the path.

William lit the cigarette and took a long drag before plopping down onto the overstuffed chair. Although he had just gotten out of bed and it was already afternoon, for some reason he felt extremely tired. He looked out into the turquoise-blue water beyond the window and yawned. The sound of a key turning in the lock caused him to turn toward the suite door just as Spike entered.

"You finally decided to take a break for a moment, huh, man?" he grinned conspiratorially, his bald head shining. "I've heard of marathons before, but I believe you and Germaine take the prize."

William gave him a laid-back, barely tolerant

smile. "I don't think you were doing too badly yourself," he replied, blowing smoke into the air. "Is Claudette still here?"

"Nope, she left last night. I hope to see her again later on this evening."

Spike smiled as he placed the bags he was holding on the table. The spicy scent of creole food and fresh fruit drifted out into the room.

"Man, I know you got to be hungry," he said, pulling several steamy containers out of the bags. "You can help me get rid of this, so you can keep up your strength," he chided.

"No, Spike. I don't feel hungry." New lines settled around William's mouth as he extinguished the cigarette in the ashtray.

Spike stopped in his tracks, one of the dishes still held in his hand.

"You feeling all right, boss?" He eyed him with concern.

"I feel okay. I'm just a little out of it, that's all," William replied.

"If I didn't know any better, I'd say the problem is you've been eating that woman's cooking." He raised his brows in an insinuating manner.

The adjoining door to William's room opened and Germaine sashayed into view.

"Bon matin," she greeted Spike, before settling like a cat in William's lap.

Germaine dramatically crossed her legs and leaned back to give William a kiss, the oversized T-shirt she wore slipping up even higher on her mahogany-colored thighs.

"How are you this morning, *mon amour?"* She ran her hand over William's hair, then cupped his chin.

William could hear his heart begin to pound

faster as he looked into her face. He had never known a woman who affected him the way she did, and he had known much prettier women in his lifetime. There was something about her that literally made his blood boil, and he was helpless to resist her charms. She was able to rouse him and keep him that way, reminding him of his younger days. But that was just it: He wasn't a kid any longer, and he could feel the wear and tear on his body that their all-night marathon had created. It was a little strange, he thought, rubbing his hand over her silky thigh. He had wanted to deny her, but he couldn't.

"I'm doing just fine, darlin'. How about you?"

"I'm doing great, can't you tell?" She gave him a meaningful, private pat.

William thought about the woman who sat on his lap, and he wondered if he should offer to fly her back to the States with him. Of course money was already no problem, and by the time he returned he would have the ruby.

It had been two days since Hawk and the woman left for the northern portion of the island. Before he'd met Germaine, William had considered following them there. Not that he planned to do any of the actual legwork himself, but just to keep a somewhat not-too-distant eye on their progress.

He had spoken to Carl earlier that day, who'd told him that the hostage, Dawn, was holding up pretty well. But there was something about the way Carl sounded that made him feel a little leery. William was glad he had given Hawk and the Russell woman only a week's time to find the gem. He had a feeling he needed to get back to the States in order to keep Carl in line.

William gave Germaine's firm hip an appreciative pat, but in doing so he noticed a small red spot high on her thigh.

"Hey, sweetheart, is that a tattoo?"

Germaine's dark gaze took on a secretive glow.

"*Oui*. Yes. Do you like it?" She leaned over and whispered the question in his ear.

"I guess I do. It's kind of different. What is it?"

"It's a ruby."

"A ruby . . ." William repeated the word, looking at Spike. "How did you decide on that for a tattoo?" His thickly lashed gaze was instantly suspicious.

"Like all women, I love jewelry, *mon amour.* I've never been able to afford anything other than this thin gold chain"—she held it out from her neck with a painted finger, her eyes doelike. "Maybe one day I'll find a man who will shower me with real jewels. It is quite common for island girls to wear tattoos of various stones. You did not know that?" she inquired innocently.

"No," William replied, sizing her up for a moment. "No, I didn't."

She placed her full lips upon his rigid ones.

"Maybe before you leave, I will have more than an empty gold chain, eh?"

William's body relaxed as he smiled at her.

"Sweetheart, there's no telling what you might get before I leave here. Maybe even a trip back to the States."

She gave him a hug and squirmed seductively in his lap, before she stood up.

"What about you, Germaine?" Spike's round

eyes looked up from a spoonful of savory sea-
food stew he was dumping in his mouth. "Care
for anything to eat?" Although his gaze reached
her face, it kept slipping down to her legs and
her thighs.

"No, I don't think so." She glanced at William
meaningfully. "I thought we'd order breakfast
in bed."

"Sure, darlin'. Order whatever you want," he
acquiesced. "I'll be in there in a moment."

The woman cast him a grateful smile before
she disappeared into the other room.

Seventeen

Hawk stood at the window of Mickey's office, while Sienna waited in an antique chair. They had said very little to one another on their way to Fort-de-France, and for Sienna it had been a most uncomfortable ride. She was thankful for Raja's sporadic guide tips, which he offered willingly as he drove them through the countryside.

Sienna tried to concentrate on the paintings and artifacts around her, but her thoughts kept straying to the man standing at the window. It was hard not to notice how the bright sunlight tinged his light brown dreadlocks with gold, and how his muscular body appeared as tense as a tightly strung cord.

"So you're back," Mickey exclaimed as she walked through the door, her arms outstretched toward Hawk for a welcoming hug.

In Sienna's estimation, Hawk reciprocated the greeting all too willingly, and she had to look away to quell the jealousy that instantly rose inside her.

"*Bonjour,* Sienna. How are you?" Mickey greeted her with a wide smile. "I couldn't wait for you all to come back to Fort-de-France. If I had known how to contact you, I would have. . . ." She rubbed her hands together ex-

citedly. "I have some interesting information.
I've met a woman who claims she knows where
to find the Passion Ruby. And she says it is on
the island."

"Is that right?" Hawk's voice lacked the enthusiasm Mickey's did. "We've also been given
some concrete information on where to find the
gem."

"You have?" Mickey looked truly surprised.

"Yes. An old Indian medicine man was pretty
sure he knew where it could be found. He said
it was being kept near a petrified forest in the
south of Martinique."

"*Mon Dieu.* My God." Mickey's almond-
shaped eyes opened wide. "That is the same
thing that this woman told me. But she says she
knows exactly where it can be found. She claims
one of the women who brought the ruby to the
island was a distant relative of hers."

"Well, if she knows exactly where the ruby is,
why hasn't she claimed it for herself?" Sienna
asked.

Mickey held her palms out from her body in
a gesture of disbelief.

"She declares the ruby is still being used in
orgiastic rituals of all things and that the people
who control it are very secretive. Can you believe
it?" Mickey raised her well-arched eyebrows in
speculation. "This woman claims that over the
years, some of the people who have tried to interfere with this group have actually disappeared. She said she wouldn't dare go in there
alone, but with someone else to help her she
most definitely would. She told me someone
very dear to her has been hurt by the power of
the gem. . . ." Mickey placed her hands upon

her ample hips. "To be honest with you, Hennessy, you know I've always had an open mind, but to hear that something like this is supposed to be taking place now, I must confess it is hard for me to believe. But the archaeologist in me says to leave no stone unturned. If it is true, I've got to see for myself. So you must let me accompany you when you go to the petrified forest."

"I think that can be arranged," Hawk replied. "When can you be ready?"

"I could go at any time. . . ." Mickey placed a newly manicured hand over her breasts. "But it is the woman whom we really need, and she says she cannot leave until tomorrow morning."

Hawk crossed back over to the window and stood in silence, while Mickey's puzzled gaze traveled from his broad back to Sienna's solemn features.

"What do you think? Do you want her to take you there?" Mickey's question was directed at Hawk.

"It's up to Sienna." His voice was distantly cold.

One of Mickey's eyebrows rose suggestively.

"Oh, I see. So now *you* are running the show. . . ." Her dark eyes gleamed as she looked Sienna up and down. "I can only guess what must have happened between the two of you, under the magical moon of Martinique, to bring about this change in power."

"Actually, Mickey, whatever may have happened or not have happened is none of your business," Sienna flatly informed her. There was no way she was going to start out taking Mickey's verbal abuse. "Hawk and I came here

together on business and that's what we intend
to take care of." She met Mickey's disdainful
gaze head-on. "As far as the woman goes, if she
can lead us to the exact location of the ruby,
yes, we can wait until tomorrow morning. We
will end up saving time in the long run."

Mickey's full lips spread like butter into a de-
ceitful smile.

"I didn't mean to offend you, Sienna. It's just
that I've known Hennessy for so long. And for
so long I've tried to wiggle my way into his af-
fections, and he's managed to avoid me. . . ."
She crossed the room and placed her arm
through Hawk's. "I'm glad to hear there's nothing between the two of you but business, as that
simply means the road is all clear for me."

For a moment Hawk's amber gaze rested on
Sienna, before he looked down at the woman
next to him.

"So it's set, then," Mickey perked up again.
"I'll put you back in the same rooms you had
a couple of nights ago, and we will all leave together in the morning."

"That won't be necessary. I've already selected
a hotel here in the city," Sienna informed her.
"Hawk, you can do whatever you like. I'll just
let you know where I'm staying, and you two
can pick me up in the morning." She started
for the door, her heart feeling as if it had
turned into a knot inside her chest.

"Wait," Hawk called, his burning gaze on
her back. "Part of our business deal is for me
to protect you. And we've already run into a
couple of incidents that prove that's something
you really need. So Mickey"—he gave her a light
kiss on the cheek—"thank you for the offer, but

I'm going to have to keep up my end of the bargain."

"*C'est la vie,*" Mickey remarked as she lifted her shoulders. "But I'm going to tell you this— and I won't take no for an answer: There is a club next to the tourist office here, which really plays some wonderful music. I want the two of you to meet me there tonight at eight o'clock, for something that we will call a pre-celebration." She closed her eyes and waved her hands. "I won't hear any excuses. I'll simply see you there." And with that, Mickey walked behind them to the door.

Sienna gave a solemn nod before she headed down the hall in front of Hawk, her eyes and her expression showing her chagrin.

"All right, Mickey," she heard Hawk reply. "We'll see you at eight."

"Here are your keys," the desk clerk informed them. "Your rooms are located next to one another on the second floor. The door between them can be unlocked if you like." He presented the statement in the form of a question.

"No, that won't be—"

"Yes, I think that would be a good idea," Hawk told the clerk, overriding Sienna's reply.

"I don't see why that's necessary," she challenged him.

"For safety reasons," he said, looking down into her flushed face.

It was bad enough that his room would be so close to hers, but to know that he would have such easy access to her quarters and she to his . . . Sienna didn't know if it was a temptation she would be able to resist.

"I'll send someone up to unlock it right away, sir," the clerk replied, a knowing smile about his lips.

Sienna stood and watched in silence as the attendant unlocked the adjoining door, then bowed courteously and disappeared out into the hall. When she was finally able to close the door behind him, she stood with her back against it for support, both mental and physical.

It was hard to be so close to Hawk without recalling when he had made love to her and the intimate words they had shared. It could be likened to the type of torture one might experience being close to a fire yet remaining determined to stay out in the cold.

Feeling an ache deep in her heart, Sienna lay across the full-size bed. Although she tried to resist, she found herself straining, listening to Hawk's movements in the room next door. As she drifted into a needed sleep, several times she thought she heard the doorknob turning and her heart began to beat in expectation, only to slow down in disappointment when the adjoining door remained closed.

Sienna's eyes were only partially open when she realized the clock said 5:32 P.M. She was surprised to find she had slept away the majority of the day. Perhaps it was the result of the injury she had recieved on the motorcycle, or perhaps it was from a night of sleeplessness, which had been spent worrying over Hawk's safety.

As she sat up on the side of the bed her stomach complained of hunger. Reaching into her knapsack, Sienna pulled out the bright red West Indian cherries Pria had packed for her. All kinds of thoughts tumbled through her mind as she ate—thoughts about Hawk, about Dawn, and about tomorrow being the day she might actually find the Passion Ruby.

Her mind drifted to the uncanny vision she had had after injuring her head. It was a most unusual experience, for it still felt so real. The effects of the incident were quite powerful, for she no longer feared she would not know what to do once she possessed the gem. Now she believed, with all her heart, that she was being guided by some invisible force. How else would she have actually seen in her mind's eye a village and a people that had been gone for a thousand years?

Sienna swallowed the last bit of the fruit, and once again she was grateful for Pria's kindness and hospitality. They had parted in friendship, with the woman giving her a dainty linen dress with small embroidered flowers and beads decorating a low neckline. She had said she never wanted Sienna to forget her.

Pria had finally told her she believed that through her vision about the village, *Ciel de Marbre,* Sienna had helped pave the way for the power from the past to flow into the present. In her eyes the success of The Walk of Faith was proof of that. She was grateful Sienna had helped her to restore her faith in her people's past and, therefore, in their future.

With care, Sienna removed the dress from her knapsack and laid it out on the bed. She would wear it to the club tonight, honoring her own journey out of a faithless past and into a trusting future. She would have trust in whatever powers influenced her life as a Stonekeeper, for she now believed the roots of her mission had an ancient, powerful origin.

As for her trust in the people and the world around her, Sienna thought, as strange as it might seem, she knew it would take more time for her to trust in them. She still held on to the painful memories of the past, and somehow the world of the Stonekeeper was easier to have faith in at the moment.

Nearly a half hour later, Sienna stood in front of the bathroom mirror drying herself with a large, coarse towel. There had been no shower cap, so she had placed her hair on top of her head to keep it from getting wet. The warm water had felt wonderful, rejuvenating. With her eyes closed, she sighed as she patted the back of her neck and behind her ears.

"Oh, here you are," Hawk said, his voice a deep purr.

Sienna turned abruptly, her eyes opening wide. She had been caught totally off guard by his appearance, and she scrambled to cover herself with the towel.

"Hawk! What are you doing in here?" she exclaimed as tiny rivulets of water streamed down her face, some of the drops becoming caught in her curly lashes.

"I knocked and knocked, and you never answered," he spoke low, "so I decided to come in and make sure you were okay."

His voice did not reveal the fear that momentarily clutched at his heart when she did not answer. Now that he knew she was safe, Hawk realized he should just walk away, but the sight of Sienna attempting to cover herself with only a towel struck one of the most basic chords within him.

A heated glint entered his amber gaze as he stared into her face. Gently, he reached out and wiped the water from the edges of her hair. Just that single contact caused a bolt of sensation inside her.

Sienna would not allow herself to nurture the feeling. Yesterday morning Hawk had promised the night would be one of love, but he had ended up deserting her, then refusing to tell her why.

"As you can see, I'm fine," Sienna managed to answer as she continued to hold the towel scrunched up in front of her. "What do you want?" She strengthened her resolve.

Hawk's eyes narrowed at her question and his gaze focused on her lips, which trembled ever so slightly.

"Don't ask me that, Sienna, for I may do more than tell you what I want. I might end up showing you" was his silky reply.

Her breath caught in her throat as he took a step toward her, and she knew if he touched her she would be gone. This lack of control was so foreign to her. Sienna had never met a man who affected her the way Hawk did.

"That's not what I meant. . . ." Her voice sounded strange, even to her own ears, and Sienna had to look away, for she knew he would see the desire in her eyes. But seconds later her hesitant gaze returned to Hawk's face, for he stood unusually still, only inches in front her.

Sienna noticed his eyes had turned a smoldering gold-green, but they were not focused on her face. Her knees felt like jelly when she re-

alized his attention was focused on the mirror
behind her, for the long glass gave him a perfect
rear view of her naked frame.

For a moment she thought of switching the
towel from the front to the back, but Sienna figured that would be an even greater faux pas. It
was hard for her dilemma not to be reflected
in her eyes, and she could tell Hawk knew exactly what she was thinking.

Suddenly, Sienna heard this erotic sound rumble deep within his throat, and her female in-
stinct told her what he was about to do. Even
before she could mouth a protest, he had taken
her in his arms.

His intensity was spellbinding as his lips
sought hers and his hands began to explore her
back, ultimately cupping the two rounded globes
that had pushed him over the edge.

Sienna's mind told her to object, to tell him
to stop, but her body became as pliable as putty
and her heart soared with the feeling of his
muscular arms about her, his strong hands ma-
nipulating her flesh.

In his vigor Hawk cupped his hands beneath
her and raised her body off the floor, molding
her against his hardness. From that moment on
Sienna was lost, and she wrapped her arms
around his shoulders, pressing herself against
him.

"Sienna," he crooned as he rained kisses on
her neck and her face. "Do you think I would
want another after making love to you? You've
gotten deep down inside me, baby," his hot
words poured into her ears, "and no matter
what it takes, I don't plan to ever let you go."

His kisses traveled downward from the tender

spot at the front of her neck and began to nuzzle the valley between her breasts. Sienna heard herself moan with delight and she laid the side of her face against his dreadlocks, his name on her lips. But through the haze of passion, Sienna thought she heard someone knocking at the door. Then again the tapping sounded, this time more insistent.

"Hawk," her voice was breathy. "Someone is at the door."

She heard him cuss beneath his breath as he reluctantly let her go. He crossed the room in a few strides. To say he was upset was an understatement.

"Who is it?" he called gruffly.

"It's hotel services, *monsieur.*" Hawk cracked the door open.

"A *Mademoiselle* Fournier has tried to call you several times from the lobby, but I believe your phone is not working. She told me if you did not answer the door, to try this room as well." He tried to peer around Hawk's body. "She says she thought you might like to go to an early dinner."

"Tell Miss Fournier I'm busy. . . ." He began to close the door in the attendant's face.

"But *monsieur, Mademoiselle* Fournier is a very influential person around town. Th-there are rumors about her, *monsieur,* strange rumors." He stopped abruptly. "I would not like to be the bearer of such bad news, seeing that she has been waiting for the last fifteen minutes."

There was a moment of silence before Hawk finally said, "Tell her I'll be down in a minute."

Sienna listened from the bathroom, her body still pulsing from moments before. In a way she was grateful for the interruption, which gave her the opportunity to clear her head and to try to rid herself of the overwhelming desire Hawk had created within her.

Quickly, she wrapped the towel around her body, tightening it in the front. Before Hawk could say another word, she had crossed the room and was standing behind the door. She pushed his hand away from the knob and opened it just wide enough for Hawk to make an exit.

"Please don't keep Miss Fournier waiting," she announced in her most syrupy voice, causing the puzzled attendant to stop in the middle of the hall.

She could see the muscle in Hawk's jaw begin to work with irritation, as he gave her a wicked eye, but it was only a moment later that she was closing the door behind him, not quite certain she had done the right thing.

Sienna stepped into the club alone. She had refused Hawk's invitation to pick her up when he had called no more than forty-five minutes earlier from the restaurant. She had insisted that she could catch a cab, and he and Mickey should go on without her, since he seemed to prefer the other woman's company to her own, anyway.

The bile still rose in her throat when she thought about it. Even after making love to her all Mickey Fournier had to do was to press him just the slightest bit, and he simply gave in to her whims.

How dare he leave her in such a tizzy! It had

taken her quite a while to calm herself. Yes, she knew it was her maneuvering in the end that had made him leave, but ultimately it had still been his choice, and in Sienna's mind—the mind of a woman in love and lust—he had chosen Mickey over her.

She walked a little farther into the dimly lit room, her eyes searching the crowd. She was surprised at how crowded the disco was at such an early hour. It was nearly packed with tourists and locals, and the dance floor was full.

"Are you looking for someone in particular, *mademoiselle?*"

Sienna turned and looked up into an extremely handsome, suave face.

"Actually, I am." Her smile was reserved. "You wouldn't happen to know a Michelle Fournier, would you? She is the curator—"

"—at the museum," he completed the sentence.

They laughed together, his teeth a pearly white against his chocolate-brown skin.

"I'm familiar with *Mademoiselle* Fournier for more reasons than one. . . ." His dark eyes hardened. "I have also seen her here tonight. Why don't you come with me and I'll escort you to her table," he offered.

"That's very kind of you. With all the people in here it would have been rather difficult for me to find her, especially since I've never been here before."

"Oh, I'm quite aware of that," he said, as he took her arm, guiding her around a very animated group. "There is no way I would have missed seeing someone so beautiful. I pride myself on acknowledging beautiful women."

"I bet you do," Sienna replied insinuatingly.

"Oh, no, *mademoiselle.*" His jet-black eyes appeared to be offended. "It is not what you think. I am a photographer by profession. It is my job to know beauty."

"I'm sorry," she sincerely apologized.

"Your apology is more than accepted. . . ." He gazed down at her for longer than was necessary. "Well, here she is."

Sienna didn't realize they were standing by the table where Mickey and Hawk were seated. Her eyes immediately met Hawk's, which were shining like yellow diamonds.

"Maybe you will allow me the pleasure of dancing with you later," the handsome man said, taking her hand and placing it against his warm lips.

"Maybe" was all that Sienna could say as she took a seat under Hawk's watchful gaze.

"Hello, Antoine, good to see you," Mickey called with a strange gleam in her eye.

The man nodded his wavy head. "I don't know if it's good to see you or not, Michelle," he said, before touching Sienna on the arm and walking away.

"Well, he wasn't exactly friendly, was he?" Mickey pushed out her bottom lip. "Maybe he's having a bad day." She brushed the incident aside and placed her hand on top of Hawk's. "So, how do you like it? The club, I mean," she had to nearly shout, because the band had begun to play again.

"So far, so good," Hawk answered, but his gaze remained on Sienna, who looked at him directly, a satisfied expression on her face.

It was the first time he had ever seen her attired this way, and Sienna was glad she had taken the time to do her best. She knew that Mickey would pull out all the stops, and tonight Sienna had determined not to be bested.

After Hawk left she had thrown on a pair of jeans and a top, then visited the store inside the hotel. She was able to buy makeup, a curling iron, and hairpins. There was even a pair of white sandals to match her dress, as well as long, exotic earrings.

It had taken quite some doing to coerce her hair into a French roll and to curl what was left on top into ringlets and bangs, but knowing what was at stake she worked at it and in the end was quite pleased with the results. With a face full of makeup and a sampling of perfume, Sienna felt armed and ready for whatever the night might bring.

"And don't we look especially lovely tonight, Sienna," Mickey commented, after becoming aware of Hawk's concentration on the other woman. "Is there some special occasion?"

"Why, Mickey, of course there is," Sienna replied in a mimicking, placating tone. "This is supposed to be a pre-celebration, remember? So I had to dress for the occasion."

Mickey smiled, but the gesture didn't reach her eyes.

"You are right. How could I forget. . . ." She caught hold of the end of a passing waiter's jacket. "Bring us champagne. Lots of it. And keep it flowing," she instructed.

The live band ended one song and started another, although they had been playing for quite some time. Still, Sienna could tell by the crowd's reaction that this one was a favorite. It

was a sensuous tune with a fast beat, causing
the dance floor to fill up rapidly.

Mickey emitted an animated squeal, before
draining her champagne glass to the bottom.

"This is my favorite of all songs, and I just
have to dance."

In an instant she was on the floor, tugging
insistently at Hawk's arm.

"Please come dance with me, *mon chou*. If I
never ask you anything else in my life, I want
you to dance with me right now," she pleaded.

She began to tug at both of his hands, wig-
gling seductively and thereby drawing an audience. Reluctantly, Hawk rose to his feet and
followed her onto the dance floor.

Sienna attempted to look nonchalant as the
music played on, but it was hard for her to pull
off the farce. She was on her third glass of
champagne, and its heady effects were already
in action.

She had never before seen Hawk dance; as a
matter of fact, she didn't think it was his style.
Yet when she threw a sly glance in their direction, Sienna could tell that he was far from a
novice. His moves were full of rhythm and fi-
nesse, and his body operated like a smooth machine. Like the congas, his hips kept time with
the beat in a rotating motion that set Sienna on
edge.

"How about that dance?" Antoine leaned over
her shoulder and whispered in her ear.

Sienna looked at the crowd on the floor, then
over at Mickey and Hawk. Mickey's hands were
on Hawk's chest as she swung her hips, and she
threw back her head in a fit of laughter. Sienna
had to admit she was a sensuous sight in her

black jumpsuit and sheer skirt, and it was obvious to her, if not to anyone else, that Mickey's private party was in full swing. She could tell from the way she dipped and swayed that she had plans for the night, and those plans included getting Hawk into her bed.

"Sounds good to me," Sienna replied, for she couldn't stand looking at the spectacle any longer. Antoine helped pull out her chair and they headed for the floor.

As sheer luck would have it, he led her to a space not far away from Hawk and Mickey, and they ended up in Hawk's direct line of vision. Secretly, she was glad, and as Sienna began to dance, her head full of champagne, she put on a mighty performance that she knew Hawk could not ignore. The spotlight shone directly on her, turning her thin linen dress into a second skin.

It didn't take long before Sienna was in the groove, reaching deep and pulling out the most sensuous of moves as the music touched her. Her shapely, thin body turned into an undulating reed, weaving in and out of the notes and all around them.

"My goodness," Antoine croned, "very rarely have I seen an American woman with such island fire."

She smiled and flirted back. "I can't believe that"—she put her hands behind her head and moved in a snakelike manner—"because we all have the same roots. I'm talking about Mother Africa, and you know how the sistahs can go over there."

Sienna moved in closer and Antoine's eyes began to gleam like black opals, at the same time

she happened to notice that Hawk's were spit-
ting gold fire.

"I take it from the way you spoke to Miss
Fournier that you're not too fond of her."

"How can one be fond of a snake?" he coun-
tered, placing his hands around Sienna's waist
and matching her rhythm.

"A snake. My goodness . . ." Sienna's laugh
was real. "I love it!" She twirled away from him,
not wanting him to get too intimate.

"She's quite an attractive snake, wouldn't you
say?" Sienna baited him.

"Mais oui, for sure. But like the beautiful coral
snake, she is just as poisonous."

The fast music ended and he walked up to
her as a slow, gutsy song took its place.

"Now this is the kind of tune that I like. The
kind that I get a chance to really feel my partner . . ." Antoine reached out for her.

"Sorry," Hawk's deep voice cut in from behind. "You won't get to feel *this* partner tonight."

"Come here, Sienna." The order vibrated
with a definite threat.

She looked into his blazing gaze and knew
this was not the time to cross him. With her eyes
downcast and her heart pounding erratically, Sienna did as she was told.

"Maybe I'll see you later. . . ." Antoine eyed
the intense man standing beside her.

"Maybe not" was Hawk's reply as he swept
Sienna into his arms.

"Now wait a minute . . ." She placed her
hands up against his chest. "Who do you think
you are? My father?" His arrogance had riled
her. "I beg your pardon. My father died a long

time ago, and I don't need you or any other man taking his place."

From the hold he had on her, Sienna could feel Hawk's body all the way from his pecs to his thighs. Slowly, his eyes narrowed as he looked down into her face and put pressure on her lower back, forcing her pelvis to become flush with his.

"If you don't need a father, you definitely need a bodyguard. That spotlight showed everything but your tonsils, baby. And what I saw was much more exciting than your tonsils would ever be."

"What?" Sienna was so embarrassed she could have crawled under the nearest table.

Hawk moved his body slowly against hers, his breathing a bit accelerated.

"You have to be careful, Sienna. Don't flaunt something you're not willing to give. But with the way I feel, I'm going to make damn sure you give that and more to me tonight."

Caught off guard by the knowledge that she had displayed far too much in public, yet feeling a tinge of excitement as a result, coupled with a floating sensation from the champagne, Sienna felt Hawk's sexy promises rain down on her like an intoxicating elixir.

"I didn't know that was happening. . . ." Her shiny, dark eyes looked up into his.

"I know that, sexy." His lips intentionally touched her ear as he spoke. "And the dance floor was so crowded, I believe I had the best seat in the house. But I intend to have the only seat for tonight's performance."

The music stopped, and Hawk followed a hot

and bothered Sienna back to the table as the band announced they were taking a break.

Sienna sat down, and it was difficult for her to raise her eyes to Hawk's face. The electricity between them was a tangible thing, and Mickey could definitely feel it. She looked at Sienna, then at Hawk.

"I guess I'm going to call it a night," she announced without her usual sugar-sweet overtones. "I will pick you up in the morning at nine. . . ." She gave them a vengeful look before she walked away.

"I think it's time for us to go back to the hotel, Sienna. We've got a busy . . . time ahead of us."

Sienna felt as if her entire body were vibrating as she met his gaze, and there was no doubt in her mind what he meant.

Immediately, her thoughts began to race, offering all kinds of excuses why she shouldn't give in to him or to herself. There was so little she knew about him, and he made sure that he kept it that way. How could she ever trust someone who was so secretive? Who refused to share all of himself with her? How could they ever have a future?

But in the end Sienna's heart spoke louder than her mind. It told her to be patient, because she knew deep within that this was a good man. But above all else she loved him, and her love for him was stronger than her pride.

Sienna nodded her agreement. Hawk took her hand and led her out of the club. Just his touch caused her heart to beat faster, and her entire being cried out for more.

When Sienna entered her hotel room, Hawk closed the door behind them. She began to walk farther inside, but he caught her wrist and pulled her to him.

"Oh no, sweet thing. I cannot wait. . . ." And his full, moist lips descended on hers. Instantly, his tongue sought out her own, caressing and coercing. His hands were hot and insistent as they roamed over her body, touching the most sensuous places, lingering there until they ventured on.

But Hawk's hands weren't the only ones that were frantic. Sienna caressed his face, his pecs, his dreadlocks.

"Oh, Hawk," she sighed. "I want you, man. Oh, God, how badly I want you."

With her encouraging words, he turned their bodies until her back was pressed against the wall, his hand searching beneath her, caressing and lifting her thigh. Seeking, his fingers rubbed against her womanhood and he discovered that she was moist, which created a growl deep within his throat.

"Mmm, my sexy woman. Now it is very clear you really do want me."

Hawk reached down and pulled Sienna's dress over her head, then stopped to discard the rest of her clothing. Sienna's hands were in his hair as she called his name.

"Hawk. Hawk. What am I going to do with you?"

"You're going to love me, baby. And you're going to let me love you."

Instead of rising, as Sienna had expected, Hawk gently spread her thighs and began to stroke the curly valley between her legs.

"You're so beautiful to me. All of you. I want to know all of you, Sienna, like I have known no woman before. . . ." His amber eyes sought out hers. "I love you, baby," he purred, his tongue seeking out the essence of her being.

Sienna's knees were like jelly and her head writhed from side to side. He had said he wanted to know all of her, and his actions did more than substantiate his words.

Hawk's quest to show his love was unrelenting and her pleasure was beyond words. Out of control, Sienna sighed and moaned sounds of ecstasy that emanated throughout the room. When Hawk finished he kissed her deeply, then carried her to the bed.

Small ripples of delight continued to flow through Sienna as she looked up at him through dreamy eyes. But she was shocked by the harshness of his features, for there was a fierceness there she had never before seen. His eyes remained fastened to her naked flesh as he undressed, and when he looked into her eyes she could feel his power.

With a jerk, he pulled her body down to the edge of the bed and hovered over her, her legs spread apart.

"You hear me, and you hear me well, Sienna Russell. From now until the sun falls from the sky, you are mine. I claim you with every power possible to man . . . and even those that are higher."

Hawk entered Sienna with such swiftness that it took her breath away, sending her on a journey that was like paradise itself. She saw hills and valleys and the waves of the deep blue sea, and when they finally climbed to the mountaintop, the peak made her shiver with icy cold and she hung there for an ecstatic eternity, before they slid down the mountain slope together.

Afterward, they embraced and stared into each other's eyes, until they drowned in their emotions. Lovingly, Sienna wiped the remaining moisture from Hawk's brow, then kissed him tenderly.

"I love you, too, Hennessy 'Hawk' Jackson," she declared.

Eighteen

Sienna turned sleepily on her side and reached out for Hawk, but he was not there. Drowsily, she sat up in the middle of the bed and looked around the room. Her clothes were strewn by the hotel door, reminding her of how their night together had begun. It wasn't until the wee hours of the morning that they had finally fallen into exhausted sleep, and she quivered inside as she remembered how wondrous it all had been.

Dragging the sheet with her, Sienna headed toward the adjoining door. When she stepped inside the other room, there was Hawk, executing his morning ritual of *hsing-i*. Grinning like a child and feeling as light as a feather, she tiptoed to the bed and sat down to watch. As Hawk did his final salutation to the sun, Sienna applauded profusely.

"You're not supposed to clap, you idiot," he said, tickling her. *"Hsing-i* is a serious thing."

He tried to make his face reflect his words, but to no avail. Sienna's laughter was so free and genuine that Hawk couldn't help but laugh himself. She tried tickling him, but his body was so tight and muscular, it was hard to find a place that would yield to her fingers. In her exasperation, Sienna struck him with a pillow.

"It's not fair, and you know it," she giggled, lashing out with the soft object with every word.

At last he caught the ball of fluff in midair and tackled Sienna on the bed. It was only a matter of moments before their tussling turned into intimate caresses and they made love again.

"Look what time it is!" Sienna exclaimed as she held her wild locks of hair away from her face a short time later. "We've only got twenty minutes before Mickey gets here."

"That's no problem for me. It's you females who take forever to get ready, no matter what the occasion."

"This female is going to prove you wrong. . . ." She touched the end of his nose with her finger, climbed out of bed perfectly nude, and began to walk toward her bathroom.

"My goodness, isn't this a change from yesterday!"

Sienna turned and looked at him, a puzzled look on her face.

Hawk snatched up the sheet, pretending to cover himself. "What do you want, Hawk?" he mimicked her. "You get out of here."

Simply amazed at how playful he could be, Sienna put her hands on her hips and stuck out her tongue.

Instantly, a lascivious glare entered his eyes. "Don't you do that!"

"Do what?" Sienna declared, a doelike expression on her face in spite of her devilish inclination. This time she slowly slid her tongue across her top lip.

In a flash Hawk sprung from the bed and was

on his way across the room, causing Sienna to squeal with shock and pure delight. She dashed for the bathroom, barely closing the door and locking it behind her.

Nearly a half hour later, a knock sounded on Hawk's door. This time it was Mickey herself.

"Good morning, Mickey." Hawk stepped aside to allow her to enter.

"Bon matin" was her short reply.

Mickey walked slowly toward a chair and sat down. Immediately, she noticed that the door to the adjoining room was ajar. Suddenly, Mickey's features grew much sterner as she looked at her watch.

"I thought I said we would be leaving at nine o'clock. . . ." She crossed her legs and began to shake the top one. "It is now ten after. I was waiting for you down in the lobby."

"Sienna should be ready soon. And from what I understand, it shouldn't take us long to get there. . . ." Hawk walked into Sienna's room and picked up his belt from the floor.

Mickey's gaze followed his every move, and when she saw him retrieve the personal article, her brown eyes filled with a vile emotion.

"I have to warn you, Hennessy, not too many men have had the pleasure of toying with me the way you have."

He stopped and looked at her.

"Let's get this straight right now, Mickey. I've always been fond of you, but I've never made any other kind of advances. Our relationship has always been platonic. I wouldn't call that toying with anyone."

"No? But you had to know how badly I wanted you. And in the beginning, I tried to bide my time after you told me about your wife. It was obvious you were not ready for another relationship. But I don't think you realize that I never forgot about you. For the past six years, you've been in my fantasies and in my thoughts. That's a long time to yearn for a man . . . especially for a woman like me."

She walked over to him, pressing her ample body against his hard one.

"There are things that I could do to you and for you, Hennessy, that would be beyond your wildest imagination. . . ." She ran her hand down his back and lightly cupped his buttocks. "You see, I've waited for you for an awful long time. I picked you out especially for me. I had plans for us and still do if you're interested."

"That's the problem, Mickey," he spoke softly. *"You* had plans for us. You never stopped to find out if I wanted to be a part of them in the way that you envisioned. . . ." Hawk paused. "You know, you will always hold a special place in my heart. You were there at a time when I really needed someone"—he touched her cheek—"but I can tell you now that that's as far as it's going to go."

"Is it because of Sienna?"

"She's part of the reason, yes."

Sienna opened the bathroom door, only to stop and stare at the scene before her.

"Bon matin, Sienna," Mickey smiled in a deceivingly satisfied manner. Then she sauntered over to the desk. "I can see you're just about ready. . . ." She halted dramatically. "Oh, *mon Dieu,* I just remembered . . ." She spun around, placing her hand up to her head. "There's something I've got to take care of back at home

before I can join you. Why don't you go to the café around the corner and have some breakfast. It is called *La Belle Cuisine.* " Mickey started for the door. "Tell the owner that I sent you, and he will fix something special just for the two of you. Wait for me there. . . ." And with that, she closed the door behind her.

"What was that all about?" Sienna asked.

"I don't have the slightest idea. At first she was raring to go, and now this."

"No. I don't mean her leaving. I mean what I saw when I came out of the bathroom."

"Oh, that. You jealous woman . . ." He grabbed her and placed his arms around her from behind. "That was my telling Michelle Fournier that I got a woman and it ain't her," Hawk announced, nuzzling Sienna's ear.

Sienna closed her eyes and smiled. She was pleased that Hawk had finally told the aggressive woman to chill out. But there was still something about Michelle Fournier that bothered her, and she wondered what Antoine had meant when he called her a snake.

Mickey walked through her bedroom door and slammed it. For more years than he could ever know, she had made plans that involved Hennessy Jackson, and now he had outright rejected her, told her they would never have a future together. And that woman, Sienna Russell, the Stonekeeper, was to blame.

She began to rummage through one of her dresser drawers, finally pulling out a small manila envelope. With care, she removed the picture she had cherished for the past six years. It was an enlarged print of Hennessy and his wife, Rashida.

Mickey remembered how she had come to have it made. She and Hennessy had known each other for several months, and they had become close friends. It had been a couple of days before she left on her emergency trip to Martinique, and they had been working in the lab. As usual, their conversation took all kinds of twists and turns, but that night Hennessy was being more open than normal. Maybe it was because she had started to show how she felt about him, and he wanted to be honest with her to keep her at bay. Whatever the reason might have been, it was the first time he had ever spoken about Rashida.

He told her they had been high school sweethearts who vowed to marry someday, and being the kind of man who kept a promise, Hennessy made her his wife after he graduated from college. They had been married only nine months when Rashida died in a car accident on her way home from the doctor's office. She had been two months pregnant.

Mickey recalled how solemn his face had been when he reached into his wallet and removed the only recent picture he claimed he had of her. It was a small photograph that they had taken after their wedding, and already it was crinkled and worn and torn on one side. Mickey had offered to have a copy made for him when she returned to Martinique, one that he could frame and display in his apartment.

At the time her heart had gone out to him, for this was a man she had come to love. Love, of all things! She had never counted on falling in love. With all the things that had come to her in life, especially when she considered the passion, she had never thought she needed or wanted love. But she had fallen in love with Hennessy Jackson and she wanted him by her side for the rest of life . . . however long that might be.

So Mickey decided to be patient and wait for his wounds to heal, for time was something of which she had plenty.

When she left for Martinique that day, there was no way she could have known it would be the last time she would see Hennessy for at least a year and a half. The timing was ironic. She had gone to the university under the guise of being a student, to seek out the crystals. Josei, the guitar player, had told her where they could be found, for along with the other powers she possessed because of the Passion Ruby, she had wanted the gift of sight. Had she been able to evoke their power as she had done countless times with the ruby, she would have foreseen the split in their destinies.

Mickey had given the original picture back to Hawk when he visited the island a year and a half later, but she had kept the copy for herself. Although, up until a week ago, they had not seen one another since he had left, she always made it her business to keep in touch, for one day she believed she would make him hers.

She stuffed the photograph into her purse and walked over to the veranda to gaze out at the sea. Ever since the day he had disappeared, Mickey had known all along that one day he would be back.

It didn't take much for her to figure out something unusual had happened, when she walked into the lab the evening she returned and found the crystals on the floor, one of them broken. She recalled looking around the room and finding Hennessy's notes still lying on one of the tables.

An unworldly glint entered her eyes as she smiled. It was almost ironic that his life, like hers, had become entangled with stones, and that he would see the Stonekeeper as his savior, while she would see her as her enemy.

Sienna Russell. The Stonekeeper, for the day of her coming had been foretold in the papers that were left with the ruby. Papers that she had guarded just as relentlessly as she guarded the Passion Ruby itself.

From the very first time she had found the papers, along with the two rubies, during an archaeological dig after a recent volcanic eruption of *Mont Pelée,* Mickey had never shared them with a soul. They were her key to evoking the ruby's power, and hers alone. A power that she had intended to share with Hennessy, but now she wasn't so certain.

Mickey's manicured fingers stroked the ruby she wore around her neck. For the past seventy years she had worn it and like its powerful counterpart, it had changed her life. Suddenly, her hand squeezed the stone until it began to tremble.

She had not made such tedious plans for her future, only for them to be dashed to the wayside because of a man's rejection. Men of all people had been dispensable, mere vessels from which the life force could be drained and used to enhance her own life.

Then she laughed out loud, drunk with her

own sense of power. She would show Hennessy and his Stonekeeper what the Passion Ruby was all about. But she would make her suffer first before killing her, and after that she would decide Hennessy's fate.

Mickey picked up the phone to call the hotel.

"This call is for you, Germaine," William remarked.

She looked genuinely surprised as she took the receiver from his hand and sat down on the bed beside him.

"Bonjour."

"Bonjour, Germaine. This is Michelle."

"Ah, *maman* . . ." She looked behind her and gave William a deceptive smile.

"I know that you cannot talk, but I wanted you to know there will be a gathering tonight, and you and your friends will play a very important part."

"I see."

"We will gather at our usual place," she informed her. "This will be the ceremony that I have spoken of before. The most powerful one ever. After tonight there will be no threat to our group or our existence as we have known it. For as long as you want, Germaine, you can remain young and beautiful, and enjoy more passion than most human beings could ever experience in several lifetimes. That is, as long as you remain faithful to me. And I know that you will. . . ." Her tone became seductive, almost hypnotic. "I will always take care of you, Germaine, and any of those who wear the mark of the ruby. You can depend on that. And you will have more than you have ever dreamed of, but I make no promises to anyone who goes against me."

"I understand."

"Meet me outside the hotel in thirty minutes, and I will give you the herbs that you will need for tonight."

"All right, *maman.*" She hung up the phone.

"So your mother still checks up on you?" William pulled her back against him, "How old are you, girl?"

"I'm old enough," Germaine smiled seductively. "You should know that by now. My mother has some things that she needs to take care of, and I'm the only child who helps her out financially," she lied. "So I'm going to meet her outside in about thirty minutes to give her a little money."

"So you mean to tell me she doesn't care that you've stayed up here for the past three days in this hotel with a man you just met? That's different from most of the mothers I know."

"I am a grown woman, William. I have always been independent, and my mother does not interfere in my affairs." She took his hand and placed it on one of her full breasts. "Speaking of staying in the hotel, I would love to get out of here today. I want you to see the southern portion of Martinique. The beaches are lovely there. And there is even a petrified forest. . . ." Her voice vibrated with an enticing excitement.

"You mean to tell me you've finally had enough?" He covered his mouth in mock shock.

"Not really . . ." She rubbed her breasts against his hand. "I thought perhaps all four of us could go down there. I know this place that is completely secluded. . . ." She began to massage his chest. "It would be a wonderful place for a nighttime orgy."

This time it was William's turn to be surprised. "You wouldn't?"

"Wouldn't what?" She put on her most innocent face.

"You wouldn't have both Spike and me?"

Germaine leaned over and placed her lips close to his. "You were the one who told me it was so very good. Why wouldn't you want me to share it with your friend?"

At first William was speechless, then he broke out in a gale of laughter. "Won't Spike be pleased to hear this. Why don't you go in there and tell him the good news?" He patted her on the rump.

Germaine started for the door.

"Hey. Hey! What about your friend? Will she be game?"

"Of course, she will," Germaine replied. "We've done this kind of thing before," she said, smiling secretly.

William watched her disappear through the door, and he knew that with this woman he had gotten more than he'd bargained for. If he had one weakness in his life, it had always been women. As long as they were attractive and willing, he was always ready. Perhaps when everything was all over, he'd spend some extra time on the island. Hopefully by then, he and Carl would have mended their relationship, and he could bring him back and introduce him to Germaine and her friend. It was too bad that he was missing out on all the fun, but someone had to stay there with the woman, Dawn. She was their insurance that Sienna Russell would deliver the ruby as she promised.

William nodded his head, feeling good about himself. When he thought about it, he was quite sure that with all the money the ruby would bring, Carl would forget the entire incident and they would get back to business as usual.

Mickey drove into Fort-de-France with Alisha Leonarde on her mind. She hated to admit it, but whenever she saw her now it bothered her. Her thin hands shook incessantly, and her mahogany face, which used to be unrivaled in beauty, was wrinkled and drawn. The only thing left that reminded her of the old Alisha, who used to live and work in her home, were her youthful green eyes.

Mickey's jaw tightened as she thought about it. What a waste! A damn waste! Alisha could have remained young and beautiful longer than most, for she of all people had been special to her. But she had decided to take her life into her own hands, operating outside of Mickey's desires. So in truth, she decided, Alisha had brought on her own demise.

Impatiently, Mickey waited outside the hotel, her mind conjuring up images of the evening to come. This would be the most powerful ritual they had ever had, and just the thought of it caused her loins to ache in anticipation.

All of a sudden her dark eyes brightened as Germaine walked out of the building and headed across the street. She was not as beautiful as the mulatto, Alisha, had been, but she was still a gorgeous woman. It had also been quite a challenge to bring her into the circle. Her former boyfriend, Antoine, had been hard to get rid of. But in the end it had all been worth it.

It had only been six months since Germaine joined their little family, but she had proven to be invaluable. Already she had garnered a new member, and with no problem at all she had captured the attention of the American who had eyes for the stone.

Arrogant Americans, Mickey thought. For years they had been nothing more than thieves. Always going into other countries and robbing them of their resources, arrogant enough to believe there would be no consequences. This time, this one would be dead wrong.

"Bonjour, mademoiselle," Germaine spoke as she approached the vehicle.

"Bonjour, Germaine," Mickey answered. "Is everything ready for tonight?"

"Yes. They will all be there."

"Good . . ." She stared into the other woman's eyes. "Tonight will be a very special night for you. I have decided tonight you will be given the eternal gift of youth."

Germaine's eyes gleamed.

"Fifty . . . sixty years from now you will look exactly as you do today. There have only been a few, Germaine, with whom I have shared this gift. Consider yourself special. . . ." Mickey touched the hand that lay against the car. "Tell your friend this will be her night of initiation. She will receive the mark of the ruby and will be permitted to be a recipient in the ritual. You have done well. . . ." Mickey reached inside her purse and pulled out a small packet.

"Here are the herbs. Use them sparingly, and I will look for you tonight."

Nineteen

The side of Sienna's face felt wet and sticky. There was a bitter taste on her tongue and her mouth felt dry. Groggily, she lifted her head and wiped away the perspiration, as her eyes opened on an unfamiliar place. She had been lying on a long seat of sorts, which was covered in a forest-green vinyl. There was a similar apparatus only a few feet away, upon which lay a brown envelope marked "For Sienna."

Totally confused, she looked out into a short hall just as the room began to rock back and forth. It reminded her of the sick feeling she had experienced while she and Hawk were having breakfast in the restaurant. Sienna could vaguely remember being thrown over someone's shoulder, but she could not recall a thing after that. Suddenly, the cold realization hit her. There was no doubt about it. She had been drugged!

The hollow sound of footsteps overhead caused her to look up. The sound decreased, then increased again, but this time it was coming from the end of the hall. Still dazed, Sienna saw bright flashes of red advancing in a downward fashion. As she closed her eyes and shook her head, trying to gain some clarity, Mickey stepped off the stairway at the end of the hall.

"So you are finally awake. . . ." She came and stood before her, dressed in a stunning red jumpsuit. "Good."

It was hard for Sienna's eyes to focus, and her tongue felt thicker than usual.

"Mickey, what happened? Where is Hawk?"

"I hope you didn't find your bed too uncomfortable," she said, ignoring her questions. "As you know I am into hospitality, although you ended up being a most ungrateful guest. Come . . ." Mickey motioned for her to follow. "Let me give you a tour of the cabin cruiser. Oops, don't forget your envelope . . ." Her eyes gleamed wickedly as she tucked the packet under her arm.

With Sienna's state of mind and the unrealistic feel of the whole situation it wasn't quite clear if she was dreaming.

"As you can see, this is the kitchen area. Nice, isn't it? And over there is what you would probably call the john. It's equipped with a shower and all. . . ." Mickey stopped abruptly and looked straight into Sienna's eyes.

"Can you believe that as a child growing up, my entire house was about the size of what you see here?" She hunched her shoulders and sighed. "I don't know how we did it," Mickey continued, placing one foot on the stairs. "You're going to love the view of the sea from here."

Sienna's grogginess was beginning to wear off, and a strange feeling was creeping up her spine.

"What is going on, Mickey? Where is Hawk?" She grabbed the other woman by the forearm.

"Get your hands off me," Mickey snapped, her eyes suddenly on fire.

Sienna stepped back, all her senses rising to the forefront. She stared at the woman in front of her, who had suddenly turned vicious.

"I'm not following you anywhere until you tell me where Hawk is."

"You're in no damn position to tell me what you're not going to do," Mickey retorted, pulling a small derringer from her pocket. "If there are any questions to be asked around here, I'll do the asking." She gritted her teeth and stepped to the side. "Now get up these stairs."

Wary, Sienna squeezed by her and began to slowly climb the short flight of metal stairs. When she reached the top it was still daylight, but the sun was on a downward slide. Even with the approach of dusk Sienna noticed the water was the most transparent of shimmering turquoise blues, and the sand on the beach, no more than a mile away, gleamed like small particles of diamonds.

There were two young, well-built men aboard the boat, who both eyed her with a distant curiosity. One manned the steering wheel while the other simply lounged against the side.

Sienna turned to face Mickey, who was staring at her wrist.

"Take off that bracelet and hand it to me."

Sienna looked down at the gift her Aunt Jessi had given her. "What good could this bracelet possibly do you?"

"Don't worry about that. Just do what I said."

Sienna's dark eyes narrowed with anger as she yielded to Mickey's demands. She watched as a satisfied, enigmatic smile crossed the other woman's features, then her expression changed to one of disdain.

"So, you want to know where Hawk is, do you? Well, first of all his name is not Hawk. It's Hennessy. Hennessy Jackson." Mickey threw her head back haughtily. "And right now he's waiting for me in a special place of mine. Probably resting comfortably in my bed, getting off on my satin sheets."

Sienna's eyes narrowed in disbelief.

"I don't believe a word you're saying."

"You probably wouldn't, you're so stupid and naive . . ." Mickey paused to let her jab hit its mark. "You actually bought that Stonekeeper story, didn't you?" she laughed sarcastically. "What did you think, Sienna? That all of a sudden you were going to be endowed with some kind of magical powers? Wo-o-o-o," she moaned, flailing her arms up and down in a ghostlike fashion. "That you had been chosen especially by the powers of the universe? Sienna Russell from Georgia," Mickey announced out toward the sea, "Mother Earth's chosen one for the planet, right? See, you're just stupid and gullible. Just like you bought that line Hennessy was feeding you . . ." She thrust the envelope toward her. "Open it."

Sienna shook her head.

"I said open it." She spaced out each word between gritted teeth, pointing the gun again.

With numb fingers, Sienna opened the packet and removed the photograph from inside.

"Hennessy didn't tell you he was married, did he? His wife's name is Rashida."

Sienna was speechless as she stared at the picture, the blood that flowed in her veins feeling like ice water.

"You see, I know all about him. And I can accept everything about him, even when he plays the kind of games that he's been playing with you."

Sienna looked into Mickey's smug features. She didn't know exactly what to believe, but the picture appeared to be proof enough that Mickey was telling the truth. With her mind reeling, Sienna tried to think clearly. But the first thought that popped into her head was that Mickey was a liar, and suddenly she could hear Aunt Jessi's words: "Follow your first mind, it will never lead you wrong."

"Well, since I'm such an insignificant person in this whole scheme of things, why do you have me out here in this boat with a gun pointed at my stomach? You are the one who is afraid, Michelle Fournier. Of what I don't know, but I plan to find out."

From a flash of unsettled emotion on Mickey's face, Sienna gleaned that she had hit her mark, and seeing that made her bolder. She determined that if she was going to end up dying on some boat without even knowing why, she would at least go down taking names.

"From the very first moment I saw you, you've flaunted yourself and thrown yourself at Hawk, but he just wasn't interested in what you had to offer. Sistah-girl, you must be one desperate woman to go to the lengths that you have," Sienna declared, eyeing her up and down. "And I know that neither Hawk nor I ever told you I was the Stonekeeper. But I'll tell you what: I am the Stonekeeper, and I'll claim it with every bone in my body if it's going to help me kick your fat butt."

Mickey was stunned at Sienna's audacity and started to sputter a response, but before she could Sienna had hurled her entire body against her, dislodging the gun and accidentally casting herself overboard.

The water was lukewarm as she continued to plummet. Moments later she was finally able to take control, and she began to swim. Panicked, she paddled upward until she saw the outboard motor of Mickey's boat, then she quietly surfaced along its side. Sienna could hear the commotion aboard the craft above the lapping water.

"Are you all right, *mademoiselle?*" a male voice inquired.

"Get your hands off me" was Mickey's heated response. "Where did she fall overboard?"

"Right here."

"Do you see her?"

There was a moment of silence, and Sienna held her breath as another choppy wave washed over her head.

"I don't see anything, and it will be dark in a couple of hours," another male voice chimed in. "Even the best of swimmers would not come out this far at *Pointe de Diamant.* The currents are strong and you would be taking your life into your own hands trying to navigate them."

"That's true," Mickey's response was unusually calm. "So let's leave her here. . . ." There was a pregnant pause. "This way the sea will do the job for me. After all, we don't want to be late for your first gathering, do we? I know you young men don't want to miss a thing."

Sienna heard laughs of acknowledgment before she quickly dove away from the outboard motor. In a matter of seconds the blades began to churn. She stayed submerged as long as she could, allowing the boat to gain considerable distance.

This time when Sienna surfaced, her heart was beating even more rapidly than before. She began to tread water and knew the man had spoken the truth, for she could feel the currents around her as the sun was sinking in the West.

Sienna's heart was in her throat as her fearful gaze focused on the distant beach. There wasn't a boat in sight that might help her, and she knew she had no other choice but to swim for the shore.

The powerful currents continued to pull at her body, the water feeling like silky shackles attempting to drag her under. Determined, she managed to evade them as thoughts of Hawk filled her mind, along with the terrible things Mickey had said.

Suddenly, a more persuasive current wrapped itself around her. Terrified, Sienna struggled against it as she cried out, "I'm not ready to die! I'm not ready to die!"

Hawk turned his face downward and felt the cool, silky smoothness of satin. His brow wrinkled at the thought. How could that be? His arm slid up toward his face, and he smacked his lips softly as he sampled the residue of an acrid taste. Abruptly, he sat up, which caused his head to swim. Images of him swinging wildly before completely blacking out flashed through his mind. When he was able to open his eyes, Hawk was astounded at the sight he beheld.

The walls of the bedroom in which he found himself were covered with erotic paintings in all shapes and sizes. There were singular nudes and couples, menage á trois scenes, and group activities with amazing explicitness. In all the paintings the subjects wore red. Astonished, he climbed out of bed for a closer look, his toes sinking into the thickest of carpets as he crossed the floor.

Having a knowledge of art, he could tell the majority of the paintings had been created by the same artist, some of them more recently than others. He wondered if they were depictions of actual happenings, because there was a striking realness about the work. One woman in particular appeared in a majority of the paintings, and Hawk felt there was something vaguely familiar about her.

Just the thought of a woman caused the fog to start lifting from his mind. Sienna! Where was Sienna?

Hawk rubbed his temples and tried to focus. Someone must have put something in the food at the restaurant, and if he had been rendered unconscious, so had Sienna. But where was she?

Hawk moved swiftly toward the door, but as he might have guessed it was locked. He turned and surveyed his prison once again, this time with full consciousness. A king-sized bed. The paintings. Erotic statues and carvings. A closet and a hope chest. Draperies. Other than that, the room was empty.

He felt no immediate threat to his safety, yet someone had gone through an awful lot of

trouble to bring him here. Was Sienna also being held in this building? And what was the purpose?

Suddenly, Hawk heard an overpowering
whooshing sound in his head. He covered his
ears to try to block it out, but in doing so the
sound only became more distinct, and he began
to hear a faint voice beneath it.

Hawk feared another attack was about to over-
come him, and he cursed the powers that be for
their awful timing. Angry, he paced the room
in an effort to ward off the onslaught. He had
to be able to help Sienna if she needed him.
Even so, he waited for the blistering pain to start
as he railed against the forces. "I will not let it
be!" But as the minutes passed the pain never
came, and the voice remained with an insistent
familiarity.

Of its own volition, a mental fog descended
about him and Hawk entered a place where he
felt as if he were drowning. He could feel himself struggling, and he had very little strength
left to fight the currents that tugged at his legs
and his feet. His nostrils burned from sea salt,
and his eyes teared from fear and exhaustion.
Still, his determination was strong as he focused
on a distant shore. Then, as clear as day, he
heard the words: "I'm not ready to die! I'm not
ready to die!"

His heart beat so fast he felt as if it would
burst within his chest, for he knew with every
ounce of his being that the voice belonged to
Sienna. It was his gift. Hawk knew without a
doubt that she feared for her life.

In an instant he was on his feet, Sienna's cry

for help still ringing in his ears. He had to get out! And he had to get out now!

With a mighty jerk he opened the draperies, but the window only admitted a limited amount of sunlight. He could tell through the dark stained glass that the sun was beginning to set, and it wouldn't be long before it was totally dark.

An icy fear gripped his heart as he thought of what it might mean, for he knew that as long as Sienna had sunlight someone might possibly find her or she might find a shore. But Hawk also knew that in the dark of night, her chances for survival were almost nil.

His tear-filled eyes turned skyward, and he trembled with the weight of his fear.

"Don't let her die," he pleaded beneath his breath. "I have never asked anything of you since my mother died, but I'm asking you now: Don't let Sienna Russell die. . . ." His heart ached from the thought of it. "I have cursed you before for what you have done to me, but I promise with every breath of life I have in my body, if you allow her to live and me to use my power of sight to find her, I will continue to be your vessel until the day I die."

A tunnel of warm spiraling air seemed to engulf him, as if to acknowledge his promise, and somehow Hawk felt as if he had been heard. With renewed strength and adrenaline, he picked up the hope chest and turned toward the window. What he saw stopped him in his tracks. The stained glass had come to life as a result of the sun's bright rays of descent, and glowing with an unheavenly light was the defined shape of a multi-faceted ruby! Yet it only halted him for a moment, for he had more important things on his mind. With all the strength that he could muster, Hawk ran up to the window, thrusting the hope chest through the glass. Prisms of blood-red shards powdered the air, and he covered his face to protect it.

Once he knew it was safe, Hawk jumped up onto the windowsill and looked down at a white sandy beach about twenty-five feet below. With his dreadlocks extending behind him and his eyes burning with determination, he leapt into the air, landing safely as he rolled in the cushiony sand.

Articles from the hope chest lay scattered all around him, and as he pushed himself up from the ground his hand came in contact with a hard, pointy object. Curious, he dug down in the sand and uncovered a crystal.

For some reason Hawk ran his hands over the rock's smooth planes, and he was stunned to feel the familiar curves of hieroglyphics. It didn't take long for him to piece it all together. It was Mickey who was responsible for drugging them. She was the woman who appeared in a majority of the paintings on the walls and who had made a stained glass window in honor of a gem. It was Mickey who possessed the Passion Ruby. Hawk's face hardened at the thought of it, for he knew she was also responsible for Sienna's situation.

As swift as a bird in flight, Hawk ran up to the side of the building, where a Jeep and a smaller car were parked. He could see two men standing outside smoking and talking. They were in a jolly, distracted mood. He wondered why they had not heard the window break, until

he caught a whiff of the smoke they were gen-
erating. And from the cigar-sized blunt they
passed back and forth, Hawk was surprised they
were standing at all.

Calling forth his ability to move swiftly and
quietly, Hawk hung close to the shadows until
he reached the cars. There he removed his Swiss
knife from his pocket and stuck one of the
blades into the tire of the smallest vehicle. Once
done, he made his way to the open-model Jeep.
Patiently, he crouched down beside it, searching
under the dashboard until he found the two
wires he knew would do the trick.

Hawk was in the Jeep with the wires in hand
before the men ever realized what was happening, and when the fire hit the engine he put
the pedal to the board, driving off in a white
shower of sand.

He drove onto the darkening road, and he
could hear the men starting the car behind him.
When they realized their tire was flat, he could
hear their cusses mixing with the wind.

Logically, Hawk had no idea where to go, but
he opened up his heart and sought the gift he
had so long denied. For a while he drove over
ground that was deeply rutted, the Jeep bumping in and out of what had to be extremely dry
soil. Even the trees in the area were gnarled and
stubby, and from the lay of the land Hawk assessed that he was in the petrified forest. A short
time later he made his way onto a road that ran
beside a beach, causing the sound of the waves
in his head to blend with the sound of the actual
water. A strong impulse to pull off the road and
onto the beach struck him, and he sat there in

the Jeep concentrating on the messages he was receiving.

Hawk no longer felt water all around him. Instead, he felt the mushiness of wet sand. His lungs burned from the residue of seawater and his throat ached from coughing. A vast wave of relief washed over him because he knew from these feelings that Sienna had made it to the shore.

He began to run down the darkening beach. With each stride he could feel that he was getting closer to Sienna, and he began to call her name.

"Hawk . . ."

At first he thought his ears were deceiving him or that the sound of his name was only in his head. But then he heard it again, truly heard it from a place outside of him, and Hawk knew it was Sienna's voice and that she was near. Finally, he saw the dark shape lying on the white sand near a boulder several yards away.

Hawk didn't know how he reached her, if he crawled or if he ran. All he knew was he was holding her in his arms, and they hugged and rocked until the need subsided. Silently, he thanked whatever powers that be for sparing her life as he kissed her face, her lips, her wet hair.

"Sienna, I thought I'd never see you alive again," he crooned, holding her wet body pressed against his.

"I had a few moments there that I thought the same thing myself," she teased, her voice raspy. "But by now I'm beginning to believe I'm too stubborn to die."

Hawk removed his shirt and wrapped it around her.

"How did you find me?" she asked, shivering from exhaustion more than from anything else.

"I made a pact that if I was allowed to find you alive, I'd do whatever I'm supposed to do from here on out." His eyes became hooded.

"And what's that?"

"I don't know yet. I guess everybody's got a job to do in this life, some responsibility they have to live up to."

"Yeah. I wonder what Mickey's is. She is the one who had us drugged. . . ." Sienna looked at him, afraid he might take Mickey's side against her.

"I can tell you the answer to that. Because I believe she was also responsible for all the other incidents that have happened since we arrived in Martinique."

"What did you do to that woman to make her want you so badly that she would do all of the things she's done, just to get me out of the way?"

"That's not her only reason, Sienna."

"It's not?" She continued to look at his troubled features.

"I believe Mickey is the one who owns the Passion Ruby."

Even in the fading light, Hawk could see the shock that registered on Sienna's face.

"Why do you think that?"

"After I came to, I woke up in this place that was filled with strange paintings. It was a bed-room with—"

"Satin sheets," she interjected.

"Yes. How did you know that?"

"Mickey told me. Even at the moment that

she was planning to kill me, she had to rub her feelings for you in my face."

Hawk shook his head.

"I think that whatever effect the ruby has had in her life, it has twisted her mind. I say that because of the paintings, and there was even a large stained glass window decorated in the color and shape of a ruby."

"Hawk, she knew all along that I—I am a Stonekeeper." Sienna still found it hard to say.

"I can believe that. The papers that were found with the ruby—which she claimed she had never seen—probably reveal all kinds of information, including the rituals on how to evoke the power of the stone. It's obvious that whatever the ruby has helped her to manifest, she is willing to kill to keep control of it."

"Well there's only one way to find out," she said, looking at her empty wrist. "I've got to get my bracelet back, and I must get my hands on the stone." Her eyes filled with determination. "Mickey's going to perform a ritual tonight, and I'm going to be there."

"Do you think you can after what you've been through, Sienna?" Hawk asked with deep concern.

"I have a bone to pick with Michelle Fournier." She sat up straight, wrapping her arms around her knees. "She's an evil woman, Hawk. It wasn't enough for her to kill me; she wanted to break my spirit and my heart before she did it."

"What do you mean?"

"She showed me the picture that you and your wife took after you got married. She said she knew everything about you, and that I was simply a game you were playing." Despite herself, Sienna's voice was choked with emotion.

Hawk reached out and touched her face.

"Why didn't you tell me you are married?" her pain-filled eyes beseeched him as a light rain began to fall.

"I'm not. Rashida died in a car accident nearly seven years ago. Mickey knew that."

"You're not?" Sienna got up on her knees.

"No . . ." he paused for emphasis, "I'm not."

"Oh, Hawk . . ." She threw herself into his arms, mixing the moisture of the rain with her kisses on his face.

He tumbled backward under her enthusiasm as Sienna continued to kiss his neck and his bare chest, murmuring how much she loved him over and over again.

"You better be careful," his voice was husky. "You know I cannot stand for you to be this close to me without wanting more."

"Hawk, Hennessy Jackson, you can never want more than I am willing to give. . . ." She straddled his thighs.

He pulled her body closer to his.

"All I could think about when I was searching for you was how much I loved you, and that I might never see your face or make love to you again."

"Well, now part of your worry has been laid to rest, and it won't take long for the other worry to be laid," she advised him provocatively.

With the light rain covering them, Sienna and Hawk undressed each other under the orange and gold light of the fading sun, each touching the other's body with reverence, knowing how close they had come to never being in each other's arms again.

Sienna wanted to show Hawk how much she loved him, so she gently pushed him on his back against the sand. Afterward, she began to straddle him, willing and ready to take control of his pleasure. But Hawk wrapped his arms around her waist and pulled her down against him.

"Let me make love to you, Sienna. There are so many men in this world who don't know how to really make love to a woman. To show her how much he cares for her totally . . . her mind, her soul, and her body." He looked deep into her eyes. "Here I am, a thirty-year-old man, and for the first time in my life I know what it really feels like to be *in* love with someone. I loved my wife, but I have never felt what I feel for you. . . ." Gently, he turned her over on her back.

"So let me love you, because I want you to know no matter who may have been in your life before me—and God knows I don't want to think of anybody coming after," he said, his eyes turning a dim green, "they will never be able to make love to you the way that I do, because no one could ever love you more."

This time when Hawk took her, Sienna felt like a flower opening its petals to the nurturing rays of the sun. The need for him was more than sexual. It was as if her body craved his to live, and he totally filled her deepest need in every sense of the word.

As he began to move in and out of her, slowly and purposefully, Sienna felt as if he opened the doors to her own private Pandora's box, the cravings and sensations she experienced so powerful that they were foreign even to her. There was a wantonness that rose and threatened to consume her, and her body lurched and expanded to satisfy the awesome drive. And as Sienna sought to soothe the savage beast within her, she awakened Hawk's primal instincts. There wasn't a place or a feeling he did not explore, a word or a sound he did not make. But in the end, when they both were reaching the point of madness bordered by bliss, Hawk's words came through with lucidity: "I'll cherish you forever, baby, for there will never be another love like this."

When their bodies had had their fill, Sienna and Hawk gazed into each other's eyes as one would stare at the nighttime stars.

"We're on the brink of something, Hawk. Can you feel it?"

He nodded slowly, his eyes never leaving her face.

"Tonight is going to be special. It's like I can feel this fire slowly rising in my veins. It's almost as if your love for me has opened the way."

"I hope you always feel this good about me, baby . . . no matter what tonight or tomorrow might bring."

Twenty

Mickey stared at the gaping hole that stood where the stained glass window used to be. She could hear the waves from the sea pouring onto the shore. Somehow the moanful noise made the room feel like a tomb. All of a sudden she felt dizzy and she hurried to the window, where she gulped large breaths of air. She needed to feel the open space, the wind upon her face.

Feeling calmer, Mickey opened her tear-filled eyes. Why had her life taken such an awful turn? With all the powers she possessed as a result of the Passion Ruby, she had learned it could not give her one of the most important things in life: It could not guarantee her love.

She looked down at her broken hope chest and all her articles spilled out on the beach. They were scattered broken objects, as were her hopes of sharing an immortal lifetime with Hennessy. She had had plans for them.

In the beginning she would not have told him he had been endowed with the powers of the ruby. The realization would have come to him naturally as everyone around him continued to age, and she and he remained forever youthful. In the end, she believed, if he had come to love her as she loved him, it would not have mattered. The important thing would have been that they would always be together.

Instead, he had risked his life to escape. Mickey looked down at the immense distance from the window to the beach. To escape from this beautiful, erotic prison rather than be an unwilling captive. She wondered if he knew it was from her whom he had escaped. Soberly, she closed the draperies and walked back across the room.

Somewhere deep down inside, Mickey knew how Hennessy had felt, for she, too, had become an unwilling captive. Prisoner of her own lust for youth and power. A prisoner of the Passion Ruby.

She turned abruptly as her bedroom door opened, then closed. She was shocked to see Alisha, standing frail and worn, a foot or so inside the doorway.

"Alisha! You know better than to come to my room without being called."

The woman stared at her with bleak eyes, her voice hollow-sounding as she spoke.

"I only come to let you know I am through takin' part in these disgustin' rites. Whatever you do you will have to do without me."

"What are you talking about?" Mickey demanded, Alisha's voice sounding eerie and making her skin crawl. "As long as I hold your life's vessel you will do what you have done every other time, and that is what I tell you to do."

"And if I refuse? What are you goin' to do to me that can be worse than I've already suffered?" Alisha's bright green eyes pierced the other woman. "If I had only known as a young girl how evil you truly were, I would never have gotten involved with you. Never have gotten involved with the ruby."

"How dare you stand there and judge me!" Mickey's anger rose. "You knew what you were doing. Just like the rest of us, you craved immortality and you willingly went along with the rituals. You were more than satisfied for years, until you decided to step out on your own. Until—"

"I fell in love with a man," she cut her off. "A man whom you didn't know about. A man whom I would not allow you to manipulate through me . . ." A hushed silence fell in the room. "You just couldn't stand it, could you, Michelle? Keepin' your youth and becomin' just about the richest woman on the island wasn't enough for you. You began to crave even more power. Power over everyone around you. And as soon as I wanted a life outside of what you have the audacity to call 'the family,' your cravin' for control was so strong, it didn't matter whom you ended up hurtin'. . . ." Alisha's thin body shook with emotion. "For all those years you were able to control my body, Michelle, but when I decided to give it in love instead of just animalistic passion, you couldn't take it. So you did what you thought you had to do, even if it meant hurtin' me and the man I loved . . . who just happened to be your brother."

Mickey's eyes gleamed with emotion. "Shut up, Alisha. I don't want to hear any more. What's done is done."

"Yes, it is. That's why I'm tellin' you I will have no further part in it. But I want to know one thing, Michelle: Did you know it was your brother who you would be suckin' the life out of when you decided to destroy me? Did you know that it was George who would turn old before his time? Or did you think that by rushin' back here from that university you would be able to reverse what you had already secretly put into motion?" Alisha crossed the room and stood in front of Michelle. "How did it feel to see your young brother . . . your only sibling . . . look twice as old as you? Did you feel powerful then, Michelle?"

Mickey couldn't stand the images Alisha's words conjured up in her mind. Grabbing the woman by her thin shoulders, she shook her violently.

"I said shut up! Do you hear me? Shut up!"

She thrust her away from her, and Alisha crumpled in a fragile pile on the floor.

Once again the door opened, unexpectedly, and Sylvie shyly stepped inside. Confusion was apparent on her face as she stared at Alisha lying on the floor. Finally, she forced her gaze away from the pitiful sight before her.

"I—I was just getting impatient, I guess, for the ceremony to start. How do I look?" She turned around and modeled the white satin gown.

"You look lovely, Sylvie." Mickey attempted a smile. "I'm sure everyone will agree. Now go back and wait in the room where I put you. Someone will come to get you at the appropriate time."

Sylvie headed for the door, but then she stopped and looked back.

"*Mademoiselle,* I cannot thank you enough for what you have done for me. And now making me a part of your special family to ensure that I will always be taken care of . . ." Her eyes were bright with emotion. "My family will always be grateful."

"I know, Sylvie," Mickey nodded. "Now go back to your place."

Quietly, the girl closed the door behind her.

"Is she fifteen just like I was when you *honored* me by bringin' me into the family?" Alisha's voice rang clear with accusation.

Mickey turned her back on Alisha and walked over to where the pieces of stained glass window still littered the floor.

"That was when I met George, remember? Although it was only eight years ago, it feels like a lifetime . . ." She ran her hand over her wrinkled face. "He had just come back from Paris, where you had sent him to school, and I was a grateful servant in your household. We had an immediate attraction for one another, but I was determined to honor my position in your home and remain in my place. But after you told me about how special I was and that you wanted me to be a part of your family . . . I thought perhaps there was a chance for George and me. And then my day of initiation came"—she stared at Mickey with ill-concealed hate—"and after that I felt as if I was no good for any man. There I was, a girl of fifteen who had more men in one night than many women have in their lifetime . . ." Alisha looked down at her hands. "So I tried to forget about George, and of course, the way you spoke of your plans for his future made me know I was definitely not the one to be a part of them. But I could always feel his eyes on me whenever he was near. . . ." She gazed into the distance. "Even then the power of the ruby was workin', makin' me more allurin', but it wasn't until I was given the gift of the red rays that he began to find me irresistible, and because I loved him, I had no power to deny him. If I had only known that I would be the one through whom his youth would be stolen, I would have stayed away from him at all costs. But you never told me, Michelle. You never told me," she cried.

"How stupid could you be?" Mickey whirled on her vehemently. "How did you think I maintained my youth? You were there on more than one occasion when a young, vigorous male entered the ceremony willingly, only to leave a mere vestige of himself. Where did you think I got the life force to keep old age at bay? I used the ruby as a transducer, drawing the life force from the men through sexual union and thereby enhancing my own. It was through young women like yourself," she continued, "and like Sylvie, in whom the life force of many men can be stored until I am ready to access it through the stone . . ." Her chocolate brow furrowed. "But then I had to come up with another way of drawing the energy. As I get older, I find it is harder to maintain my youth. My need is so great, even the strongest of males could die with just one encounter. Unless there was one who also shared the power of the Passion Ruby . . ." She looked at the draperies that billowed ever so slightly from a sea breeze passing through the broken window. "Then it would be different."

"Why couldn't you just have been satisfied with a longer life?" Alisha shook her head sadly. "No. You had to live forever. Well, I am tellin' you, Michelle, I am not goin' to participate in anything that opens the life that I have lived to that girl," Alisha challenged her. "Not tonight. Not ever."

"You must," Mickey demanded. "It is the only way this rite will work. The one who holds the rank of the second must be initiated as a virgin. Sylvie cannot be brought into the fold without you surrendering your hold on the energy."

"I'd rather die first." Alisha drew herself up off the floor. "With how I feel now, death would be better than this. . . ." She began to walk toward the door.

"All right, if you decide to bring on your own death, you are sentencing George to death as well."

Alisha turned to face Mickey, her eyes filled with torture. "You wouldn't! He's your brother."

The emotions on Mickey's face were a battle between love for another and self-preservation.

"To save myself, I would."

Alisha's chin dropped to her chest, and in that second she appeared to age ten more years.

"I will not let George die because of me." She stared down at the plush carpet beneath her feet, then turned her lifeless eyes in Mickey's direction. "I still love him, Michelle, even though it's been years since I've seen his face. . . ." She paused. "But I know each time he looks into yours, he wants to strike back for what you have done to his life," Alisha continued, loathing filling her green gaze.

"When he was truly a young man you found out his weakness and you fed it, providin' him with any kind of sexual partner he desired. You thought it would be a way for you to control him." Alisha grew silent. "You were right. He would die rather than admit his bisexuality to the world." She stepped inside the doorway. "The best thing you ever did for me, Michelle, was to tell George that I was dead. Living here in isolation for the past three years has been hard, but far better than seeing George as I am now." She looked at Mickey one last time. "You see, with all that I know, I love him more than life itself. But that is something you will never understand."

Mickey watched her close the door behind her. Alisha, there is one thing you said that was not true, Mickey thought. I do understand what it means to love someone, but not more than life itself.

"Shi-it, this is one strange place. And it looks like it's connected to somebody's private property. I hope they don't discover us at an inopportune time," Spike said as he looked back at the rocklike trees behind them, his feet finally sinking into smooth sand.

"If I didn't know what a good cause I was coming out here for, I don't think you could pay me to be here. Man, this is one creepy place."

"I'm with you on that, Spike," William agreed, but when he looked around and saw Germaine standing completely nude, bathed in a glow of orange and gold, and Claudette almost there, he didn't care how unnatural the setting felt.

William and Spike began to shed their clothes as quickly as humanly possible, as the two

women encouraged them with promises and
jeers. Waving what appeared to be red bandanas
above their heads, they enticed the two men as
they advanced farther down the beach.

Spike was the first to take off in an animated
trot behind them. Even William's cool stride resembled more of a run than a walk as the
women disappeared behind several huge boulders. But when the men arrived, the only sign
that the women had ever been in the area was
their footprints upon the sand.

For a minute or so they looked around in silence, feeling rather silly standing there nude
on the beach. Up to that point William had
called Germaine's name in playful tones, but as
the minutes passed he began to get impatient.

"Germaine, goddammit, where are you?"

"Big man, I'm right over here." Her voice
sounded smooth and seductive. "I can see you
but you can't see me."

"Yeah, and I'm already tired of this game."

"Well, let's play another one, William. And
you, too, Spike. A game where we get to blindfold you and make the two of you big, strong
men completely vulnerable to our whims."

William turned abruptly as her voice sounded
clearer, and to his surprise she was standing behind him, as if she had appeared out of thin
air.

"I don't like the idea of being blindfolded on
some secluded beach in Martinique. If I had to
drive back to the hotel right now to save my life,
I wouldn't know where in the hell to start. You
could be setting me up for a robbery or anything
else," William informed her.

"If I were going to rob you, I have had more

than one opportunity to do it over the last three days. On top of that, you've been plenty generous with me, William. It's not your money that I want."

She struck a match and pretended to inhale from a hand-rolled cigarette as she walked toward them, Claudette trailing close behind. Germaine sandwiched herself between the two men, who both turned to face her as she blew the strangely aromatic smoke in the air.

"You aren't afraid of what we may do to you, are you?" she asked as her body moved to an inner, provocative melody, and Claudette ran her hands over William's and Spike's bodies.

"Should we be?" William queried as he looked down into her hypnotic eyes.

"Hell, no, I'm game for whatever you got in mind," an enthusiastic Spike chimed in.

"Well, I guess we'll both have to play with Spike, then. You'll just have to be an observer. Even though I guess that could be stimulating, in the end it could be quite frustrating as well."

Germaine acted as if she were about to turn her back on William, but he caught her by the shoulders.

"There's no way I'm going to allow him to have all the pleasure. Count me in."

Germaine's and Claudette's eyes met for a moment in a clandestine look of triumph, before they directed the men to get down on their knees to enable them to tie on the cloths.

"There you are," Germaine cooed as she tightened the knot. Afterward, she stuck the cigarette up to his mouth. "Now, take a slow pull of this, and I assure you, you will be in for the experience of your lives."

Neither William nor Spike were strangers to marijuana, but they had never tasted or smelled smoke like the kind Germaine offered. Immediately, the herbs created a light-headed effect, as the two women led the men back into a natural alcove between the rocks.

"Spike, if you ever tell anyone back home about this, you're going to be one unemployed son of a bitch."

"I won't say a word if you don't," Spike replied as the feel of silk entwined one wrist and then the other. "Damn, this is getting to be real kinky," he smiled.

The feel of several pairs of hands applying a fruit-scented oil on his body assaulted his senses, and Spike shivered from the contact.

"William, man, you're gonna have to wait your turn. I got both women working on me."

"I don't know how that could be. . . ." Wrinkles formed on William's brow. "I know there has to be more than one person over here oiling me down."

No sooner had the words issued from William's lips than he felt both his arms being extended out from his body by means of the satiny shackles. In seconds, his arms were being held tautly over his head.

"What the hell is this?" he exclaimed. "Germaine, you all are taking this a little far, aren't you?" he spoke into the darkness.

"You can say that again. My arms are going to be too tired to do anything worthwhile after this," Spike agreed, as nimble fingers untied the blindfold behind his head.

"Now I guess the real fun begins. . . ." He blinked several times, pleased at the thought of seeing what pleasures the women had in store for them. But the sight he beheld made his jaw drop down so far that it locked, as William yelled out in astonishment beside him.

"What is this?"

About ten women and six men stood completely nude in front of them, except for a red cord they wore tied around their waists. Their well-developed forms gleamed as if they were made of polished woods, their skin tones ranging from light pine to ebony. Candles had been stuck into crevices between the rocks, and a large center stone had been covered with a shiny red cloth.

William couldn't believe his eyes, and for some reason he looked down at his feet, which had also been restrained by silken cords. Strange patterns had been drawn near his feet with a variety of crimson petals. It reminded him of a trail of blood against the sparkling white sand.

"Germaine," he screamed, "who in the hell are these people?"

"We are the family of the Passion Ruby," a sonorous female voice spoke from behind him.

William jerked his head from side to side in an attempt to see who had spoken, but the restraints curtailed his body movements and he was forced to wait impatiently to see the bearer of those words. Finally, a well-endowed female dressed in a robe of the thinnest red chiffon stood in front of them, examining him from head to foot.

"For the last five hundred years, the Passion

Ruby has passed through the hands of many people. It has been a bearer of good for some and evil for others. But I doubt that there have been many ignorant enough to crave her simply for her financial worth. . . ." Mickey stared directly into William's eyes. "So, you are interested in possessing the Passion Ruby, William Curtis." Her lips turned a cynical smile. "I will gladly show you what it means for the ruby to possess you . . . to possess your very soul."

"Who is this crazy bit—"

William's words were cut off by the sensuous sound of a slow drumbeat, and his attention was drawn to the group of women who had formed a large semicircle on the ground. They sat with their legs crossed in front of them, a set of bongo drums on their knees.

William didn't know if it was the result of the glow from the setting sun or the smoke that he had inhaled, but all their eyes were focused on him and Spike, and they appeared to gleam with a bizarre inner light. He noticed how the men simply stood to the side, almost as if they did not know what to do with themselves. Some wore surprised expressions on their faces, while others snickered in anticipation of things to come.

Then a figure clothed in a red hooded cape appeared. Slowly, she walked toward the covered stone, holding a candle before her, and she was followed by a body that William knew well. Although Germaine was nude, as she had been minutes before, this time her body had been painted in the strangest fashion. William's eyes narrowed as he watched her advance, her breasts, stomach, and buttocks painted red, while a shiny crimson mask covered her face and a red leather sheath dangled from a cord she wore about her waist.

In a swaying, lunging fashion she followed the figure, eventually taking the candle as the person climbed on top of the covered rock. It was then that William realized the hooded figure was a female, for her breasts pointed to the sky like small mountain peaks as she reclined on the stone, the robe falling open, joining the flow of red satin that was already there.

As familiar as William felt he had become with Germaine's body, he was virtually stunned by the creature who moved before him now. Her frame was so fluid it appeared to be boneless, and despite himself he marveled at her grace.

William watched as she kept perfect time with the hypnotic beat, slithering and undulating on her knees, her back, her sides. In the midst of such a display she continued to hold a lit candle in her hand, dramatically lighting the candles that circled the bottom of the altar rock.

William looked over at Spike, whose large eyes appeared even larger as he watched the scene around him. Slowly, he turned and gazed into his boss's eyes.

"What the hell are they doing? And what do they plan to do to us?"

"I don't know," William replied. "But this is going to be my last time ever taking up with a woman from any island."

He was more frightened than he cared to admit as he watched Germaine dip her hand into a large chalice and begin to make her way toward them. First she swayed and bowed in front of him, her beautiful eyes focused on his face.

But from the look she carried, he was not sure if she was aware of who he was.

"Germaine. Sweetheart. You've carried this game far enough. I'm willing to give you anything you want if you just stop everything right here. I've got to say, you're scaring me, sugar."

But Germaine gave no response. Instead, she twirled her head as if it were on a gyrator, before she moved over and repeated the acts she had performed in front of Spike.

"I don't think she heard you, boss," he said, his frightened eyes staring at the woman in front of him. "Or she just don't give a damn. But I'm gonna tell you this right now: The next time you decide to go on a trip, you can just leave me in good old Atlanta, down in my neighborhood, College Park. With all the stuff I've seen go on down there, I ain't never seen no shit like this."

Germaine spun her head again, then she suddenly blew a red powder into Spike's face. For a moment he coughed and sputtered from contact with the substance, but his reaction did not last long. A stunned, dazed look replaced it, accompanied by the dawning of a strange smile. But Spike was not alone in his seduction, for a small red cloud seem to descend from the rocks above, engulfing the cluster of unsuspecting male participants who stood idly by.

William thought he had been frightened before, but now he could actually hear his heart beating as he watched Spike's transformation. Within moments, his companion's expression had changed from one of scared skepticism to one of pleasurable acceptance. He had heard tales of island magic, of people becoming mere puppets to the whims of others; now, to his dismay, he was actually seeing living proof.

William watched with a tightness in his chest as Germaine removed a shiny dagger from the sheath she wore and, with practiced swipes, rhythmically cut the silken cords that bound Spike's hands and feet. With the drumbeat steady and sure behind her, she replaced the knife in its covering, stretching out her arms toward Spike in a welcoming fashion.

For as long as William had known him, his employee had always been a man quick on his feet, but there was no evidence of that agility now. He appeared to sway like an errant tree caught in a wind storm as he followed Germaine's wordless command.

It was clear to William that Spike no longer had a mind of his own, and with something approaching terror he watched his friend progress toward the altar. The intensity of the drumbeats seemed to announce an even more unworldly scene to come and William swallowed hard, fearing what his part in the bizarre ritual would be.

Five more women painted in a similar fashion to Germaine's appeared, their arms beckoning to the intoxicated males. They advanced toward them wearing lopsided smiles of euphoria and anticipatory looks of delight. Now the drumbeats were joined by the players' voices, which created a keening vibratory sound, and it was obviously a call to action, for the new arrivals began to dance.

To William they resembled red, swirling dervishes, creating mad circles around their chosen partner. Maybe it was a result of the red powder, but for some reason the men felt compelled to follow their circular movements, until their bodies began to resemble spinning wheels. But what was most frightening for William was to see Spike under the spell, for he was compelled to follow every twist and turn Germaine created with his body, until he became drunk with the motion.

Suddenly, the music stopped, leaving the performers' voices so high-pitched that William longed to cover his ears. With astonishment, he watched as each man fell to the ground in a dizzy stupor.

"They are now ready to give of themselves to benefit the power of the ruby," Mickey announced close to William's ear, frightening him all the more.

As if guided by her pronouncement, a sexual frenzy began, creating a collage of undulating, moving body parts. It was shocking to see, for the men were no more than tools, the women controlling the entire act. Again and again they were forced into orgasm by the voracious females, until their bodies and their mouths cried out in agony for release.

William felt the urge to regurgitate rise in his throat, for it was not a pretty sight. The men had been turned into mere vessels of unwilling energy, the women into sexual vultures.

"Now, you must be wondering why I have spared you from this part of the ritual. . . ." Once again Mickey spoke near his ear. "These are merely the preliminaries, dear William. A collecting of the energies that will soon be stored inside the Passion Ruby. But perhaps in your greed, you never wondered how the ruby got her name. The ruby is able to hold unbridled animalistic passion of humans like them. Like you and like me. It is literally an energy, *my* William, one of the most powerful energies on earth. Through it human life is created, and through it human life can also be prolonged. . . ." Mickey stepped in front of him and looked deep into his eyes. "But in order for one life to be extended, another must be extinguished. Annihilated through the very act that creates a life . . ." She ran her hand down his face. "I'm going to enjoy making you the medium through which my youth is nourished and through which Germaine can start her voyage to immortality. But as a result of that, my dear William, you will lose your life. . . ." She smiled wickedly.

He slumped into a dead faint.

Twenty-one

"Goodness gracious. This is unreal. They're all practically nude down there!" Sienna proclaimed, her mouth wide open. Then her expression changed to one of earnest intent as her gaze fell on the woman who wanted to take her life. "And there is Mickey Fournier."

She looked back at Hawk as he advanced behind her. Under the circumstances, Sienna wasn't too sure that his presence was a good idea. Feeling a bit uncomfortable, she turned back to survey the unusual gathering and was stunned when she recognized another player.

"Hawk! That's one of the men who was at Aunt Jessi's house!" Sienna exclaimed as she found a comfortable place on the opposite side of the boulders.

Hawk joined her, lying flat against a convenient stone.

"You're right! That's William Curtis, and the other large man, lying away from the group, is his counterpart Spike."

"I wonder how they became a part of this?" Sienna's eyebrows furrowed.

"Evidently not too willingly," Hawk replied, "or William would not be tied, spread-eagle, with those bindings."

For a moment they lay beside one another, quietly observing the clandestine spectacle. Sets of women pulled barely conscious men away from the altar. Once done, they assembled themselves in a neat half circle. It was apparent they had the timing down to a science, for no sooner had they become settled than the light from the setting sun created a concentrated beam through an opening at the top of the alcove. The result was a powerful ray, illuminating the covered altar where a woman lay.

Sienna and Hawk watched as a thin woman dressed all in white, her back facing them, emerged from behind two large boulders, carrying a black pillow upon which sat an extremely large red stone. She advanced timidly, every once in a while turning her head in Mickey's direction. An elderly woman dressed entirely in red brought up the rear.

The entire scene was amazing, but the stone itself was the most astonishing sight of all. Sienna had never envisioned a gem of such magnitude, and it was difficult for her to tear her gaze away.

As she watched, the bearer of the gem entered the ray of light, which caused the stone to glitter majestically. The setting sun's luminary finger caressed the ruby, and a vibrant scarlet light emanated forward and backward from the gem, creating a radiant ruby-colored cylinder that seemed to blend and stretch with the shape of the ray. The vermilion light illuminated the face of the woman lying on the altar and totally changed the color of the bearer's dress from white to red. The color of the ruby was so rich, it deepened the shade of the elderly woman's dress to maroon.

"My God. Look! The Passion Ruby!" Sienna's voice was full of awe, and as she spoke Mickey's voice rang out below.

"The light and power of the ruby has no beginning nor end."

"It is the power of creation," one woman stood up.

"It is the power of youth," another stood and spoke.

"It is the power of prosperity," the cycle of standing and speaking continued.

"It is the power of life."

"It is the power of death."

When the chant was completed, each woman entered the ray, bathing in its red glare.

Mesmerized, Sienna watched as Mickey stuck a long, thin object into the flame of one of the candles below the altar, until the small head of it burned bright red.

"The mark of the ruby is the mark of life. . . ." She held the object up within the ray, at the same time that Germaine took hold of her wrist. Together they touched the tiny brand to the thigh of the woman lying on the stone. Claudette flinched ever so slightly before replying.

"It is the mark of the family."

Sienna heard a loud gasp, and suddenly the ruby began to wobble on the pillow. For a moment all eyes were upon the bearer, whose shoulders had begun to tremble visibly.

"It is the lifeline of the family," Mickey chanted as she glared at the distraught female.

With reverence, she took the pillow from her hand and handed it to Germaine.

Sienna watched as Mickey and the woman in red began to unfasten the ties that held up the white gown. But no sooner had the bearer realized what was about to happen than she clasped her arms across the gown that hung at her breasts.

"What are you doing, *Mademoiselle* Fournier?" Sienna heard the vaguely familiar voice question.

"It is time for you to join the family, Sylvie." Mickey attempted to pry the girl's hands away from her body. The woman in red dropped her hands to her sides, and she stood as still as stone.

Sylvie's head turned helplessly from side to side as she looked at the women around her.

"I've changed my mind, *mademoiselle*. I don't want to be a part of this. I am frightened," she cried.

"It is too late to change your mind, girl," Mickey spoke harshly as she tugged at her gown.

Hawk reached out to stop Sienna as she stood, but his foot had become caught inside a crevice.

"You heard what she said, Mickey. Let go of her."

Countless pairs of eyes turned in Sienna's direction as she made her way down the boulders and onto the beach.

"She's just a child, Mickey. An innocent child." Sienna walked into the clearing. "Although I know innocence is something you forgot about a long time ago."

The anger that passed over Mickey's face

caused it to look distorted, before a vengeful
smirk rose to her full lips.

"And so the Stonekeeper has been delivered
unto us again. . . ." She touched the silver bangle that she wore upon her wrist. Outside of
Sienna, the woman dressed in red was the only
one who seemed aware of what Mickey's pronouncement meant.

"So you're here to fulfill your destiny,
Stonekeeper," she pronounced the word with
spite. "You are here to take away all that we
have strived for . . . eternal youth and prosperity." She turned to the women of the circle.
"She is here to rob you of your futures. Will
you allow her to do that?" she asked incitingly.

"No," one woman shouted, followed by another, then another. Soon they were all in agreement and they began to advance on Sienna,
picking up stones and sticks along the way.

Sienna's eyes opened wide with fear as she
turned to face them. She was shocked by the
inhumane look reflected in their gazes.

"Do not listen to her, my sisters," another
voice rang out from behind her. "I am Alisha
Leonarde. I am of the second rank. I am the
first of you to have ever joined the circle. Many
of you may not recognize me, but it was only a
few years ago that I was as young and beautiful
as you. . . ." They all turned and listened as
she spoke. "It was Michelle Fournier who stole
both of those thin's from me. Stole them because I chose to have love in my life outside of
the evil that has entered this circle."

"Be quiet, Alisha," Mickey hissed between her
teeth.

Alisha ignored her warning as she continued.

"They weren't the only thin's that she stole from me. Like many of you, and like this young girl who came to live in her household unsuspectin'ly, she promised me a life of beauty and prosperity, but she stole my innocence in the process. I lost it and my self-respect here amongst these stones"—she pointed to the alcove. "But most of all, she has turned all of us away from what women were born to be: lovin', sensitive bein's. She has turned the most beautiful act in the world into somethin' vile and evil. . . ." Her eyes focused on Mickey. "Instead of love, we have nothin' but nights of insatiable passion with men we do not know. Instead of families with husbands and children in our futures, our lives will probably be long, but they will also be empty. It is a shame, Michelle, for it didn't have to be this way. . . ." A tear trickled down Alisha's withering cheek. "You took the rituals of the Passion Ruby and twisted them to suit your own means. It was because of your insane quest for immortality that this has happened. Had you truly followed what was written as the old ways, so many of us could have been happy usin' the power of the stone."

Suddenly, it was silent on the beach as all the members of the circle turned their gazes toward Mickey.

"What do you young women know about a life of need? A life of loneliness? Because of me you have wanted for nothing. . . ." Mickey took the gem from the pillow and stared down into it. "This world is a man's world. Since time immemorial, a woman's value has been determined by her youth and her beauty, not what's in her head, not what's in her heart. . . ." She raised her eyes to the crowd. "I did not make the rules, I simply

found a way to get around them. And I will not
let any of you cheat me out of what I have worked
for for so long. . . ." Mickey pulled the dagger
from Germaine's sheath and grabbed Sylvie
around the neck, her elbow under her chin, the
ruby in her hand.

"There is more than one way to gain immortality through the power of the ruby. I don't
need any of you. . . ." She began to back away,
with the terrified girl in tow. "All I need is the
freshly drawn, death blow blood of a virgin and
the dying rays of the sun. . . ." Mickey raised
the knife above the girl's head.

"For God's sake, Mickey. Don't do it!" Hawk
cried out from above, feeling helplessly caught
within the crevice, his fingers working to untie
his shoe.

A moment of lucidity entered Mickey's de-
ranged eyes as she turned them in the direction
of the voice of the man she loved, and that was
all Sienna needed. She lunged forward, grabbing Mickey's hand that held the knife.

"Run, Sylvie! Run!"

It was a battle of strength—Sienna's against
Mickey's. In a way good against evil, as the women
around them stood rooted in terror and shock.

Mickey's eyes gleamed bizarrely as she stared
into her adversary's face, and within their depths
Sienna could see the source of her hatred was twofold. She wanted her dead because Mickey believed
she was the Stonekeeper, but even more so because
of her love for Hawk.

Mickey's lust for Sienna's blood was stronger
than her desire for the stone, and she allowed
the gem to drop to the ground between them.
A second clawlike hand joined Sienna's around

the dagger and the blade teetered in the air above their heads. But Mickey's date with insanity gave her unnatural advantage, and as she bared her teeth in a diabolical grin, she began to force Sienna down to her knees and onto her back. Finally, Mickey wrenched her hands from Sienna's grasp and turned her head to the star-filled sky in demented glee, for she knew she had won as she raised the knife and brought it down.

Like a movie in slow motion, Sienna could hear Hawk shout her name, and she knew her moment of death was at hand. With all her heart, she called on the powers that be as she desperately reached for the ruby. Instinctively, she placed it in the middle of her breasts against the mark of the crystal, just as Mickey plunged the dagger toward her chest.

No sooner had metal met stone, breaking the blade, than the earth began to tremble beneath them. The ruby began to feel hot to Sienna's touch, and images of her entire ordeal, from Aunt Jessi's funeral up to this very moment, flashed within her mind and her heart. In an instant, Sienna experienced all of her thoughts and feelings, along with those of the people whose lives she had touched and who had been touched by the stone.

As she opened her eyes the sky seemed to tremble above her, and for the first time she was aware of the screams of panic around her. She didn't know when Hawk had reached her side, but she could tell from the expression on his face that he, too, had been touched by the power of the stone. He appeared to be frozen in the depths of its power, a look of realization upon his face.

With the ruby clutched against her chest, Sienna sat up to look within Mickey's astonished gaze as a fissure opened up the earth between them. Mickey's expression turned to terror as the edge of the opening expanded, cutting away the earth beneath her. With a scream unlike any Sienna had ever heard, Mickey slid into the crack, her fingers clutching at the very edge.

Without hesitation, Sienna threw the ruby into the earth and she grabbed for Mickey's wrists, for she could not bear to watch another human being die. Using all the strength that she could muster, she tried to save her, but it was not to be. As Mickey slipped from Sienna's grasp their eyes locked for the last time, and as she plunged into the darkness her lips formed the words "*Merci,* thank you for releasing me," before the earth closed around her. The only thing that remained was the crack in the earth, which was quickly being covered by sand, and Aunt Jessi's silver bangle, which had slipped into Sienna's hand.

Finally, Hawk was released from the stone's grip, and with his eyes as bright as yellow diamonds he placed his arms around Sienna. There was no need for words. Nothing either could have said would have done justice to how they felt. Up to the very last moment Sienna had doubted her legacy as a Stonekeeper, and it had been an act of self-preservation that had ignited the power within her, that elongated moment when nothing else would suffice but the will to live itself, and that will had been enough to open the door.

Sienna took Hawk's hand and placed it on her cheek. "Are you all right?" she asked, concerned about the change she saw within him. For more than a week now, she had known Hawk to be a man who held a tight rein on his emotions, but from the light she saw within his eyes, she knew a crack had been made in his armor. An opening that would allow a hint of compassion in his life, for himself and for others.

"I'm all right, baby," he spoke slowly. "What about you?"

Sienna nodded her head and drew a deep breath as Sylvie ran up to her and hugged her about the waist. Alisha touched her arm with tears in her eyes.

"The island of Martinique has many stories, as many as there are flowers. . . ." Her smile was forlorn. "Tonight another story will be added to the garden. This one will make us look deeper within ourselves, acknowledgin' our weaknesses, but at the same time nurturin' the bud of faith and hope within us all. From it we will learn it's never too late to take action. It's never too late to change."

"Hey, what about me?" William called from behind them, his eyes large and frightened. His hair was practically white. "All this talk about change and everything. Are you going to leave me here like this?"

Hawk walked over and stood in front of him.

"It may not be too bad of an idea, unless you promise to drop the trumped-up charges against Sienna."

"Look, after what I've seen here tonight, I don't want to do anything to upset Ms. Russell. Do I look like a fool to you?"

Hawk did a deliberately slow assessment of his nude predicament.

"I wouldn't ask that question right now if I were you."

By now the women of the circle had donned their normal clothing and had begun to quietly file by Sienna to give her words of thanks.

Suddenly, a loud moan emanated from somewhere behind her, and as she turned she noticed Spike raising his head up out of the sand. With his eyes bloodshot and out of focus, he looked at William. "What the hell happened, man? Did I miss anything?"

Sienna and Hawk looked at each other, finally breaking out into a gale of laughter.

Turning to a still dazed Spike, Hawk replied, "No, man, you didn't miss a thing."

Twenty-two

"And so this is Hawk . . ." Dawn placed her hands on her hips, tilting her short cropped head to the side.

Sienna's smile spread from ear to ear as she ushered Hawk into her living room, where Dawn was standing.

"You've got it. I'm Hawk." He extended his hand in welcome.

"I don't want no handshake." She looked up at him with an attitude. "After all you two have been through, you better give me a hug. . . ." She embraced him warmly before they sat down.

"So what's this that I hear from Carl? He says he let you go the day that William and Spike arrived in Martinique."

"O-o-oh," Dawn shook her head. "Thank God he did. During that first day, I thought I was going to lose my mind. But he let me go, just like he told you. And he went and filed his own report with the police. I tried to contact Sienna by leaving messages at the museum, but as you know it did little good."

"That's why the authorities were waiting for William Curtis and Spike when we arrived at Hartsfield International Airport, " Sienna added with satisfaction as her eyes caressed Hawk, who sat next to her on the couch.

The couple smiled at one another, their gazes holding for just a moment.

"Well, I guess it's about time for me to be getting out of here," Dawn announced abruptly, a knowing smile upon her lips.

"Dawn!" Sienna exclaimed. "You just got here no more than thirty minutes ago. Let's sit and talk for a while."

"No, no. I got something to do. You know with your being gone for a week, The Stone-keeper didn't run itself. I'm in the middle of finishing a few things. . . ." She got up from the chair. "I don't want my stuff to be half baked when you come into the shop tomorrow," she said, turning to Hawk.

"It was really a pleasure meeting you, Mr. Hennessy 'Hawk' Jackson," she smiled.

"Same here," he stood up and replied.

Sienna stuck her index finger up in the air, motioning to Hawk. "Be right back."

Hawk nodded his head in acknowledgment, then his amber eyes immediately began to survey Sienna's place.

Sienna was glad to have Hawk in her home, and she couldn't help but smile as she opened the door for Dawn, although she didn't want her friend to think she was happy to see her go.

"Girl, you know you don't have to leave right now," she whispered. "Hawk and I will have plenty of time together," Sienna insisted.

"Girlfriend, from the way you and that man were looking at each other, I don't even want to stand in the way of progress." She looked at Sienna meaningfully. "M-m-mm, must be love."

"You got that right."

They laughed quietly together as Dawn bounded down the stairs.

"I'll talk to you tomorrow."

Sienna waved and smiled before closing the door.

When she reentered the room Hawk was standing at the cold fireplace, looking at the pictures she had on display. He was dressed in a dark purple knit T-shirt and jeans, and Sienna couldn't help but notice how they fit his lithe frame perfectly.

"Are these your parents?" he asked, pointing to a young, smiling couple in a pewter picture frame.

"Yes, they are." Sienna picked it up, giving the familiar photo a closer inspection.

"And this must be your Aunt Jessi. . . ." He slipped his arm around her waist as he took down an enlarged Polaroid shot.

Sienna smiled. "It's the only picture that I have of her. I took it with a camera that I bought from a garage sale given to benefit the orphanage."

"Well, that's some gleam in her eye," Hawk remarked.

"It is, isn't it?" Sienna seemed to notice it for the first time.

"Turn around here . . ." He placed his hand on her chin, focusing her eyes on his. "Let me see. Mmm-hmm, you've got it, too. You must get it after you've become a bona fide Stonekeeper by deed. . . ." His expression was serious, then he winked at her. "But I don't know about you. You had quite a bit of fire in those baby browns the first time I met you." He touched her nose, and they hugged lovingly.

"Hawk . . ." Sienna said his name softly as he held her in his arms, "Sylvie called me. . . ." Silence hung between them. "You know, even though I was in the middle of everything that went on that night on the beach, I don't believe I will ever be able to tell anyone what happened without them thinking I'm crazy. But when I really think about it, I actually fulfilled my mission." She looked up into his face, her dark eyes full of awe. "I returned the Passion Ruby to the earth. . . ." She spoke in a breathy whisper. "Sylvie says George and Alisha have completely regained their youth. It had to be the result of Mickey's life being taken. All of their life force must have returned to them from her. . . ." She paused thoughtfully. "Sylvie also told me they plan to marry now."

"That's wonderful," he replied.

"Is it really?" She leaned back to look up into his face.

"Yes, I think so." His brows furrowed. "Why did you ask me that?"

"I don't know. . . ." She looked at him and began to pull away. "You're such a strange man."

But Hawk held her to him, "If I'm strange, baby, it doesn't have anything to do with my feelings for you." He looked deep into her eyes.

"Are we going to be able to make this work, Hawk? You know, we're practically strangers."

"Sienna, from what I've seen and experienced over there on that island, I believe we can do anything we want to do. All we have to do is want it bad enough. . . ." He drew her to him and kissed her deeply. "And I want you. More than I've ever wanted anything in my life."

"Hawk . . ." Her curly lashes covered her eyes for a brief moment. "Will you ever tell me your secret?" Her voice was almost a whisper.

"I promise to tell you everything, Sienna, when I truly understand it myself."

Sienna took a deep breath, and she knew from the look in his eyes it was the best he could give her for now.

Silently, she touched his face, a slight smile upon her lips, then she took his hand. Sienna led him down the hallway to her special place, closing the door behind them.

Dear Friend,

I want to let you know that you haven't heard the last from Sienna Russell and Hennessy "Hawk" Jackson. You'll be able to be swept away along with them in their next adventure, which involves an emerald. It's all part of a series that I call the Gemstone Collection. Together we all can experience the height of love and adventure through these stories.

Let me hear from you, and help me get back to you quickly by enclosing a SASE to the following:

Eboni Snoe
P.O. Box 800028
Roswell, Georgia 30075-0001

Peace & Happiness
Eboni Snoe